Alf glowed with pleasure. "Now you dance." He took Seth's large hand and placed it in Rose's.

When she slipped her hand into his, Seth straightened and hesitantly began guiding her in wide circles.

"See? I told you. You're dancing." Alf was jittery with excit

"We've m Rose comment

Seth didr queezing her hand oser, he said, "Maybe two, or dare I hope, three?"

Her heart fluttered out of all proportion to the words he'd spoken, words she wasn't sure how to interpret. Caught up in the spell of the moment, she couldn't think how to answer him.

Just as the music ceased, she heard him mumble, "Well, two anyway."

As she moved toward a vacant seat, the next dance began.

"Quite a lad," Seth said, sitting down beside her.

"He adores you, Seth." *As do I.*

Books by Laura Abbot

Love Inspired Historical

Into the Wilderness
The Gift of a Child

LAURA ABBOT

Growing up in Kansas City, Missouri, Laura Abbot was deeply influenced by her favorite literary character, Jo from *Little Women. If only,* Laura thought, *I could write stories, too.* Many years later, after a twenty-five-year career as a high school English teacher and independent school administrator, Laura's ambition was unexpectedly realized. When she and her husband took early retirement and built their dream home on Beaver Lake outside Eureka Springs, Arkansas, he bought her a new computer and uttered these life-changing words: "You always said you wanted to write. Now sit down and *do* it!" Happily, she sold her first attempt to Harlequin Superromance, a success followed by fourteen more sales to the same line.

Other professional credentials include serving as an educational consultant and speaker. Active in her church, Laura is a licensed lay preacher. Her greatest pride, however, is her children—all productive, caring adults and parents—who have given her eleven remarkable, resilient (but who's prejudiced?) grandchildren, including at least three who show talent in writing and may pursue it as a career. Jo March, look what you started! Laura enjoys corresponding with readers. Please write her at LauraAbbot@msn.com, referencing the book title in the subject line.

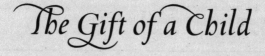

The Gift of a Child

LAURA ABBOT

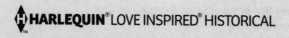

HARLEQUIN® LOVE INSPIRED® HISTORICAL

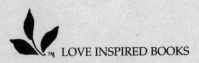

LOVE INSPIRED BOOKS

Recycling programs
for this product may
not exist in your area.

ISBN-13: 978-0-373-28280-7

THE GIFT OF A CHILD

www.Harlequin.com

Printed in U.S.A.

Whoever welcomes one such child in my name welcomes me.

—*Matthew* 18:5

My beloved brother Chuck took the time to
read an early manuscript of this story aloud to his
dear mother-in-law, Olene Roberts, now legally blind.
This book is dedicated with love to them both
for their encouragement and welcome suggestions.

Chapter One

Cottonwood Falls
May 1873

Sunbeams danced across the altar. The pump organ filled the church with a soothing prelude. But in a place where she should have been at peace, Rose Kellogg bowed her head in shame. An unwelcome emotion rioted through her. There was no avoiding the issue or assigning a different name to her feelings. She was guilty of envy. Worse yet, it was her beloved sister she envied.

She and her younger sister Lily had always been best friends. Never had she coveted Lily's dolls or wished she had her honey-blond hair and flawless complexion. When they had lived at Fort Larned, Kansas, where their father was post surgeon, Rose, the plainer of the two, had understood that Lily, not she, would receive the attentions of the young officers. Nor had she resented her sister's opportunity to spend months with their wealthy aunt in St. Louis. Even when Lily had married handsome Caleb Montgomery, Rose had rejoiced in their happiness, content in her role as her widowed father's housekeeper.

At the ripe old age of twenty-seven, she had made peace with the fact it was unlikely she would ever marry.

Caleb and Lily sat in a front pew, Lily cradling their toddler daughter, Mattie. Behind them sat Caleb's father Andrew, his sister Sophie and his older brother Seth, a gentle giant of a man who doted on Mattie just as Rose did. She watched Lily brush a hand across Mattie's light-brown curls. To escape from her thoughts, Rose nestled closer to her father. What kind of person begrudges her sister her happiness?

Twisting her hands in her lap, she uttered a silent prayer. *Lord, forgive me the sin of envy. Help me to accept with grace the path You have given me.* Rose knew the prayer should end there, but she couldn't help adding to it. *And, Lord, somehow, if it be Your will, send me a child of my own.*

Pastor Dooley's voice interrupted her reverie. "Let all the little ones come forward." The minister then seated himself on the altar steps. Some youngsters bounced to the front, eager for attention, while others clung to a parent before leaving the safety of the pew. An older girl took Mattie by the hand, led her to the front and settled the child in her lap. Mattie clapped her tiny hands in delight.

After the minister welcomed them all by name, he opened his Bible to Jesus's words. "'Suffer little children to come unto me, and forbid them not: for of such is the kingdom of God. Verily I say unto you, Whosoever shall not receive the kingdom of God as a little child shall in no wise enter therein.'"

Pastor Dooley closed his Bible, his gaze roaming from adult to adult. "My friends, what riches we see here." He gestured at the children. "Innocence, vitality, possibility. These boys and girls are not nuisances or burdens as the disciples at first suggested, rather each is a cherished gift from God."

Rose gripped her hymnal against the stabbing ache in her chest. *A cherished gift from God.* A gift she was to be denied.

Dimly she heard the minister urge the congregation to accept the kingdom of God with the innocence and enthusiasm of a child. Then he dismissed the children to their families. When Mattie faced the congregation, her blue eyes widened as she spotted Rose. She hurtled past her parents and into Rose's arms. "Woze, my Woze. I seed you!"

Rose curled the girl into her lap, fighting sudden tears. Mattie leaned back with a contented sigh and began sucking her thumb. Looking over the child's head, Rose saw Lily beaming at her. Then Seth Montgomery caught her eye, and the comfort of his broad smile and approving wink settled her nerves. She had Mattie. Granted, she was not a daughter, only a niece, but she was a gift from God. For Rose, it would have to be enough.

The following Saturday, Seth Montgomery, mending a harness in the barn, was startled to see his sister, Sophie, marching toward him with fire sparking from her eyes. The eleven-year difference in their ages had never daunted her when she wanted to charm him into doing her will. She stopped in front of him, tapping her toe. "Seth Mayfield Montgomery, what is this?" From behind her back, she pulled a white shirt, smeared with grass and mud stains.

"Seems to be my Sunday-go-to-meeting shirt."

"Seems?" She tossed it into his lap. "Today is Saturday, and wash day, as you well know, is Thursday. Furthermore, I found this poked under your bed." She shook her head. "I am not your maid. I pity the poor person you marry."

His mind turned to the women Sophie had tried to foist on him—the overbearing schoolmarm with the stubby legs and the Widow Spencer, agreeable enough to look at despite being five years older than him, and who needed a stepfather for her five unruly children. Then there was Rose Kellogg, a fine woman and excellent cook, but she was more friend than prospect.

Besides, he had reconciled himself to bachelorhood. Life was simpler that way. Less prone to complications and the kind of hurt he had witnessed in his father as a result of his mother's untimely death.

Seth reluctantly picked up the shirt. "It's a mess," he admitted.

"It looks like you wore it to wrestle a calf."

He didn't figure it would help his cause to admit that that was precisely how he had soiled the shirt. "I'll stay home tomorrow."

"Oh, no, you don't. Surely you don't want to miss the ice cream social fund-raiser for the Library Society after services."

Despite his aversion to large community gatherings, his mouth watered in anticipation. "No, I guess not."

"Let's make a deal. You need a clean shirt and I need a ride home from town late tomorrow afternoon." She paused as if gathering courage. "After the social, I've been invited for a buggy ride."

He restrained the growl rumbling in his chest. "Buggy ride? With anybody I know?" The fight seemed to go out of her, replaced by an imploring look. Seth sighed. "I should've known. It's Charlie Devane."

"I like him, Seth. Please?"

He could never deny her anything, even as an irrational protective instinct warred with the reality that she was twenty-one years old. "Do I have a choice?"

"Not if you want a clean shirt by tomorrow morning." She took the garment from him and started toward the house. "It's a lovely day," she called over her shoulder, "so when my chores are done, let's ride out to check on the cattle."

Hardly had he finished the harness repair, when Sophie came flying out of the house wearing her riding skirt with britches showing underneath, a plaid flannel shirt, boots and one of his father's old felt hats. "I've attended to the shirt, the stew is simmering and Pa's working on the ledgers, so let's go."

"Saddle up, then." He glanced at the sun, reckoning they'd have three hours or so of riding. He was eager to check on the calves. His brother, Caleb, had commented the other evening about seeing more coyotes than usual. There was much beyond their control in ranching life—predators, storms, prairie fires, rustlers—but he wouldn't trade the challenge for anything.

He had just saddled his pinto, Patches, when Sophie trotted up, mounted on her black mare, Mandy.

"Race you to the creek," Sophie hollered, and before Seth could collect himself, she was ahead of him. Her hat blew off, held only by the string tie, and her carroty-red curls glinted in the sun. After catching up to her, Seth spurred his horse, reaching the creek first.

"You didn't give me a fair start, but I won anyway."

She loosened the reins for Mandy to get a drink. "Men like coming in first." She grinned impishly. "Maybe I let you."

"When did you start paying attention to what men like?"

"I've lived with them my whole life. I would never have gotten my way without exploiting the habits of you males."

Seth mustered a wry grin. "Charlie Devane has his work cut out for him."

They rode side by side to the far pasture. Some cows rested by the small pond, while others grazed, their calves following closely. The rain of the previous night had washed the landscape in vivid color. Seth pulled a small notebook from his pocket and made a notation of the number of calves. Three new ones since his last visit.

"It's beautiful," Sophie said, taking in the panorama. "I liked Missouri," she said, referring to where the Montgomerys had lived until after the War Between the States, "but this is special."

By way of answer, Seth merely grunted. Not all of his memories of Missouri were positive. School, for instance. He'd never been the student Caleb was. Things didn't come as easily to him. Nobody had ever called him "stupid," but the message had been communicated just as effectively through his schoolmates' stifled giggles and eye-rolling. His face still burned when he recalled standing at the blackboard agonizing over his spelling while the rest of the class stared at him. Maybe he could've endured that, but being a head taller than his peers, and gangly at that, had been another source of embarrassment. He still remembered the school-yard chant directed at him:

Goliath, Goliath, you standeth so higheth.
You almost can toucheth the sky-eth!
Giant, giant, GIANT!

Before she died giving birth to Sophie, his mother, and later his father, had assured him his size was an enviable characteristic and that rather than academics, his strength and his talent for making things would be the envy of others. He never quite believed them.

Preoccupied with the past, he hadn't noticed his sister ride off toward the spring hidden beneath the limestone ledge at the boundary of their property. By the time he joined her, she had dismounted and was hunkering near the spring studying something on the ground. "Look, Seth. This is strange."

He hopped off Patches, squatted beside her and immediately saw the source of her curiosity. In the damp ground around the spring pool was a recent set of footprints. Before the rain a few hours ago, the soil had been dry. "Boots. Somebody's been here."

"That's not all. Look here." Sophie pointed to a couple of prints half obscured by the mud near the flowing water. "They're tiny."

Seth squinted. "Sure are." The thought of a child wandering around the place conjured the unwelcome image of a ravenous coyote.

Sophie looked up. "Who do you suppose?"

"Drifters, maybe. Indians passing through. Hard to tell." He got a drink, then mounted his horse. "Let's ride home along the creek to check for campsites."

The sun beat down as they made their way back to the house, alert for hoofprints or other evidence of unwelcome visitors. Nothing. Seth couldn't help thinking of Sheriff Jensen's recent warning concerning unsavory elements in the territory. Even though the footprints suggested a single adult and a child, not a gang, the idea of strangers on their property was unsettling.

The next day after church services, folks gathered on the banks of the Cottonwood River at the base of the main street where the Library Society had erected tables in preparation for the ice cream social. A warm breeze whispered through the leaves of the trees bordering the water, and lilacs perfumed the air. Families were still arriving, spreading quilts on the ground. Some children scampered across the grass chasing rubber balls, while others rode on the merry-go-round or played on the seesaw.

Smiling with satisfaction, Rose watched her friend Bess Stanton approach. A widow and former Civil War nurse, Bess had recently relocated from Maine to be near her sister and had volunteered to help Rose organize today's event.

"Looks like a success," Bess said. "Thank you for asking me to help."

"I couldn't have done it without you." Rose hoped to soon introduce Bess to her father. Their war experiences should give them a great deal in common and she could perhaps be of some use in easing Papa's case load.

When two o'clock approached, the crowd moved toward the bandstand where the Library Society president would make a short speech. At least Rose hoped it would be short. Too long and they risked melted ice cream.

As Rose and Bess made their way closer to the bandstand, Rose saw Lily and Caleb before she spotted Mattie. Rose held out her arms, but to her surprise the child scampered right on past her. "Unca, Unca!"

Seth stood just behind Rose. He knelt down as Mattie approached, a broad grin on his face. "Come to Uncle Seth, sweetheart," he called. And that's exactly what she did—catapulting herself into his arms. The sight of the trusting little girl in the big man's arms made Rose smile. Seth's tenderness, which seemed incongruous with his brawny build, was one of the reasons Rose liked him so much.

Lily and Caleb joined Rose in admiring the tableau. "I've never seen my brother so besotted," Caleb said.

Lily laced her arm through her husband's. "You're pretty besotted yourself, Captain."

Just then the mayor called for order. Blessedly, he was brief in his introduction of the Library Society president, Willa Stone, who thanked everyone for coming out to support the efforts to begin a library with their donations. She concluded by saying, "If you ladies serving the ice cream will move to your places, the feasting can begin."

The applause was robust, and on every side, children broke away from their parents to line up with their spoons and bowls. Rose moved among the servers, helping wherever there was a delay. Her hair had come loose around her face in the effort of scooping. Finally there was a lull, and she wiped her forehead on her sleeve.

"Is there any more?" She looked up to see Seth

standing before her, holding out his bowl. "I liked the sample."

"Second and third helpings are our specialty," Rose answered, "Provided, of course, that you make it worth the Library Society's while."

"I wouldn't short you ladies for anything."

Rose dug deep into the freezer can she had brought and piled his bowl with rich chocolate ice cream. "You fancy chocolate?"

"Yes, ma'am, but then I always fancy your cooking."

Rose hoped he thought her blush resulted from the heat. "Thank you." He seemed reluctant to leave, but neither managed to find the words to prolong the conversation, so when the pastor's boy arrived for seconds, Seth turned away, and for some reason, Rose felt disappointed.

After the ice cream and cookies had been served, the men and boys decided on a baseball game while the women gathered to visit. When Willa Stone approached and asked Rose to accompany her to the church to help count the donated monies, Rose was thankful for the reprieve. Listening to the chatter of her friends concerning pregnancies, teething and patterns for children's clothing had left her feeling awkward. Where did a childless spinster fit into such conversations?

When she and Willa returned with the news of an astonishing total of $31.80 in contributions, those within earshot applauded even as others gathered their belongings, exchanged farewells and made their way toward their homes. Lily sought out Rose to give her a hug. "Everybody is talking about what a success this was. You deserve much of the credit."

Rose took a moment to bask in the compliment

before shrugging. "I only did what anyone would've done." She watched her sister join Caleb and Mattie in their buggy. When they rode off, Rose wrapped her arms around herself, swallowing the lump in her throat. The bustle was over.

Some of the men were dismantling the tables while a few of the townswomen folded tablecloths and disposed of trash. Rose willed herself not to feel a letdown. She had anticipated this occasion with delight, but now that it was over, she would go home to an empty house.

At noon, her father, the town doctor, had received an urgent summons from a man whose wife was experiencing a difficult labor, so he had been forced to miss the social and had not yet returned.

Rose moved among the stragglers, thanking them for their efforts. At last, she reluctantly made her way home, where only Ulysses, her large gray tomcat, would offer companionship. Reaching the house, she glanced at the sun, an hour or two short of setting, and decided to fix a glass of lemonade and rest a while on the front porch.

She settled herself in the wicker rocker and sipped her lemonade. Rose reflected that after years of looking out on a dusty cavalry post, it was pleasant to live on a tree-lined street where she could study the neighbors' houses and watch the passing pedestrian and horse traffic. Off in the distance rose the clock tower of the nearly completed county courthouse, modeled on the French Renaissance style. Three stories high, it was built of native limestone blocks quarried nearby, hand-cut and then transported by wagon to the site. Rose was still awed by such architectural grandeur here on the prairie.

Ulysses lazed on the floor beside her. She had found him cowering under the back stoop the day they moved into the house, his gray fur tangled and one ear missing a small chunk. At the fort, they had never had a pet, so she had enjoyed fattening up Ulysses.

"Afternoon, Miss Rose." At the sound of the male voice, the cat skittered off into the yard.

Lost in her thoughts, Rose had not noticed Seth Montgomery coming up the walk.

He stood awkwardly, one foot on the first porch step. "You mind if I sit a spell?"

"Please." Rose gestured to a straight-backed wooden rocker. "You're always welcome." Seth removed his hat, and the two sat wordlessly until Rose asked, "What occasions your stay in town after the ice cream social?"

"No occasion, really. Pa rode on home, but I'm waiting with the buggy for Sophie."

Rose was never one to pry, but something in Seth's tone impelled her to inquire. "What delays your sister?"

Seth shuffled in his chair, then stretched out his feet. "I may as well say it." The man could never be considered garrulous, and he was clearly uncomfortable. Rose waited. Finally he blurted, "Charlie Devane."

Rose stifled a chuckle. "And the two of them—?"

"On a buggy ride. Together." His face clouded over. "I reckon maybe he's courting her."

"Your sister is quite attractive. Something like this was bound to happen sooner or later."

"Later."

Rose couldn't help herself. She laughed out loud. "Dear me," she sputtered when her breath returned, "you are one protective brother." Then, in that same instant, she sobered, remembering her own older brother, killed at the Battle of Lookout Mountain.

Seth grinned sheepishly and hung his head. "It's stupid of me, but I'm hard put to picture our home without Sophie."

"Change is difficult."

The creaking of the rockers on the wooden floor filled the silence.

He looked up. "Maybe like it was for you when Lily spent those months in St. Louis with your aunt."

"Exactly. I didn't know how I would manage without her. We'd never been apart."

He folded his hands across his chest, lacing his fingers. "Same with me when Caleb left for the war. But Sophie? She's been with us since the day she was born."

"I can't imagine how difficult it was for you when your mother died. It's a wonder you didn't resent Sophie."

"Couldn't. Pa said God sent us Sophie to love."

"And you have. All three of you."

"There're seasons in life. You can't work the land and not recognize that fact. The same way I'm never ready when winter comes, I reckon I'm not ready to let Sophie go."

Rose had a sudden intuition. "Seth, I hope you know that you have a whole family that cares about you. Your father, Caleb, Lily and Mattie. Pa and me. Whatever happens with Sophie and Charlie, we're here."

"I appreciate that."

Out in the street, a wagon rattled past bearing a whole passel of children, laughing and hollering. "Look at that, would you?" Rose said.

"Carefree times."

Rose detected sadness in his voice. "But not carefree times for you?"

He stopped rocking. "No, ma'am. I worry about how my father and I will manage."

"Without a woman, you mean?"

"Exactly. We menfolk are skilled at farming and ranching, but we're no housekeepers."

She was touched by his vulnerability. "You've just named the solution."

He sat forward. "I have?"

"A housekeeper. You and your father could hire a woman to perform domestic duties."

The relief in his face amused her.

"I've pondered that idea. It's a better solution than marrying just any woman."

"Seth. When you marry, it should be for love."

"I know that in my head, but sometimes my worries get the better of me."

"My mother had a saying that might help. She would always remind us, 'All will be well. All manner of things shall be well.'"

Seth fixed his eyes on hers and reached over to cover her hand with his own. "I pray it may be so, Rose." He lingered a moment, searching her face as if some elusive answer could be found there. Then, abruptly, he stood, gathered up his hat and bowed. "Thank you for your counsel. I'll think on what you've said."

Rose got to her feet and walked with him toward the street, as always impressed by his tall, hard-muscled frame. Unlatching the gate, she turned on impulse and said, "If circumstances such as today's bring you to town again, you are always welcome here." Unexpectedly her heart beat a little faster. Usually the two of them were surrounded by family, but something was different about today. She realized she had treasured the time alone with him.

He doffed his hat and started off down the street. Although she couldn't be certain, she thought she heard him mumbling under his breath, "'All manner of things shall be well.'"

Lost in his thoughts, Seth was hardly aware of driving the buggy and was letting the horse find the familiar way back to the ranch. When Sophie had returned to the livery stable with Charlie, she had seemed downright giddy, and his sister was never giddy. He couldn't wait to get her safely home, far from the man who clearly had designs on her. Yet Seth knew he couldn't shield Sophie forever, nor discount the dreamy look on her face.

They were halfway back to the ranch when he finally said, "Is Devane sweet on you?"

Sophie turned and studied his face. "Sweet? What if he is?"

He shrugged and fixed his attention on the road ahead.

She poked him in the arm. "Seth? Wouldn't it be all right if I liked Charlie and he returned the sentiment?"

"I guess, if you're happy." He didn't want to interfere with her pleasure, but his stomach was in a knot.

As if sensing his discomfort, she squeezed his arm. "For the moment Charlie and I are just friends. I'm in no hurry for anything more."

Her words did nothing to diminish the growing realization that his sister was an adult and their time together as a family under one roof was limited.

Sophie changed the subject. "I hope you weren't bored waiting for me."

"I saw Rose sitting on her front porch, so I passed a bit of time there." For some odd reason, he was unwilling to relate much of anything about their conversation.

"Was Ezra home?"

"No."

He had the distinct impression Sophie was smirking, but all she said was, "Rose is a wonderful person."

"And a great cook." His stomach growled with the memory of her chicken and dumplings, not to mention today's chocolate ice cream.

Sophie snuggled next to him and closed her eyes, a contented smile playing over her lips. Seth figured he didn't want to know whether she was thinking about Devane.

Lulled by the steady trot of the horse and the dimming light, neither said anything further, which suited Seth. He appreciated silence. He'd noticed that this afternoon with Rose. She wasn't one of those magpie women like the Widow Spencer. By contrast, when Rose did open her mouth, she made good sense. A man didn't feel like a boorish oaf around her. It dawned on him that'd he'd felt more comfortable with her than he usually did with women. He liked the way her freckles highlighted her blue eyes and the fact she wasn't one of those women all caught up in looking fancy. No, Rose was different. Restful, that's what she was. Restful.

After eating a light supper, Rose picked up her crocheting and settled in her usual chair by the stove. Ulysses cuddled by her side. She needed to feel a living thing, to know there was a buffer for her sudden loneliness. She had been surprised when Seth had stopped by. He was a man of few words, unlike a certain sergeant she could name whose glib tongue and false heart had taught her a harsh lesson. Seth's concern for his sister was laudable, but she worried about his dependence on her. Seth was older than Rose and, like her, probably set in his ways. No housekeeper would ever fill the gap if Sophie left to be married.

As the room darkened, she set aside her crocheting but didn't stir to light the lamp. The house was still, save for the ticking of the clock and Ulysses's contented purr. It had been a long day, but Rose fought sleep, still caught up in the remembrance of her time with Seth and the catch in her breath when he had laid his hand upon hers.

Finally, though, she roused, feeling the need for a bracing cup of tea. When she filled the kettle, she noticed the wood fire in the stove was reduced to embers. Pulling a shawl around her shoulders and carrying a lantern, she went out the back door toward the small barn behind the house. Night had fallen, and quiet, broken only by the occasional barking dog, had descended on the neighborhood.

Inside the barn, she placed the lantern on a hook near the door and made several trips carrying kindling into the kitchen. Then she returned for the lantern. Picking it up and preparing to leave, she was overcome by the eerie sense she was not alone. All the talk of drifters had made everyone skittish. It occurred to her that she was virtually defenseless in the darkened barn. She should scurry inside the house and bolt the doors, but before she could act, she heard a sound coming from the haystack at the back of one of the horse stalls. A high-pitched hiccupping, followed by a soft sigh. She steeled herself, knowing she had to investigate. Holding the lantern high, she tiptoed toward the sound. What she saw on the bed of hay nearly caused her to drop the lantern.

It couldn't be. Not here. Not in her barn.

She knelt beside the figure of a little boy not much older than Mattie. He was fast asleep, his thumb in his mouth, his long, dark eyelashes closed, his chest rising and falling with his breathing. But what was on that chest was the most surprising of all. Rose raised the lantern to better read the note pinned to his tattered little shirt:

PLEEZ. TAKE KIR OF ALF. I KIN'T DO IT NO MORE.

Rose's hands shook. She couldn't grasp the miracle of it. Tears moistened her cheeks, yet she was oblivious to them. She kept staring at the child. Finally, she stood and set the lantern back on the hook.

Returning to the boy, she gently gathered him up in her arms and carried him into the house, all the time marveling at the loving God who had answered Rose Kellogg's prayers.

And then her heart skipped a beat as she suddenly strangled on a new thought. Dear God, her gain might surely be some family's worst nightmare. When she gazed once more into Alf's peaceful face, she made a vow. Despite what tomorrow might bring, for tonight she would love him.

Chapter Two

Rose brushed straw and grass from Alf's grubby clothes and laid a soothing hand on his forehead, brushing away his crow-black hair. She knew soon enough her father would return and questions would abound. For now, though, she treasured this time with "her boy," as she already thought of him. "Suffer little children to come unto me," Jesus had said. Rose lifted her eyes heavenward. "Thank You," she murmured, her eyes filling with tears of joy.

Every now and then, Alf shifted in her arms and then, with a sigh, settled back to sleep. Rose knew she needed to think beyond the present moment. Reason cried out that she shouldn't become too enamored of the boy. Someone who loved him must be wild with worry. Yet, for this wonderful moment, he was in her care. What could she feed him? How would she clothe him? How would he react to the bath he so desperately needed? Her thoughts raced with plans. He could sleep in the trundle bed in her room and surely friends and neighbors would help supply his immediate needs. But that meant telling them about the foundling. Sharing him. All the more reason to cherish this quiet time together before the world intruded.

She must've dozed because the next thing she knew, a hand had settled on her shoulder. "Rose, my dear." Looking up, she saw her father gazing down at her with love and concern. "What have we here?"

"Oh, Papa. It's Alf." She moved her arm so he could read the message.

"How did this come about?" Ezra knelt and gently ran his hands over the boy's body while Rose explained about finding the child in the barn.

"I've been thinking that whoever left him knew from the sign out front that you're a doctor. Or somehow knew we would care for him."

Her father rose to his feet. "And so we will until we locate his people. Sheriff Jensen must be notified."

Rose's breath caught in her chest. So long as she had forbidden herself to form those words in her brain, she had maintained hope. "Please, Papa, must we?"

"You know we must." He sank wearily onto the divan, removing his spectacles and rubbing his eyes. "We do not know what extremity led someone to leave him here, nor how we might help such a person overcome the obstacles preventing them from caring for the tyke. For now, though, we will do all we can to restore this little one to health and security." The clock chimed one, and the two sat in silence until Ezra roused himself. "We all need to sleep. In the morning, I'll examine the boy, and we'll figure out what to do for him until he's returned to his family."

Rose stifled a sob. "Papa, please, can't we keep him? Someone purposely has entrusted him to us. He's the answer to my prayer."

Ezra's voice was husky when he answered. "My dear, I have suspected your need for a child. You will be a wonderful mother…some day. But you will court greater hurt if you become overly attached to this little lad. We cannot predict how his story will end."

"I know you're trying to spare me heartache, Papa. But, you see—" she stood, cradling the child "—I can't help loving him."

Her father shrugged in dismay. "Oh, Rose" was all he managed to say.

"If you will pull out the trundle bed, Alf and I will retire. In the morning, I would appreciate your help bathing him and examining him further."

"Of course." Ezra squared his shoulders. "And after that, I will go to the sheriff."

Never had Rose's intellect so warred with her emotions. Yet she knew her father was right. If Alf was not to be hers, the separation needed to come quickly. Otherwise, she understood that with each passing day, the little boy would become more firmly grafted to her heart. Surely God would not be so cruel as to take from her this gift so wondrously bestowed.

Sunlight filtering through Rose's bedroom window woke her from fitful dreams. Disoriented, she gasped in recognition when she saw the small boy sitting cross-legged on the trundle bed, weaving and reweaving strands of the afghan fringe through his little hands. "Alf?" she said quietly. Ducking his head, he cringed, shrinking in on himself in a self-protective fashion. His cheeks were rosy from sleep. He waited still as a statue, like a wary animal daring her to approach. She slowly sat up, then faced him, her hands outstretched in invitation. Finally he turned his head and cautiously stared up at her through long, dark lashes. When she gathered him in her arms, he stiffened but did not resist. She sensed he was a child who had been schooled to keep quiet and attract little notice. "Alf," she said again. "I won't hurt you. You are safe."

He relaxed against her. "Nawah," he said in a cracked voice.

She had no idea what the nonsense syllables meant, but she decided to answer in kind. "Nawah," she crooned. "Nawah."

He laid his head on her shoulder and began sucking his fist.

"Oh, little one, you must be hungry." She stood and still clutching him to her, managed to put on her wrapper. "Let's see what we can find."

In the kitchen, her father had already stoked the fire and was boiling water on the stove. Rose had an inspiration. "Nawah," she said to Ezra, who raised his eyes speculatively.

To her surprise and joy, the boy pointed at Ezra and whispered, "Nawah."

Catching on to Rose's ploy, Ezra looked straight at the child and said, "Nawah, Alf."

"Alf," the boy echoed as if commending the older man for his acumen.

Rose gently set the boy on her father's lap. "Let me get him some bread."

Rose sliced a thick piece, buttered it and slathered on some plum jam. Alf picked up the bread and attacked it as if he hadn't seen food in days. How distressing to think he'd been ill fed, Rose thought, as she quickly set a skillet on the stove for ham and eggs and poured a glass of milk, which she handed to her father to give to the boy.

"Nawah is a Pawnee word of greeting," Ezra said.

"How do you know that?"

"From the occasional Indian I treated at Fort Larned."

"Do you think he's Pawnee?"

"From the looks of him, I'd say he has at least some Indian blood." Her father rolled up one of the child's pant legs. "See these bruises? I reckon he's had some tough times lately."

Rose gasped at the thought that just came to her. "Do you think someone's abused him?"

"Possibly. Or maybe he's been out on the prairie for a time. Hard to tell."

The mere thought that the child might have been mistreated roused Rose's ire and concern. "He could be safe with us, Papa," she said in a not-so-subtle attempt to avoid the inevitable actions her father had planned.

Ezra held the glass of milk and guided the boy's hands around his so that he could drink. "Please, no arguments. We are obliged to do what we must to locate the parents or relatives."

Tending to the eggs and ham sizzling in the skillet, Rose bit her lip lest she scream out her opposition. Alf slithered from her father's grasp and walked across the floor to her, clutching her around the knees with his jam-sticky hands. "E-nah?" he said. Then he moved toward the door, crying more insistently, *"E-nah?"* Rose looked helplessly at Ezra.

"I think he's looking for his mother. As I recall, *E-nah* is Pawnee for 'mother.'"

The boy pounded on the door, repeating his cry. Rose approached him and led him back to the table, where she sat down, pulling him into her lap and uttering soothing sounds.

Ezra stepped to the stove and dished up the food. As Rose spooned egg into Alf's mouth, his trembling subsided and then he said another word: "Good."

Relief flooded Rose. The boy might know more English than she had first thought. "Yes, good," she echoed.

Ulysses came into the kitchen, pausing in the doorway to stretch, yawn and lick his lips.

Alf watched the animal warily. Ulysses paused at the table, rubbing his furry back across Alf's leg. The boy recoiled in alarm, but when Ulysses repeated the motion, he leaned forward to watch. "Cat," he finally said, then turned to look at Rose. "My cat?"

"Our cat," Rose gently corrected. "*Our* cat."

After breakfast, with great difficulty, Rose and Ezra succeeded in divesting the boy of his threadbare clothes and getting him into the wash tub. His limbs displayed bruises, both old and new, and his skinny body suggested poor nutrition. After wrapping him in a warm towel, Ezra proceeded to examine him while Rose stood anxiously by.

"For the hardships, of whatever kind, that he's had to endure, he's in fair shape," he said. "Medically, he's a trifle malnourished and his growth is a bit stunted for a boy I'd guess is around four. He seems somewhat detached emotionally, but fear will do that. I suspect English has been his second language, thus affecting his facility in it. For as long as we have him, he will need lots of love and attention."

Rose could do that. But she quailed at her father's words, "For as long as we have him." Right then and there, she made a bargain with God. *You have given this child into my care, Lord, and I will tend him with all my heart and soul. Help me to be part of Your greater plan for Alf and to accept Your will for him.*

As she carefully redressed Alf in his tattered clothes, her father picked up his hat and turned to her with words that scalded her ears. "I'm off to the mercantile store to find some new togs for the little feller. After that, I'm obligated to notify Sheriff Jensen."

Rose shrugged, unable to summon words of farewell.

Seth glanced with satisfaction at the lumber stacked in the wagon. Last week he'd hired two more ranch hands, necessitating an addition to the bunkhouse. Before he hauled his load home, he needed to stop at the mercantile to pick up items for Sophie and Lily. Entering the store, he was greeted by Horace Clay, the proprietor. "What brings you to town, Montgomery?"

"We needed supplies from the lumberyard. No way, though, would the ladies let me escape without filling their list." Reaching in his pocket, he handed Clay a creased piece of paper.

Scanning it, Clay nodded. "Shouldn't take long. Make yourself at home."

Seth looked around, uncomfortable in the cramped space crowded with bolts of cloth, tobacco tins, cosmetic potions and ladies' fineries. After walking aimlessly up and down the aisles, he decided to wait on the bench out front. When he opened the door to leave, he was nearly bowled over by Doc Kellogg.

"Whoa, Ezra. What's your rush?"

"Sorry, Seth. I don't mean to be rude, but I'm in a hurry."

Clay looked up from filling Seth's order. "Doc, can I help you?"

"I certainly hope so." He glanced around uncertainly. "Do you carry any ready-made children's clothes?"

Curious about the doctor's request, Seth edged closer.

"Not many. Some dungarees and shirts. A few pairs of shoes. What size?"

When Ezra shrugged in bafflement and held his hand thigh-high, Clay rounded the counter and led him toward the back of the store. "Let's see what I've got."

Seth scratched his head. He'd rarely seen the doctor so agitated or secretive. After a few minutes of mumbled conversation, the two men reappeared with a stack of clothing and one small pair of shoes. "Lemme get Doc fixed up," Clay said, "and then I'll finish your order."

When Ezra turned around with his wrapped bundle, he ducked his head at Seth in a follow-me gesture. Once outside the store, Ezra mopped his brow, then looked straight at Seth. "We've got us a…situation. One Lily needs to know about today. Can you get her a message?"

"Sure can. Is it anything I can help with?"

The older man sighed as if considering options, then spoke quietly. "Before you leave town, stop by the house. You'll see."

"Certainly."

Without saying more, Ezra walked quickly away. Seth watched him, puzzled by their exchange, then went back inside the mercantile to claim his packages. Climbing into the wagon, he guided his team toward the Kelloggs' home. Leaving the wagon by Doc's barn, he knocked on the kitchen door. Ezra answered and ushered him inside. "We had a visitor last night," he said in a neutral tone.

Just then Rose entered the room carrying a thin, raven-haired boy who buried his head in her shoulder when he saw Seth. Surprised by the sight, Seth turned to Ezra. "A patient?"

"In a manner of speaking."

"He's more than that." Rose looked at her father as if daring him to contradict her. "This is Alf. He's been given to me."

"Temporarily. For safekeeping," her father said.

Seth sank into a chair, discomfited by the uncharacteristic tension between father and daughter. "Where did he come from?"

"God," said Rose at the same time her father said, "A desperate parent."

Seth looked from one to the other, confused. "What's going on?"

Rose and her father joined him at the table. The boy took a peek at Seth, and Rose bent her head, kissing the top of his head. Then she looked up. "I found him." In words laden with wonder, she explained about the note.

"Alf," Seth said, nodding. "A strong name."

Again the boy peeked at him. "Nawah," he said in a tiny voice.

Seth looked quizzically at Rose, who nodded encouragement. "Nawah," Seth said.

"Big," the boy answered.

Seth couldn't help himself. He laughed and spread

his arms wide. "Big? Yes, I'm big." Impulsively he slipped to the floor, sat and folded his knees to his chest, making himself as small as possible. "Little."

The boy eyed him as if trying to decide whether he was friend or foe.

"Little man now." Then the boy smiled.

Seth would never be able to explain what happened next, but to his astonishment, Alf wriggled from Rose's grasp, edged toward him and sat facing him, mimicking his position. "Boy. Little, too."

Seth nodded, then, seized by an inspiration, hooked his hands under the child's arms, stood and lifted him above his head. "Now the boy is big."

This time Alf giggled aloud, and in the background Seth heard Rose gasp. "I don't believe it," she said. "You have a magic touch with him."

Lowering Alf and cradling him to his chest, Seth was overcome by an emotion he couldn't name—part protectiveness, part an inexplicable kinship. He pointed to Alf and repeated his name. Then he pointed to himself. "Seth. I am Seth."

Alf eyed him curiously, then stroked Seth's trimmed beard. "Sett. Big. Little. Good." Then he squirmed around in Seth's arms to look at Rose and Ezra. "Sett," he said decisively, as if introducing the man to them.

In the next half hour, Seth heard the full story— Alf's discovery, their concern for his safety and health, the need for clothing and Ezra's plan to notify the sheriff. Seth noticed Rose's frown when her father mentioned the sheriff. From her earlier comments, he had deduced she hoped to claim the boy as her own.

Before Seth rose to leave, he set Alf down and knelt to be nearer eye level. "Alf, I am happy to meet you.

Miss Rose will take good care of you." Then he stood and picked up his hat.

Alf waved at him. "Bye."

Ezra, too, picked up his hat. "Rose, I'm off to see Lars Jensen now."

Seth could hardly bear to look at Rose, whose wistful expression tore at his heart.

When the two men reached the barn, Ezra laid a hand on Seth's shoulders. "You will let Lily and Caleb know. Rose will need Lily's advice."

"I'll go there directly."

The older man's shoulders slumped. "I know what Rose wants, but I can't ignore the ramifications of what has happened. I must inform the sheriff."

Seth nodded at his wagon. "Can I give you a lift? I'll pass right by the office."

"Wouldn't say no," the doctor said.

The two men fell silent as they rode along, each lost in his own thoughts. Before they reached their destination, Seth wondered whether the footprints he and Sophie had discovered several days ago might provide helpful evidence. One adult. One child. He turned to Ezra. "I'm coming with you."

Midmorning of the next day, Rose heard a buggy pull in front of the house and out stepped her sister. Picking up Alf, she raced outside. "Lily, oh, Lily." Overcome by emotion, she couldn't go on, burying her head in her sister's embrace.

In Lily's eyes she read all the concern and love she had expected. "This must be Alf," Lily said. She grazed a hand over the boy's head. "A wonder." She held out her arms, but Alf remained stubbornly in

Rose's grasp. Lily turned and lifted a basket from the buggy. "I've brought a few play things. A set of blocks, a book of nursery rhymes and a wooden wagon model." She looped her hand through Rose's free arm and started toward the house. "I think what we should do is make a list of his needs and solicit our friends and neighbors."

"But no one knows he's here yet." Something clenched inside Rose. She wanted to keep Alf a secret for a bit longer and avoid sharing his story with the curious and the critical.

Lily raised an eyebrow and chuckled. "Darling Rose, you know better. Seth said Papa was at the mercantile and that they both went to the sheriff's office. Believe me, the word is out. I'm just relieved to get here in time to fend off all the folks who will be stopping by to hear about Alf."

Rose kissed the top of Alf's head. "So soon?"

In Lily's expression, she read sympathy tinged with reproach. "The child is yours for now. I have a suspicion what that means to you. What you would like to see happen." They had reached the front door, and Lily turned to her. "Rose, I will tell you what Mother would say. This little boy is God's own child. Right now, He is using your hands and heart to tend him. Pray for His will to be done for Alf…and for you."

Rose acknowledged the truth of her sister's advice, but it would be difficult to be patient, hoping that the sheriff never found Alf's parents. She cringed—that was an unworthy sentiment. How could she wish that a child be permanently separated from his mother and father? That was a sin even beyond envying her sister's good fortune in giving birth to Mattie. Was she acting from purely selfish motives? Just then Alf left her embrace to run across the floor to pick up Ulysses.

Lily chuckled. "My, that cat has certainly taken to your boy."

"As have I," Rose murmured. In that moment, she felt a ray of hope. Surely God wouldn't give her Alf just to rip him away from her. The God she worshipped would never be that heartless.

Chapter Three

Carrying Ulysses with him, Alf retreated into a corner of the kitchen, his back turned on Rose and Lily, his attention centered on the blocks Lily had given him. He made not a sound, only occasionally turning his head as if to assure himself Rose was still in the room. Rose fixed tea for herself and her sister, then joined Lily at the kitchen table. Lily pulled a piece of paper and a pencil from her pocket. "Let's make a list of the boy's needs. I know others will want to help either by sewing or passing along hand-me-downs." She licked the pencil tip and began. "Undergarments, trousers, shirts, stockings…" Her voice faltered. Rose stared off in the distance, knowing she should be contributing to the list but unable to think. Her sister gripped her forearm. "Rose, are you all right?"

Rose's eyes filled with tears and she nodded at the boy quietly building a wall of blocks. In a whisper she said, "It's hard to plan, when he may be taken from me at any moment."

"You must care for him gladly for as long as you

have him." Lily eyed her with concern. "It's only realistic to assume his parents will be found."

"I know." Rose struggled to explain. "Sheriff Jensen came yesterday morning after Papa and Seth informed him of our situation. He asked all kinds of questions. How had I found the boy? Had I noticed any strangers skulking about in the past few days? Had the boy said anything to provide clues?" Rose pulled a handkerchief from her pocket and swiped at her tears. "He searched the barn, examined the note, then tried to talk to Alf, who buried his head in my shoulder and wouldn't even look at the sheriff. All the while I wanted to stop the investigation, to beg the man to leave us be."

"Oh, Rose. I know how attached you've become to Alf, but he is not yours."

"But in my heart he is, Lily, he is." She lowered her voice. "Did Papa tell you we suspect he's been mistreated?"

"If that is so, let us hope such callous, unworthy parents will not be found."

"I pray that may be the case."

"Sheriff Jensen is only doing his duty, Rose."

"I know that. He's already notifying law enforcement offices throughout the region and is having one of his deputies draw up and distribute posters." She caught her breath. "I can't bear to think of Alf's picture on display all over the territory."

"But if it helps?" Her sister gazed into her eyes, as if by a look she could force reason.

"You think I'm being foolish."

"Not foolish, my dear. I know you already love the boy, but I don't want to see you get your heart broken." Lily paused, as if garnering resolve. "You've always been the more practical of the two of us. You know a search is the right and necessary thing to do."

Rose bit her lip, her emotions at war with her intellect. Finally, she nodded. "It's so hard."

"I understand, but in the time you have with little Alf, you must live as Mother always did."

Rose paused to reflect on her precious mother and her difficult last days at Fort Larned. The influenza had ultimately carried her off. Yet even at the last, she'd admonished her daughters with the words Rose now repeated. "We only have today. Live each moment fully."

"Exactly. That advice served Mother well and it has served us well."

For the first time since Lily had arrived, Rose managed a smile. "I'll try."

"All right, then." Lily picked up the abandoned list. "Sunday clothes. That's a must. You will want to show off Alf next Sunday at services."

From the corner came a loud crash followed by a feline shriek. "Gone!" Alf cried. Sure enough, the wall had been destroyed. "I'll do it again."

Rose watched fondly as he began reconstructing the wall. "I hope it will be as easy for us to help him rebuild his life."

"It is in God's hands, Rose, one day at a time."

The next Sunday was a lovely day, the hint of a breeze ruffling the ladies' bonnets and the fragrance of flowers and newly mown grass mingling in the air. As the congregation gathered before the service, many were still talking about the previous Sunday's ice cream social. Ezra, Rose and Alf had taken advantage of the temperate weather to walk to the church.

Yet far from relaxing, Rose clutched Alf's hand and prayed for his smooth introduction to the townsfolk. Over the past few days Bess Stanton, Willa Stone, Horace Clay's wife Essie and a few others had stopped by the house to welcome Alf and to bring gifts of clothing, toys and food. Rose hoped their generosity was a harbinger of things to come this morning.

No sooner had she and her father settled in the pew with Alf huddled between them, than Rose became aware of discreet stares, a few audible *tsks* and condemnatory looks on the faces of Chauncey and Bertha Britten, sitting directly across the aisle. Then with no attempt to lower her voice, Bertha punched her husband in the side and said, "I declare. What does Rose Kellogg think she's doing bringing that half-breed in here?"

Anger and defensiveness overwhelmed Rose, and she longed to call the woman to task. How dare Bertha speak so uncharitably, and in church of all places. Before she could act on her impulse, the congregation rose for the opening hymn, "Savior Like a Shepherd Lead Us." Rose choked on the line "much we need thy tender care," thinking of Alf and his need of "tender care." Then, as if her mother were whispering in her ear, the words "Trust in the Lord always" rose in her heart, defusing her anger.

During the pastor's sermon, she found herself watching Seth Montgomery, as usual seated near the front with his family. She had been unprepared last Monday for the way he had so immediately gained Alf's trust. If she hadn't already witnessed his devotion to Mattie, she would never have believed the man could've intuited what Alf needed. The little boy interrupted her reverie by crawling onto her lap and sitting back against her chest, solemnly studying his surroundings. Then smiling, he pointed and called out, "Sett!"

The Brittens glared at him and Rose heard a few shushes, but Seth turned around, his eyes sparkling, and waved at Alf. "My Sett," the boy mumbled before settling contentedly against Rose. "Big."

Leaving the church after the service, the Brittens skirted Rose and Alf, as if fearing contamination. When Bertha passed by, she hissed at Rose, "What are you thinking? You, an unmarried woman!" Once again, Rose barely withheld her retort, saved from injudicious action by Seth, who gathered a delighted Alf in his arms and led them out to the churchyard.

Fuming, Rose turned to her father and Seth. "Did you hear Bertha?"

Ezra nodded. "You'll have to expect some of that from the more judgmental folks."

"Rose, don't waste your energy on them," Seth advised, all the while jouncing Alf in his arms.

"Sett. You, me. Big!"

In response, Seth lifted the boy skyward and whirled around to Alf's delighted laughter.

Seth's playfulness had settled Rose's blood pressure. He seemed the most even-dispositioned of men. She couldn't think of a time at their family gatherings when she had ever seen him out of sorts. Quiet, yes. Content to observe, but never surly.

Lily, Caleb and Mattie approached, and when Seth saw them, he lowered Alf to the ground, where he stood clinging to Seth's leg. Rose held her breath, praying Mattie would not be jealous of the boy and the attention he was receiving from her beloved uncle. She need not have worried. Mattie toddled toward Alf, flung her arms around him and laughed gleefully. "Brudder," she said.

Startled, the boy extricated himself from her grasp. "Alf," he said by way of correction.

Lily leaned over. "Alf is not your brother, Mattie. He is your friend."

Mattie shook her head stubbornly. "Brudder." Then she took hold of Alf's hand. "My Alfie." And off she went, with her new playmate in tow.

Before the adults could take chase, Seth held up his hand. "Let me. You visit." With long strides he caught up to the children and steered them toward a patch of grass under a large elm tree, where he sat down, a child balanced on each knee. From a distance, he appeared to be telling them a story. .

Lily slipped her hand into Rose's. "That's quite a picture."

"Seth must be touched by fairy dust. The children adore him."

Lily looked pointedly at Rose. "He's lonely."

"Yet he seems content with his lot."

"That's what he wants us to believe. He would never have any of us worry about him."

Rose heard the hint of concern in her sister's words. "And yet you do worry…"

"He needs a life of his own. He will make some woman a devoted husband." Lily hesitated, then shocked Rose with her next words. "Are you interested?"

What was Lily suggesting? Why, Rose had never in her wildest dreams considered the possibility. If she had ever confessed her unfortunate experience at Fort

Larned while Lily was away in St. Louis, her sister would know better than to indulge in such romantic fantasies on her behalf. But that phase of her life was closed, and it was better no one in her family knew of it. "Lily, Seth is like family. I could never think of him as a potential suitor even if I were so inclined, which I'm not. Besides, he doesn't lack for women who are interested in him. Look." She pointed to Seth, who had now gathered a group of children around him. Standing among the youngsters was the Widow Spencer, a Cheshire cat grin dominating her face.

Lily followed her gaze. "She's not his type."

Rose hoped Lily was right because that woman was looking for a provider, not a sweetheart, and Seth deserved a sweetheart.

Lily squeezed her hand. "A piece of advice, sister." She smiled as if she knew a secret. "Never say never."

After their parents had collected the children, Seth stood and stretched, a feeling of contentment blooming in his chest. He customarily avoided idle chitchat, but, for some reason, with children, he was downright talkative. He couldn't get over how attentively they had listened to his story about Noah and the Ark. When Rose arrived to collect Alf, he didn't seem to want to part company. "Sett? You come, too?"

Seth explained that he was with his family and couldn't stay. Rose hoisted Alf on her shoulder, and the little fellow kept waving as they walked away.

Seth remained under the tree, trying to determine why the sight of Rose with the little boy moved him so profoundly. Rose was attentive and loving with the child, and he knew she would move heaven and earth if she could assure Alf's permanent well-being and happiness.

A memory swept over him, one that threatened to unman him—his mother's presence was so real he felt as if he could reach out and touch her. He longed just once more to hear her say, "My wonderful Seth, my dear boy, I love you so." Just once more to wrap his arms around her neck and inhale her special cinnamony fragrance. But she was gone, and he had never quit missing her.

That must be why the sight of Alf and Rose moved him so. Seth worried, though, that the day would come when Rose would have to relinquish Alf to his parents. She would be devastated. "Are you coming home with us?" Caleb clapped a hand on Seth's shoulder. "Sophie's going to be disappointed if her roast is overdone."

Seth shook his head in mock despair. "Heaven forbid. Isn't Charlie Devane invited to partake of our Sunday dinner?"

Caleb laughed. "You know very well he is. Our sister has been slaving over the stove for days now."

"Is a burnt roast enough to discourage him?"

"Do I detect the words of an overprotective big brother?"

"You do."

Caleb dropped the playful tone. "She's a woman, Seth. With a mind of her own. This day was bound to come."

The brothers started walking toward the wagon. "That doesn't mean I have to like it." Seth mused that it seemed like only yesterday he had tended his baby sister, changing her nappies and feeding her oatmeal when his father had been paralyzed by grief.

"No, it just means you need to worry about your own life, not Sophie's." He poked Seth in the ribs. "I saw the Widow Spencer eyeing you—like you were a prize bull at a cattle auction."

Seth groaned audibly.

They were nearly to the wagon, when Caleb asked, "Did you speak with Lars Jensen today?"

"I was busy with the children. Why?"

"He's called a meeting for Wednesday late afternoon to discuss the drifters and gangs moving through the territory."

Any lingering euphoria Seth had experienced with the little ones faded with the thought that danger could be lurking on the vast prairie, threatening those he loved.

Rose awakened Monday morning to the patter of rain on the roof, which in a matter of minutes, grew in intensity to a fierce downpour. Rivulets streaked the window panes and thunder rumbled in the distance. She left Alf sleeping and dressed quickly. In the kitchen she stoked the cookstove with kindling from the wood box, fed Ulysses and put on the kettle, all before mixing up pancake batter. Her father arrived just as the coffee was ready. "Some storm," he said, blowing on his scalding drink.

While her father read his daily Bible lesson, Rose finished her breakfast preparations. She worried about the way he pushed himself and wished he could find some help. Lily had filled that role before leaving for St. Louis, but Rose had never had her sister's knack for medicine. As she poured batter into the skillet, she remembered that she had not acted on her hope that Bess Stanton might be of use in her father's practice.

Rubbing his eyes, Alf stumbled into the kitchen, his hand-me-down nightshirt hanging around his ankles. "Rain," he whispered.

Her father set his spectacles aside and held out his arms. "Naweh," he said. Alf climbed into Ezra's lap, hiding his face. "Did the thunder wake you?"

"Loud." The boy's voice was muffled.

"You're safe here with us," Ezra reassured him.

"E-nah?" Rose barely heard the word, but she had grown quite familiar with it. Often in his sleep, Alf would cry out for his mother. She hoped he had had one who loved him, even as she would never understand how a caring parent could've abandoned the boy.

After breakfast, she helped him dress while her father went out in the deluge to make house calls. Alf would have to play indoors, so she settled him with the blocks he seemed to love. She was amazed by the concentration with which he constructed a high wall and then knocked it down, only to begin the whole process again. She set up the ironing board and hummed along as she bent to the task. The periodic collapse of the block wall and the hiss of steam were the only sounds until she became aware that each time Alf knocked down the wall, he muttered, "Good."

Rose laid the iron on its rest and went over to the boy and sat on the floor beside him. "It's a very fine wall," she said.

"No." He put another block on top. "Cage."

She was puzzled. Where would he learn such a word? *"Cage?"* Then just beyond the wall she saw the small rag doll she had given him. She picked it up. "Who is this, Alf?"

He didn't look up, just continued placing block on block. Finally he mumbled, "E-nah," then grabbed the doll from her and put it on the far side of the wall. "Cage," he said again. Then added more loudly, "Stay there."

Rose felt her heart pounding. "Was your E-nah in a cage?"

As if he hadn't heard her, Alf triumphantly destroyed the block wall. "Good." He picked up the doll and handed it to Rose. "Run away."

Could it be that somehow he and his mother had been held in jail? By whom? Where? The answers would have to be coaxed from the boy over a period of time. Rose sighed, praying for the patience to let the boy progress at his own pace. What she wouldn't give to know about his past.

With a flash of inspiration, she remembered the sack of marbles one of the soldiers had given her father in gratitude for his recovery from malaria. Rose led Alf to a chair, then slowly opened the bag. Twenty or more marbles of varying colors nestled inside. She quickly retrieved several cereal bowls, then showed him the contents of the bag. Withdrawing one agate, she said, "Green," and placed it in a bowl. Next, she found a blue marble, and mouthing the color, she put it into a second bowl. She handed a black marble to the boy, who studied it intently. Rose pointed to the first bowl. "Green?"

He shook his head vehemently.

"Blue?"

"Not blue," he said, pulling a third bowl toward him.

"Black," Rose instructed, saddened to think no one

had taught him his colors and unsure how much English he'd heard from his parents.

Just before twelve, the back door opened, and Ezra stepped inside, raindrops pooling at this feet. He took off his broad-brimmed hat, shook it and hung it on the peg inside the door. "I feel like Noah."

Alf looked up. "Noah. Sett told me. Big boat." Then he went back to sorting marbles that Rose had found for him and repeating the colors under his breath.

Ezra took off his spectacles and wiped them on a kitchen towel. "The marbles. What a good idea."

Rose wanted to tell him about her morning, about the hint Alf had given concerning what might have happened to him and his mother, but before she could begin, her father thrust out a letter he must've picked up at the post office. "Mighty big news," he said. "It's from your Aunt Lavinia."

My dear Ezra,
As you know, Henry died this past autumn, and it has been difficult to adjust to his absence. I continue with my social engagements and charity work here in St. Louis, but my heart is no longer in them. It was our custom to summer in Newport with dear friends, but I find that prospect daunting without my husband. In casting about for an alternative, I have hit upon a solution. Other than the months Lily lived here with us, I have scarce spent any time with the only family remaining to me—you, Rose and Lily. And now little Mattie, my great-niece!

Through the auspices of a Kansas agent, I have let a house in Cottonwood Falls for the

*months of June through November and should
arrive sometime during the first week of June.*

*I know this may seem sudden and presumptu-
ous, but I am curious about the West and about
my family's circumstances. I will wire you with
details of my arrival by rail. My maid will be accompanying me, and I trust someone can meet
us at the depot.*
Ever your affectionate sister-in-law,
Lavinia

Rose was stunned. Cottonwood Falls, Kansas, was a
far different place than the cultured environment of St.
Louis. She scanned the letter again. "Does Lily know?"

He shook his head. "When the weather clears, we
will go to the ranch to tell her."

"Papa, I don't mean to be rude, but it is difficult to
picture the woman I remember from my childhood and
that Lily has described spending time on the prairie."

"I agree," her father said. "But she is your mother's
only sister, and we will do our best to make her welcome. Your mother would've wanted that."

Just then Alf dropped a marble that clattered across
the floor. "Yellow," the boy hollered, leaving the chair
to collect the elusive marble.

"Yellow?" Ezra said. "Yes, sir. What a bright boy
you are."

Rose handed the letter back to her father. Aunt Lavinia had always been a distant, though imposing figure to her, moving in a sophisticated world beyond
Rose's comprehension. Lily had thrived in that world
for a time until its glitter faded. But for herself? She
could not imagine any point where she and her aunt

might find something in common. She already felt intimidated and Lavinia hadn't even arrived.

Then her breath stopped. Alf. What would her aunt think of the boy? Would Lavinia Dupree, like the Brittens, condemn their family for taking him in?

She drew a deep breath and lifted her chin. She would do whatever was necessary to shield Alf from criticism. Slowly she became aware of her father's compassionate scrutiny. As if he'd read her mind, he simply said, "Reserve your judgment, Rose."

Chapter Four

Seth stood in the back of the Grange Hall late the following Wednesday afternoon, studying the restive crowd congregated there. All eyes were on Sheriff Jensen. Rumors concerning cattle rustlers, thieves and isolated bands of renegade Indians operating in east central Kansas had stirred concerns among the county citizenry.

Caleb, standing beside him, punched him in the ribs. "We need a plan. We can't be leaving Lily, Mattie and Sophie unprotected. Until we're assured the problem has been addressed, one of us or a hired hand should be near the houses at all times."

Before Seth could agree, the sheriff stepped forward and signaled for quiet. "Lots of information has been going around, some of it accurate and some, pure rubbish. I've called this meeting to tell you what we know and what you can do to help. I believe the recent incident where somebody stole tack out of Hank McGuire's barn is an isolated case. However, it suggests a need for vigilance on all our parts. From time to time, we have men, some desperate, some organized, crossing this region and bent on no good."

"Gangs, you mean," the owner of the general store called out.

The sheriff clenched his jaw. "Now, Horace, that's a bit of an exaggeration. Certainly some folks down on their luck make their way through the territory. Three fellas were apprehended last weekend in Council Grove, suspected of robbing stores. Unpleasant as this news is, most vagabonds are homeless and looking for work. Yes, some gangs operate throughout the West, but none have been spotted in Chase County."

"It's a bit hard to tell the difference—drifter or robber," muttered Chauncey Britten, the undertaker.

"No worry which one when they finally need your services," one wag shouted to the enjoyment of the crowd.

Sheriff Jensen again signaled for attention. "Here's what I propose—that those living in town be alert to strangers and inform my office when anyone you don't know rides into town. As for those of you living beyond town, instruct your hands to keep an eye out and be ready to notify your neighbors if you see something unusual. What we don't want is folks going off half-cocked and creating trouble."

A beefy, red-faced farmer jumped up. "So we're not supposed to protect our property?"

"That's not what I said," the sheriff responded. "Caution is warranted, but take action only if you feel your property or family are imminently threatened. If at all possible, before you do anything, notify us."

"Ride eight miles to you while some renegade roams my ranch?"

"Git off your haunches, Jensen, and git rid of these varmints!"

The cries from the audience were taking a toll on the sheriff, who was a better lawman than speaker. As the hubbub continued, Seth felt Caleb stiffen beside him and knew his brother was about to intervene. Sure enough, Caleb raised his hand and cut a swath toward the front of the room, much as he must have led a cavalry charge. He strode right up on the platform. Seth followed closely behind to support his brother. "Folks," Caleb said in a commanding voice, "this is just the kind of mob reaction that'll get us in trouble. Let's back off and think about this."

"The situation calls for a united approach," Seth added.

Amid some grumbling, the men reluctantly took their seats, and Seth heard one say to his companion, "Might as well listen to the Montgomery boys. They generally make sense."

When the group calmed down, Caleb continued. "We all know Lars Jensen is a conscientious sheriff. Nothing has happened here to cause us to mount some aimless posse. Be reasonable. Many of you have been residents of Chase County for several years or more."

Seth picked up the thread. "Haven't we been satisfied with our law enforcement? Lately we've had one incident. No physical harm was done, and the guilty party didn't loiter in these parts, I suspect because we have a no-nonsense sheriff. Now, then, let's do as Jensen advises. Be watchful, notify him of any concerns and do our best to protect our womenfolk and children from rascals, but also from baseless fears."

The meeting closed with general agreement and a few apologies to the sheriff.

Afterward, as Seth and Caleb rode side by side toward home, Seth thought about Caleb's leadership. Although his military service had resulted in horrific experiences, it had also matured his younger brother. When their paths diverged, Seth gave voice to his observations. "Caleb, you did a good thing back there. We don't need mob thinking."

At first, he thought Caleb hadn't heard him, but then his brother answered him in a grim voice. "No, we don't. I've seen what a mob can do. Nothing uglier." He flipped the reins to steer his mount to the right. "Good night, Seth." Then he trotted off, without a backward glance.

Seth watched his brother until he was out of sight. There was much he didn't know about what Caleb had endured during his military career. It was painful to remember the eighteen-year-old who had ridden off to war with the enthusiastic patriotism and naïveté of youth. Seth continued to feel guilty that he had not joined the conflict, but his role at the family gristmill in Missouri had been critical.

Supplying the troops was a form of service, too, but it had spared him from the brutality and bloodshed in which his brother had, perforce, been engaged. The wonder was that Caleb still had his feet so firmly planted on the ground.

Although Caleb had told him few details of his army experiences, from things Lily had said, Seth believed his brother had spoken more openly with her and that such confidences, coupled with Lily's understanding, had been redemptive.

The setting sun lighted the trail back to the ranch. In a way, he envied the closeness of Lily and Caleb. It seemed they could talk about anything. They must have deep trust in one another, he reflected. He himself wasn't much of a talker. Would there ever be a woman in whom he might confide his guilt concerning the war? His concern for Sophie? His sorrow at the death of his mother?

Not likely.

He was almost home before a sudden recollection speared his defenses. Rose Kellogg. A week ago Sunday. He'd talked with her about Sophie…about his mother, hadn't he? Why her? He shook his head in bewilderment and spurred his horse. Such confessions made him feel exposed. Weak. It wouldn't happen again.

Settling comfortably in the saddle, he studied the rolling hills, veiled in twilight shadows. He didn't know what it was about the land but it awakened deep feelings in him, probably born of his boyhood on their Missouri farm. From the blossoms of spring to the berries of summer to the tart apples of autumn, the place had been his kingdom. He and Caleb helped with whatever chores small boys could perform, then fished in the river, rode their ponies or aimed slingshots at hapless birds. A long time ago. Before the War Between the States. Years before they moved west to start the ranch.

Boyhood freedoms were one thing. It was more difficult to think about the time his mother died…. Baby Sophie. By all rights, he should have hated her. She'd taken his mother. But Pa never saw it that way. He'd gathered Caleb and him around the crib the day after their mother's funeral. "Boys," he'd said in a choked voice, "your mama is gone, but she left us this gift from God."

After that, there was never any question. Anybody who remotely threatened their sister met Caleb and Seth's wrath. But that didn't happen often. Sophie was too loveable. She'd never in her life met anyone that didn't interest her. Seth groaned. Charlie Devane. A talented construction man, courteous with a ready laugh. Why did thinking about the fellow cause him to grind his teeth? Even if he didn't want to admit it, he knew, of course. Sophie liked Charlie. Really liked him. Seth always thought of her as his little sister, but she was of age. She could marry.

He was stabbed by a pang of loneliness. Home without Sophie would be like sunshine blotted out by clouds. He didn't want to think about it. He wouldn't. Instead, he would focus on…the cattle herd. Calves. There. That was a safe topic. Something over which he could exercise some measure of control.

Yet to his chagrin, cattle didn't fill his mind at all. Instead, his thoughts once more turned to Rose Kellogg, to the blush suffusing her face when he complimented her cooking.

Rose. A safer topic than Sophie, for sure. Wasn't it?

What with the rain on Monday, followed by wash day, it was Thursday before Rose, Alf and her father could manage the drive to Lily's. At the previous night's meeting, Caleb had told Ezra about a hired hand with a nasty lingering cough, so the trip had a twofold purpose—to offer medical advice and to plan with Lily for Lavinia's upcoming visit.

Lavinia and Henry Dupree had treated Lily to fine

dresses, elegant social activities and the cultural outings for which she had longed. At one point Rose had feared she would lose her sister to the charms not only of metropolitan life but to the courtship of wealthy Lionel Atwood. Only later had Rose learned that Lionel, aghast at Lily's rushing to the aid of a former slave who had been run over on the street, had spurned her, accusing Lily of publicly humiliating him. Rose sniffed. Good riddance.

She herself barely remembered Lavinia Dupree. Only once could she remember her aunt visiting her mother's parents and the Kelloggs in Iowa. A girl of about twelve at the time, she remembered being told to be on her best behavior and speak only when spoken to. She recalled her mother talking about Lavinia's wealthy husband and elegant home, seeming wistful about the divergence of their paths.

It was nearly noon when the buggy crested the hill behind Lily's home. Breathing in the fresh spring air and reveling in the miles of prairie grass dancing in the breeze, Rose thanked God once again for bringing her and Papa here to reunite with Lily and her family. And now, Alf completed the circle. "Bird!" Alf squirmed in her lap and pointed to a fence post where a hawk surveyed the countryside.

"That's right. A bird. His name is Mr. Hawk."

Alf turned to her with a puzzled look. "Mister? He's not a man."

Ezra chuckled. "Smart, that boy."

Rose joined in the laughter. "You're right, Alf. I suppose his name is just 'hawk.'"

"Hawk." Alf nodded several times as if to fix the information in his brain. "Bird," he said in summary.

As they approached the barnyard, Lily walked toward them holding Mattie, scattering the chickens pecking in the dirt. "What a treat! We're so glad to see you."

Ezra helped Rose and Alf to the ground, then embraced Lily. "I'll be back after I check on Caleb's patient. Is the fellow in the bunkhouse?"

"Yes. Caleb is with him. I fear he is worse this morning."

Mattie wriggled out of her mother's arms and ran to embrace Alf. "Brudder. I see you."

The adults smiled indulgently. No amount of correcting Mattie about the meaning of *brother* had changed her response to Alf.

Alf backed off, eyed the little girl and then pointed to her dress. "Blue," he said proudly. "Blue shirt."

Mattie looked down as if she had never noticed her frock. "Dress, Alfie, dress," she corrected. "Blue dress."

"Lemonade, anyone?" Lily gathered the children and led them into the kitchen. Rose took a lingering look at the neat, fenced yard, the large vegetable garden and sturdy stone dwelling. Lily was blessed by her surroundings.

Inside, Rose settled at the table while Lily produced a doll and a few tin soldiers for the children, who were soon lost in a world of make-believe.

"At last night's meeting, I presume Papa told Caleb about Aunt Lavinia's upcoming visit."

"Yes, I can't wait to talk about it. Truth to tell, I'm completely flummoxed by the news. It's so out of character for her. I know she must miss Uncle Henry, but she thrives on the fashions and social events she can find only in a city. The picture of her out here on the frontier both worries me and makes me chuckle. The very idea of Lavinia Dupree wearing a homespun dress!"

Rose mustered a wan smile before speaking. "She has rented a house and is bringing her maid."

"So she'll be quite near you and Papa."

"That's exactly what I'm afraid of. I have no idea how to talk with her. My experience is so limited." Then Rose moved to the crux of the matter. "And what if she's horrified by the idea of my taking in Alf?"

Seeing her sister's distress, Lily leaned closer and covered Rose's hand with her own. "I'll be the first to admit that Aunt Lavinia can appear imposing and judgmental. Yet, in many ways, I think you may find her demeanor a mask concealing a generosity of spirit."

"I hope you're right. Perhaps I'm overprotective of Alf?"

"As you certainly should be. As we all are where our children are concerned. Alf is doing well, isn't he?"

Rose smiled, warming to the topic of her boy and his progress with speech and the clear evidence of his intelligence. "His sores and bruises have healed under Papa's care and every day he comes out of his shell a bit more."

"I can see that." Lily nodded to the corner of the room where Mattie and Alf were acting out some play-let of their own devising.

Just then, Ezra entered the kitchen and moved to the pump to wash his hands. His expression was grim.

"Papa?" Lily said by way of inquiry.

"Your man has pneumonia. If he responds to treatment, he has a chance. I've given Caleb instructions. Only time will tell."

Lily stood up and moved to the larder. "I've made some cornbread and have beans to warm up for a meal before you return to town."

Over lunch, Ezra recalled some memories of Lavinia and underscored Lily's urging of patience. "We mustn't for a moment forget," he said, "that regardless of the situation, the woman is grieving. Both the life-long relationship, whatever it may have been, and her position in St. Louis society. We cannot know exactly what impulse has led her to Chase County, but we are her only family and we *will* welcome her."

On the way back to town, Alf drowsed in Rose's lap, and Papa seemed miles away, perhaps concerned with a patient or lost in memories of Mama and Lavinia. Rose's eyes were drooping when she was brought to awareness by the sound of horses approaching. A jolt of fear wound through her as she remembered what Papa had said about the men's meeting the night before. Beside her, Ezra sat up straight and, shading his eyes, squinted at the road ahead. Finally he sighed in relief. "It's Sophie and Seth."

Sure enough, racing toward them were the brother and sister, initially oblivious to the buggy. Then Seth wheeled his horse and held up his hand to halt Sophie. The pair trotted slowly toward the buggy. "Sorry for alarming you," Seth said, doffing his hat.

Sophie grinned. "Me, too. It's just as well, though, because Seth was winning our race." She swatted her hat at her brother.

Rose studied Sophie, confident and comfortable in her unconventional riding skirt and dust-covered boots.

Watching the two riders so at ease with one another, Rose had greater appreciation for Seth's concern about Sophie's ultimate departure from the ranch.

The cessation of buggy movement roused Alf. "Sett!" He stood up and held out his arms.

"Ready for a horseback ride, Alf?" Seth spurred his horse to the side of the buggy and glanced quizzically at Rose, as if asking for permission. She nodded.

Seth plucked Alf out of the buggy and settled the boy in front of him. "Horse! Horse!" Alf waved delightedly to Ezra and Rose. "Brown, white," he crowed. He patted Seth's leg and then stroked the horse's neck. "Big. Sett big. Horse big."

Unaccountably, Rose blinked back tears. Her boy looked so happy, and Seth held him as if he were a bundle of gold.

Sophie pulled her mount alongside Seth's. "Are you ready, Alf? It's gallop-a-gallop time." She winked at Rose and trotted ahead of Seth and Alf. When Seth followed, Alf's delighted giggle filled the growing distance to the buggy.

Grinning, Ezra patted Rose's leg. "We'd best follow. I doubt Seth and Sophie are planning to go clear into town. Nice of them to give Alf a ride, though."

"We'll probably never hear the end of it."

"Right. 'Big. Brown. White. Horse.'"

Rose nodded, silently filling in another of Alf's new words, a word that was becoming increasingly important to her, as well. *Sett.* She drew herself up short. It was nonsense to dwell on such foolish notions and risk jeopardizing a perfectly good friendship.

Chapter Five

Seth relinquished Alf into Rose's care, and he and Sophie turned for home, trotting side by side. Seth could tell his sister was itching to say something, and the urge finally got the best of her. "Well, now, brother dear, what was that all about?"

Seth pulled his hat down over his eyes, determined to avoid his sister's knowing smirk. "I have no idea what you're talking about."

"Balderdash. You're quite attached to that little fellow. And he to you."

"So?"

"You'll have to be careful not to let him down. In his young life, he's probably had more than his share of disappointments." She waited, as if permitting him the opportunity to think about his role. "To prevent that from happening, you'll have to spend a good deal of time with him."

He knew what she was going to say before she said it, and sure enough, the next words out of Sophie's mouth were "and with Rose."

He grimaced. The situation was a double-edged

sword. On the one hand, Sophie was right. He was attached to Alf. He liked the boy. But if he was honest, he also liked Rose and found himself thinking about her way too often. To put an end to Sophie's probing, he responded, "I'll spend time with them when it suits my convenience, but I won't be making any special trips to town."

Sophie shot him a skeptical look but had the grace to keep her mouth shut the rest of the way back to the ranch.

The silence, instead of comforting him, was unnerving, especially since now, as if the power of suggestion held sway over him, all he could think about was Rose. She was a good woman in every way. He liked talking to her and watching her being such a caring mother for Alf. He squelched the longing rising deep in his chest. He so wanted to be someone's father, but he'd long ago decided he couldn't do that to himself or to some innocent woman, no matter how much he loved her. He'd watched his own mother die giving birth. He'd witnessed his father crumple at her bedside, wailing out his pain.

Marriage was serious business and it didn't always end happily. Oh, he entertained fantasies about having the kind of union Caleb and Lily had, but fate was capricious. There were no guarantees. It was cleaner, simpler to live the bachelor life, enjoying other people's children without any of the responsibility. That way he could be at peace with the God he often questioned and avoid causing pain for others.

Seth saw his father waiting for them at the barn. After they'd stabled their horses, Sophie hurried into the house to begin dinner preparations, but Andrew laid a hand on Seth's shoulder. After discussing the herd and the upcoming banknote due date, his father came to the point. "You're mighty fond of that little Alf." When Seth merely nodded, his father went on. "Children take to you. Have you thought about settling down, getting married?"

Seth groaned, suspecting his father and sister had been discussing his single state, and that they were in cahoots. "Yep. I reckon it's not for me."

There was no escaping his father's steely gaze. "Why not?"

Seth struggled for words, then simply shrugged.

"It's because of your mother."

Seth swallowed, unable to speak.

His father planted his hands on his son's knees. "Look at me. I know what you're thinking. You were there that night. You saw something no small boy should ever witness." Andrew heaved a deep sigh. "It was horrible and made no sense, but sometimes bad things just happen. Whatever you may think, though, God didn't fail us. He sent us beautiful Sophie." He leaned back then, folding his arms across his chest. "I don't know much, son, but I know this. Love is worth the risk. You've always shied away from that risk."

Stunned, Seth realized this was more truth from his father than he'd ever heard. "I don't want to hurt anybody," he said.

"Can't promise that, Seth."

Maybe if he weren't so methodical, dissecting everything. If he could ever, just once, be passionate about a woman, then…but that was foolishness. He had no idea even how to court one. "It's just who I am, Pa."

His father stood up and pulled his pipe out of his

shirt pocket. "Maybe, maybe not. Be open, son. God has great things in store for you." Andrew struck a match on his boot, then puffed on his pipe, the savory tobacco aroma filling the air.

Seth wanted to believe his father, but it was difficult. "Best get washed up," he said, then walked toward the house, all the while sensing his father's eyes on his back.

Friday was baking day and after wiping down the table, Rose stood back in satisfaction, inhaling the yeasty smell of bread and surveying the pastries in the pie safe. Alf sat contentedly munching on a warm slice lathered with apple butter and sprinkled with cinnamon. Rose placed her hands in the small of her aching back and stretched, then took off her flour-dusted apron and turned to Alf. "How about a walk around town?"

He clapped his sticky hands. "See some horses?"

Rose laughed. "Yes, indeed, but first finish your bread so you can wash up."

The boy took another big bite and looked at her with sparkling eyes. After he'd finished, she washed his hands and face, and they set off down the street. For Alf, exercise was not the point of their excursion—it was discovery. First he hunkered to examine a woolly caterpillar, then skipped on down the street to pluck a dandelion from a neighbor's lawn. "Here, Rose. I give you a posy." Rose smiled, knowing no exotic orchid would ever be as beautiful.

Along the way they stopped to visit with several friends. But spotting Sheriff Jensen striding toward them, Rose stepped into his path and with trepidation asked the question looming over her every thought. "Any news concerning Alf?"

He removed his hat and with a slight bow said, "Nothing yet. Sorry."

After they parted, Rose sighed with no small amount of guilt, grateful that the lack of news ensured her continued care of Alf.

Later, at the corner of Broadway, Bertha Britten approached, her black hat perched just so on her massed hair, one spindly arm hooked into the handle of a shopping basket. Head down, as if on an important mission, she nearly ran into them. "Bertha, good afternoon."

The woman stopped dead in her tracks and stared at Rose. "I'm sorry. I don't have time to palaver. I'm in a hurry."

Alf tugged on Rose's skirt, "I seed this lady before."

"Yes, in church. Bertha, you remember my Alf."

Inexplicably, Bertha's face turned red. "Of course, I remember, but I hardly think he's 'your' Alf. Why, you're not even married." She hoisted her basket in front of her chest like a shield. "Now, excuse me, but I have other things to do." She brushed past them, *tsking* as she went.

Rose sagged against a hitching post. Alf sneezed, then tugged on her arm. "That's a mean lady. C'mon. Get away." When Rose looked down, his little face was one big frown. She took a handkerchief from her pocket and wiped his nose.

"She could have been nicer, but we're not going to let her ruin our day, are we? Look over there." She pointed to the livery stable where two horses were just being saddled.

"Horses!" He broke away from her. "Sett!"

"Oh, no, honey. Those horses are for other men. Seth is working at the ranch."

His eyes widened in disappointment. "Far away?"

"Yes, but you'll see him Sunday at church."

"Sunday. Sett. Good." He swung her hand back and forth as he led her to study the horses. "Big horse. Brown. Little one. Gray." He stared at the horseflesh with all the interest of a livestock broker.

Finally Rose succeeded in dragging him away, but not before he'd sneezed several times. Dust from the livery, no doubt. She wanted to go by the nearly completed courthouse, which loomed impressively above the prairie. Just then, though, in the shadow of a basement door overhang, she noticed a couple, oblivious to the world, entwined in an embrace.

Rose stopped in her tracks, aware of a strange tingling in her chest. Once she had known such stolen moments, had felt whiskers caress her face and had melted through and through as warm lips sought hers. What a fool she had been, actually picturing herself swept into the dashing sergeant's arms and carried off to a future of loving nights, of babies, of actually daring to think of herself as desirable. And maybe he had cared for her. More likely, not. Loneliness can make a man do strange things.

She would never forget her humiliation that day at Fort Larned when she had wandered into the sutler's just at mail call and seen one of the officers waving a letter and calling out, "Hey, Sarge, lucky you. Here's a letter from your wife."

Men. Strange creatures. Not to be trusted. That had been the lesson of that black afternoon. Never again would she put herself in the situation of appearing so foolish, so gullible.

Alf pulled her out of her fog. "I'm gonna go see that lady."

Still lost in the past, Rose was puzzled. "Go see who?"

"Horse lady." Alf wrenched away from her grasp and darted across the still barren courthouse lawn. "There!"

Rose scurried after him, but then stopped as the embracing couple broke apart. *Horse lady,* of course. Sophie. Slowly Rose started forward. Alf flung himself into Sophie's arms, while Charlie Devane stepped back and swiped a hand through his hair, as if composing himself.

Oh, Seth, Rose thought as she moved quickly toward the trio, *no doubt about it. These two are passionately in love.*

Once again Seth had to admit his sister could sweet-talk him into anything. Being thrown from a bronc, though, might be easier than watching Sophie stroll toward the river with Charlie Devane, picnic basket in hand on this Sunday afternoon. It confounded him that his father seemed to take this budding romance in stride.

So, more fool he, he'd once again agreed to wait in town to fetch his sister. Fortunately, Ezra Kellogg, overhearing Sophie's request at church, had invited him home for Sunday dinner. Given the prospect of spending time with Rose's cooking and Alf, he hadn't needed further persuasion.

Even from the Kelloggs' front porch, he could smell

the tantalizing aroma of roast chicken. Ezra greeted him at the door and ushered him into the parlor, where Alf sat on the carpet beside a stack of blocks. "Sett?" The boy let the block in his hand drop to the floor and held out his arms to Seth as he ran toward him. Seth settled in a wooden armchair, cradling the boy against his chest, unfazed by the gray cat who jumped up to join them.

"Alf seems powerful fond of you," Ezra noted, sinking into the rocker.

"He's special," Seth commented, feeling the boy's small hands gripping his wrists.

"It's good for him to have a manly influence beyond his tottering old grandpa."

"I can't help wondering where he came from. What he's been through."

"We may never know," the older man said. "My prescription for him is love and coddling, and Rose is doing a pretty good job of that."

Talk then turned to the pastor's sermon and speculation about Ulysses S. Grant's presidency. All the while, Seth could hear the clink of china from the kitchen. After a few minutes, Rose, her face flushed, summoned them to the table. As Seth set Alf down in his chair, he wiped the youngster's runny nose with his bandanna.

The meal lived up to its promise, and there was little conversation until they were all satisfied. When she cleared the table, Rose paused at Alf's place. "Aren't you hungry, dear?"

Seth noticed then that the boy had succeeded in making a lake of his mashed potatoes and gravy, into which he'd stirred small bites of chicken, but had eaten little.

Alf hung his head. "Don't want food."

Rose set down his plate and put her hand on his forehead. "Papa, do you think he has a bit of fever?"

Ezra got up from the table and took the boy in his arms. He, too, laid a hand on Alf's forehead. "Perhaps." He examined the glands along the boy's chin line and looked deep into his eyes. "How do you feel?"

Alf snuggled against the doctor, his eyes at half-mast. "Sleepy."

"Maybe he overdid at church," Rose suggested, her face drawn.

"In that case, it's nothing a good nap won't cure," Ezra said, carrying the boy into the bedroom, trailed by Rose.

Restless, Seth moved into the parlor and sat in an armchair. Surely this was a spring fever. Nothing to be concerned about. Yet his mind defied him as his thoughts turned to the time they had almost lost Sophie when she was a little older than Alf. He now tried to console himself with the knowledge that most childhood illnesses could be survived. Quietly, Ezra reappeared. "He's asleep. Rose will be out shortly." He consulted his pocket watch. "While Alf rests, I'm going to work in the garden."

Feeling out of place, Seth got to his feet.

"No, son, please stay. Perhaps you can divert Rose while the boy gets the rest he needs."

After Ezra went out the back door, Seth waited, wondering how he could possibly be company for Rose.

Finally she glided into the room and sank into a rocker. "He's asleep, though fitfully."

Her high-collared apple-green dress set off the depth of her troubled eyes, and he resisted the urge to take her hand and tell her all would be well. He didn't know that, and even if he did, he hadn't the right.

They passed a few moments in silence while Seth struggled for a conversation topic. He finally spoke. "I understand from Caleb that your Aunt Lavinia will be arriving shortly."

The minute he saw Rose's shoulders droop, he knew he should have come up with some other opening. "You don't seem happy with the prospect."

Rose, usually so calm, almost serene, worried the buttons on her shirtwaist with her fingers. "Lily is pleased, but my memories of my aunt make me…" she hesitated "…apprehensive."

"How so?"

Rose levered herself up from her chair and paced the room as she answered his question. "She is a grand lady, Seth. Her life has been so different from ours, from my mother's." She straightened an antimacassar on the back of the settee. "She has never known want. Her house is the stuff of fairy tales. The time Lily spent in St. Louis accustomed her to Lavinia's ways, but I have little idea of what is motivating her to come."

Sensing there was still more Rose needed to say, Seth waited. She made another circuit of the room before returning to her seat. Taking a deep breath, she looked him straight in the eye, and in a hushed voice said, "Seth, I'm scared."

"Tell me about it." He clenched his hands in his lap, feeling out of his depth with female confession.

"It's Alf. I can handle whatever opinion Aunt Lavinia may form of me, but I'm terrified she will reject Alf. After all, he is of mixed parentage, and as several people in town take pains to point out, I am an unmarried mother. Neither of those circumstances, I'm sure, would meet the standards of high society."

"Caleb has told me about your aunt and her airs, but he also told me of her role in convincing Lily to accept his marriage proposal. Surely she is coming to Cottonwood Falls to be with family, so why would she immediately reject any of you? You may have to give her time. Give yourself time, too." Seth let out his held breath. No expert on relationships, who was he to offer advice?

Rose leaned forward. "Of course, you're right, but I have such a sense of God's will at work in my life with Alf."

"God's will." Seth couldn't refrain from a sardonic smile. "In your case, I'm sure He is at work for good." He censored himself before other words gushed forth.

Rose cocked her head as if hearing a new sound. "Seth? Can you question Him?"

"I can and I do."

"Your mother? After all this time?"

Seth fought the need to leave the room. He had never once spoken his doubts aloud. "You can't know what it was like to stand in that room and watch my mother's life ebb away even as I promised God anything to save her. Or to see my father collapse like a reed in a tempest. Where was God then?" He swallowed several times to choke back the flood of emotion threatening to overcome him. "My father has always said Sophie was a gift from God. That is the only explanation that helps me maintain even a shred of faith. I go through the motions of belief, but I struggle always."

Rose came to him and knelt in front of him, her hands on his knees. When she looked at him, her eyes brimmed with compassion. "What a burden you've shouldered. There is so much we cannot understand, so much that seems cruel and purposeless. When my brother, David, was killed in battle, the senselessness of it shattered our family, but without our faith, we'd have been totally lost." She sat back on her feet, her hands now folded in her lap. "The Bible gives us comfort in such moments. 'For now we see through a glass, darkly; but then face to face…'"

In an effort to return to some semblance of normalcy, Seth leaned over, grasped her hands and, as he stood, helped her to her feet. She mustered a smile and said, "Perhaps even Aunt Lavinia is part of God's plan."

"Yes, even Aunt Lavinia. Just let her try to criticize Alf." He grinned. "She'll have me to deal with." Yet the attempt at lightening the mood failed when he looked down at Rose's hands in his—so warm and small, roughened by work, yet so endearing. The tightening of his chest came out of nowhere, and in every sense, he felt as if in the grip of a power beyond his control.

Perhaps sensing his discomfort, Rose slipped her fingers from his and once again sat down, letting the silence continue before saying, "May I pray for you, Seth? For belief? Faith?"

All he could do was shrug. "Can't hurt."

Then, as if the sun were breaking out of storm clouds, she smiled and said, "God is working in your life, Seth, even now. One day you'll see." Then she changed the subject to the continuing progress on the courthouse and her recent encounter with the sheriff, but after a few minutes excused herself to check on Alf.

When she returned, her brow was creased with

worry, and Seth jumped to his feet. "I must summon Papa. Our little boy is burning up."

A sort of paralysis came over Seth before he collected himself. "You go to Alf. I'll fetch Ezra."

A few minutes later, bending over the boy, the doctor called for cool cloths, which Rose hastened to prepare. "Is there anything I can do?" Seth asked helplessly.

Ezra looked up, peering over his spectacles. "You go on and collect your sister, son. We can handle this. If we need more help, Rose's friend Bess, who I understand is a nurse, can help us."

Walking toward the livery stable, Seth's thoughts raced. Concern for Alf. His own total loss of self-control in telling Rose about his mother's death and his subsequent questioning of God. The way the woman unerringly pulled from him thoughts and feelings he had worked so long and hard to keep buried.

Why now? Why Rose?

Despite all his good intentions that he needed no woman in his life, something else filled his thoughts for the rest of the day and into the night. Rose's tear-washed blue eyes, so full of…he could only call it love. And her dear hands nestled in his. Fitting his.

Rose sat motionless, eyes fixed on her boy—his hair damp and matted, his eyes glassy and his lips parched. The grandfather clock struck twice, disturbing the silence of the night in which the only other sound was Alf's raspy breathing. She and Papa had done what they could to make him comfortable—a tepid bath, a tonic of honey and water, even ice chips from the spring house. Yet, in the last hour, the boy had become more agitated, an intermittent cough disturbing his rest. Rose knew she would soon have to awaken Papa and put voice to the fear gripping her heart in a vise. Whooping cough.

More than once with neighbors' children, she had heard that unmistakable sound—the strangled, unearthly cough as a little one struggled for breath. She gripped the side of Alf's bed, willing it not to be so. Such a diagnosis was all too often a death sentence. As she had done throughout the evening, she lifted her face heavenward. "Lord Jesus, please bring Your healing powers to bear on Alf. We love him dearly and he has so much more life to live, if that be Your will. I pray You to spare him." In her heart, she also heard her mother's caution: "Thy will, not mine, be done."

Just then Alf was seized with another paroxysm of coughing, and as soon as he lay back, eyes closed, Rose knew she must summon her father, who had left the bedside only an hour earlier.

Ezra, apparently having heard the cough, appeared at the door, his nightshirt hanging at his knees.

"Oh, Papa, it's the cough," Rose whispered.

Ezra picked up his stethoscope from the bedside table and bent over the child, listening intently. "He is mightily congested." He moved to the head of the bed. "Get another pillow. We'll prop him up to relieve the pressure on his lungs."

Around three-thirty in the morning, their ministrations continuing, Alf fell into a troubled sleep, occasionally crying out "E-nah" or "Rose," and even once, "Sett."

Exhausted, Rose slipped to the floor, her head resting on Alf's bed, her prayer now reduced to "Please, God, please."

An hour or so later she was abruptly awakened by the sound of hoofbeats. Groggily, she lifted her head, checking to be sure Alf was still asleep.

Soon after, she heard the back door open and her father's whispered greeting. Who? She couldn't puzzle it out.

"E-nah." A mumbled cry. Rose felt Alf's forehead. Still hot. *God, where are You?*

Her father appeared at the door. "Any change?"

She shook her head in despair. "He hasn't coughed quite so much, but when he does, it's like a spasm."

Her father placed his hands on her tight shoulders. "Can you get some rest?"

"I won't leave him, Papa."

"In that case, perhaps you could use some additional help." He nodded at the doorway, where, to her amazement Seth stood, dwarfing the room.

She stared at him, as if he were an apparition. "What...?"

"I couldn't rest. I had such a strong premonition about Alf, so," he shrugged, "here I am."

With the dullness of her mind, she could hardly credit his appearance. He had ridden from the ranch to be with Alf, the boy he held in such affection. Rose remained on the floor but nodded to a chair on the opposite side of the bed. She watched through reddened eyes as Seth settled by the boy and laid his big hand on the tiny forehead. "Hot" was all he said.

Ezra took in the situation and then moved to the door. "Call me if anything changes."

Cradling Alf's tiny hand in his, Seth sat still as a stone, his chiseled face stoic.

In that moment, a melancholy filled Rose, so overwhelming that she could find no hope. In desperation, she reached across the bed and gripped Seth's hand. "Pray, Seth," she whispered urgently. "I no longer have the words."

Just before she lay her head back on the quilt, she noticed the panic in the big man's eyes. He began to form the words "I can't" before he hesitated, bowed his head and squeezed her hand in reluctant acquiescence.

A long silence filled the room until Seth finally spoke. "Lord, You and I have only a nodding acquaintance, and I don't know how to do this, so I'll just offer what's in my heart and let You do the rest." He lowered his voice then and filled the room with soothing words. "We love Alf and figure You sent him to us for some purpose beyond our understanding. Please help him now. Remove this illness from him." Then his voice grew husky and Rose could barely hear him. "And, Father, I beg You also to help Rose. She is a fine woman, a sheep of Your flock and a wonderful mother. You took my mother from me. Please do not take this little boy who has endured so much from Rose." Seth hesitated, then added, "I guess that's it, Lord. It's in Your hands. Amen."

In her last moments of consciousness before falling asleep at her boy's bedside, Rose managed a wry smile. Seth could demur all he wanted, but the man did know how to pray.

Chapter Six

Rose woke with a start the next morning, a shaft of sunlight falling across her face, Ulysses curled around her feet. *Alf?* The boy lay on his side, a cloth on his forehead, hands clasped to his chest, knees bent. Struggling to her feet, Rose became aware that sometime in the night, a blanket had been placed over her shoulders. Now she and Alf were alone in the room, his gentle exhalations filling the silence.

A wisp of memory pecked at her. Had Seth been here? Surely she had dreamed it. She glanced around, seeing no sign of him. Yet she was certain he had prayed over Alf. Then she remembered. Claiming restlessness and worry, he had ridden into town. How long, she wondered, had he sat with the boy while she slept.

In his sleep, Alf's dark lashes stood in sharp contrast to his pale skin. Rose laid a hand on his shoulder, needing the reassuring physical connection. From the kitchen came the smells of coffee and bacon, and she realized she was ravenous.

Just then Bess Stanton appeared in the door extending a large, steaming cup. "Good morning, my friend.

Here's a quick tonic." She handed the coffee to Rose, who took a grateful sip. Then before Rose could ask the questions flooding her brain, Bess supplied the answers. "First of all, your father thought you might need help nursing Alf, so Seth fetched me. Second, while the patient still has some fever, he is much improved. He is still coughing, but neither your father nor I have heard the kind of gasping coughs associated with whooping cough. Although he will need several days of bed rest and care, Alf probably has the croup and should recover with time."

"Thank God," Rose whispered, her eyes filling with tears of gratitude. She took another sip of coffee while Bess straightened Alf's covers.

"Now as for you, missy," Bess rounded the end of the bed and put her arm around Rose, "I am here to assist for as long as you need me. You cannot permit yourself to get worn out. That helps no one."

Once more the thought occurred to Rose that if Bess stayed to help, she and Ezra might discover ways to forge a medical partnership. "If you're certain it is convenient for you, I would welcome your support and expertise."

"That's settled then. Now, let's get some food into you."

Bess served Rose flapjacks and bacon, then left to sit with Alf. Ezra sat across the table, the lines of his face etched with exhaustion. He'd finished eating but set down the weekly newspaper he'd been reading when Rose joined him. "A long night, daughter."

"For you, too. Bess seems confident Alf will recover."

"I agree, but it will take time." He removed his spectacles and rubbed his eyes. "Your friend Bess seems knowledgeable and competent."

"I'm glad you sent for her."

"Well, you've been dropping so many hints about how helpful she might be to me that I decided to test the proposition."

"And?" She paused, a forkful in the air.

"So far, so good." He winked at her and put his glasses back on his nose. "Young Montgomery was helpful, too. You didn't relax until he came."

"I don't understand why he was here."

"Never underestimate urgings that come from God."

Rose guided the fork to her mouth and chewed thoughtfully. Had it, indeed, been God who had roused Seth to action? "I think he cares a great deal about Alf."

"He's a lonely man, Rose. A childless one with an enormous heart."

"Alf will be pleased to learn Seth came on his account."

Her father folded his newspaper, then looked at her, a glint of amusement in his blue eyes. "Alf is part of it, but I suspect not all of it."

Rose trembled as she comprehended the unspoken implication, but before she could quiz her father further, he'd gathered his hat and exited the back door. She sat in stunned silence, absently stroking Ulysses whose purrs failed to soothe her. Surely Seth's visit had nothing to do with her.

After breakfast, she and Bess gave Alf a sponge bath and changed his nightclothes. Listless, he watched them with big dark eyes. "Sick," he said. "Cough."

"Yes, but you're getting better. You were quite ill

last night. Mrs. Stanton and I are taking good care of you."

"Sett, too."

"Yes, Seth, too." Rose was surprised. Alf must've awakened at some point during Seth's vigil.

"Sett singed to me."

The idea of that giant of a man sitting tenderly by the boy's bedside singing lullabies rocked her. Looking now at her boy, Rose realized that on top of everything else, Seth's prayers had borne fruit.

Bess bustled about folding linens and towels before approaching Alf. "How does your throat feel?"

"Hurts."

Rose watched while Bess fluffed the pillows and then helped Alf drink a spoonful of the cough preparation she had made for him. In a few minutes he closed his eyes and was soon fast asleep.

The women tiptoed from the room. As they tidied the kitchen, Rose asked Bess about her life in the East.

"My husband and I lived in Maine. When he was called into service for the Union, I was restless, and since we had not been blessed with children, I vowed to do what I could to help. Nurses were needed, and as I had always been the one to tend to sick family and neighbors, I volunteered to work in field hospitals." She paused, as if recalling painful images from the past, the sunlight highlighting the silver in her hair. "It was heartbreaking but necessary work. When my husband was killed at Gettysburg, all I wanted to do was run home and bury myself in grief." She turned to Rose with a sad smile. "But I couldn't. Those wounded soldiers had wives and sweethearts who were counting on me to restore their menfolk, even as mine would

never be restored. How could I turn my back on them?"
She shrugged.

Rose marveled at her resilience and faith. "I sense
that purpose would make everything better here."

"Oh, yes. I'm pleased that your father called on me
to help with Alf."

"He's tired, Bess. The strain of his practice is taking its toll. I will encourage him to welcome your assistance." Rose moved a stack of clean plates into the
cupboard. "How long do you think it will be before
Alf is recovered?"

"A week, more or less."

Thinking aloud, Rose said, "He should be well, then,
when Aunt Lavinia comes."

"You're having company?"

Rose filled Bess in about her aunt and the surprising journey she was making to Kansas.

"My, she will discover Cottonwood Falls is quite
different from St. Louis."

"How will she react to our frontier ways?"

Bess untied her apron and laid it on the back of a
chair. "We'll just have to think about what might entertain her. To begin with, we can invite her to the Library Society meetings."

"Lily says she's not much of a reader."

Bess raised one eyebrow. "Oh, really? Think about
it, Rose. How many of our members are genuine stu-
dents of literature? A few, I'll grant you, but most come
for the refreshments and gossip. And then there's the
Courthouse Ball. We could use your aunt's help to
make it as elegant as possible."

Rose was confused. "What ball?"

"It's just been announced. It is to be quite the grand

affair in celebration of the completion of the court-house. Along with several others, I have been asked to serve on a committee to plan the event scheduled for mid-October." She clapped her hands enthusiastically. "It's going to be quite wonderful."

Rose wasn't much for gala festivities. She'd always left such occasions to Lily, yet she, along with the entire community, would want to honor the courthouse completion. "Those activities should offer at least some diversion for Aunt Lavinia."

Bess eyed her speculatively. "You sound apprehensive. What is it, Rose?"

"I fear she shall find me wanting." Turning away, Rose stared out the kitchen window, unwilling for Bess to see her level of distress.

Her friend came to her and put an arm around her shoulder. "Why would you say such a thing?"

"I am a simple person. She's elegant and proper. Alf is my world. How can she possibly accept a half-breed foundling?"

Bess squeezed her shoulder, then began talking softly. "It occurs to me that some powerful impulse within your aunt is bringing her here. You are family, and I suspect she is in dire need of all of you. You have nothing of which to be ashamed, quite the contrary. You have saved Alf from we know not what. Leave it to God time to work in your aunt's heart."

A variety of emotions warred within Rose. "You're suggesting I show her love, rather than being defensive about Alf...or myself."

Bess pivoted Rose around so they faced one another. Holding her by the upper arms, the older woman smiled gently. "You will know what to do and how to be patient while God does His work within Lavinia."

Rose bowed her head and whispered, "Thank you."

The moment was broken by the sound of coughing coming from the bedroom. "Don't be alarmed," Bess said, as she turned toward the bedroom. "This is natural and will pass."

Rose trailed her down the hall, praying silently for Alf's recovery and in thanksgiving for Bess.

Folderol. That's what it was. Folderol. Seth had no understanding of why the farm wagon wasn't good enough for Lily and Rose's Aunt Lavinia, but, no, Lily had insisted and, of course, Caleb was putty in his wife's hands. Two buggies. One for Caleb and the grand lady, and one for him and the maid. Seth had been dragooned at the last minute when Ezra had a call over Elmdale way and couldn't be back in time to meet the train. Fortunately the travelers had sent ahead the bulk of their baggage, already ensconced in the fine house Lavinia Dupree had let. Seth fumed. He had work to do on the ranch. This errand was a nuisance, but then, his brother asked so little of him. Besides, he was curious.

So here they were at the end of this first week in June, lined up by the tracks at the new Strong City railroad stop just a little ways from Cottonwood Falls. Caleb seemed calm, but Seth's nerves were ajangle, a condition exacerbated by the thrumming of the tracks and the long whistle as the locomotive neared, belching and screeching as it pulled into the station and hissed to a stop. Stepping down from the passenger car was a slightly built young woman with rosy cheeks and curly blond hair trailing from beneath a straw hat. Before

even looking around, she held out her hand and assisted
an older woman from the train. There, in all her glory,
stood Lavinia Dupree. Seth's jaw gaped. Never had
he seen such richness of material or so ornate a trav-
eling costume. The hat alone must have weighed five
pounds. As if making a grand entrance at the opera,
the woman walked toward his brother, holding out her
hand. "Caleb, dear boy."

"Aunt Lavinia, I hope I may call you that. We are
delighted to welcome you to Kansas."

"Certainly, 'Aunt Lavinia.'" Only then did the
woman look at her surroundings. Then with a sniff,
she merely said, "Kansas, yes. Well, we shall see."

Caleb turned to Seth. "May I present my brother
Seth Montgomery."

Lavinia Dupree eyed him up and down. "You're
a rancher, too." Her tone suggested he might reek of
dung. "And this," she said with an airy wave of her
hand, "is Hannah Foster, my maid."

The younger woman had retrieved their valises and
waited two or three steps behind Lavinia. She simply
nodded.

Caleb motioned toward the rudimentary depot. "Perhaps you ladies would like to wash up before we start
for Cottonwood Falls. Let us take your bags. Our buggies are over here."

During the two-mile ride, Seth could not imagine
what his brother was finding to say to Lavinia. Thank-
fully, he had been blessed with Hannah, who was full
of questions about the countryside and her new town.
Seth had heard enough about Lavinia Dupree from
Rose, Lily and Caleb to be dumbfounded that she
would deliberately choose to come to an environment

so alien to her own, where she might find shortcomings at every turn. But she was Rose and Lily's blood relative, and surely that blood would ultimately tell.

His generosity of spirit lasted only the better part of an hour. Before going to the leased house, it had been decided to stop first at the Kelloggs', where Lily was waiting, so that the family might welcome Lavinia together. Spotting the doctor's buggy out back, Seth was relieved Ezra had returned from his call.

As Caleb handed Lavinia down, she glanced around and Seth heard her remark, "How quaint everything looks." *Quaint!* Seth rolled his eyes. Cottonwood Falls was not some jolly little village existing merely for the amusement of tourists.

Just then, the front door opened and Lily came running out, followed by Ezra. Rose, however, waited in the shadows of the front porch, holding Alf. Seth watched as Lily embraced her aunt and then as Ezra picked up his sister-in-law's hand. "Lavinia, you honor us with your visit."

After Lavinia introduced Hannah, Lily laced her arm through her aunt's and started toward the house. "Please come inside. Rose has made some delicious lemonade and shortbread to welcome you. I'm sure you must be famished. And thirsty, too."

Trailed by Hannah and the men, they were nearly to the porch when Lavinia stopped. "Rose. Where is Rose?"

Seth watched Rose, still shrinking in the shadows, willing her some confidence. "Here I am, Aunt Lavinia." Still holding Alf, Rose stepped into the sunlight. "We hope you had a satisfactory trip."

"I'm here. That's the main thing," Lavinia said, dismissing the question. "It has been a long time since we visited back in Iowa," she continued, eyeing Rose with a birdlike tilt of the head. "You're quite a young lady now. That's to be expected, I suppose."

"Fifteen years makes a difference," Rose responded with asperity.

Then, as if just noticing Alf, Lavinia moved closer and looked down her nose at the boy. "Who in the world is this?" Her tone suggested some lower life form.

"This is…" Rose sounded tentative, but then seeming to gain courage, she continued "…this is my Alf." She glanced down at the boy. "Say hello to Aunt Lavinia."

Alf looked at Rose as if checking to be sure he had interpreted her request correctly. "Hello, 'Vinia."

Ignoring the lad, she stared at Rose. "*Your* boy? What can you possibly mean? Why, look at him."

Ezra sidled up to Lavinia. "Alf is a foundling. Rose has been good enough to take him in and care for him. We are all quite fond—"

Before the doctor could continue, Rose took a step forward. "Aunt Lavinia, this boy needed a family. Now, we are his family. We love him and hope you will be able to love him just as you love the rest of us. Now, if you'll excuse me, I will set out the refreshments." She and Alf circled the group and disappeared into the house.

Seth felt like applauding. Despite her apprehensions about her formidable aunt, Rose had openly expressed her love for Alf. What Rose couldn't have known was that he would also see to it that Alf would never experience rejection or judgment. Not if he could help it.

Over the lemonade and shortbread, it was all he could do to keep from staring at Rose. In her defense of Alf, her cheeks had bloomed and her eyes sparkled. She had never looked lovelier nor had he ever been prouder of her. Because of Alf, of course.

Rose took her time pouring the lemonade, dawdled passing around the tray of shortbread and all the while prayed she would not be faced with further conversation with her aunt. Just as she had feared, Lavinia had wasted no time conveying her disapproval of Alf's presence among them.

She was finding it hard to squelch her anger and maintain a facade of good manners. She glanced at Alf, sitting at Seth's feet where he quietly played with his marbles. Both he and her father had counseled her to give Lavinia a chance, but it was hard. Sighing, Rose picked up Ulysses, dragged a chair from the kitchen and sat just inside the parlor door listening to Lily's lilting voice. "Aunt Lavinia, we will be so pleased to introduce you around, and we're hoping you'll participate in some of our local activities."

"And what might those be?" their aunt asked.

When Lily outlined some of the possibilities, all Lavinia said was "How charming," her words suggesting ill-concealed boredom.

When Ezra asked about the train trip, Lavinia proceeded to compare the railroad line unfavorably with those she had taken with her husband to the East. "Why, the heat and cinders were not to be borne."

Caleb tried to placate her with the fact that the West had only very recently been opened to rail travel. Seth kept his head down, a hand on Alf's shoulder. Hannah cowered next to Lavinia on the settee. Only Lily and Ezra seemed remotely at ease. Finally her father asked the question on all their minds. "Lavinia, I'm curious. Cottonwood Falls is a far different environment from what you are accustomed to. We are pleased you are here, but wonder how we came to have you."

Lavinia hesitated, then looked around the room as if trying to formulate a sensible response. A brief frown crossed her face, replaced almost immediately by her usual unruffled expression, but in that instant, Rose perceived a slight gap in the woman's confidence. "Family, of course," she said with an encompassing wave of her arm, "but something more. An interest in seeing for myself the frontier so captivatingly described by gazetteers. Henry and I had always hoped to make this trip. After his death, I realized I needed a change of scene. What better place?"

"I see," Ezra said.

Then, to Rose's amazement, Seth turned to look her aunt in the eye. "So what is your impression thus far?"

For once, her aunt seemed at a loss for words. Then, drawing herself up, she said, "I am reserving judgment. I will have more to say on the subject after I get settled in my house. For now, it all seems very…open. The town itself is, well, quaint."

At that last word, Rose noticed Seth's jaw working. *Quaint?* Well, no doubt it was, especially compared with St. Louis.

Then Lily saved the day. "Aunt Lavinia, I'm sure with time you will come to find the town enchanting and the countryside a place where nature beautifully expresses her many moods." Then she stood and nodded to Caleb. "Our travelers are no doubt tired and eager to go to their house and get settled for the evening."

Taking those words as dismissal, everyone stood and gathered their belongings. As she moved toward the door, Lavinia paused in front of Rose. "Thank you for the refreshments. They were most welcome."

From her words, Rose gleaned at least a modicum of approval. "Lily and Father will follow you with a chicken potpie and some greens I prepared for your dinner."

Her aunt arched her eyebrows. "Greens? Surely you don't mean dandelions." Then she swept past, leaving Rose feeling foolish for ever having assumed a shred of affirmation.

Nearly everyone was loaded into the buggies, including Ezra's, for the short ride to Lavinia's house. Only Rose and Alf remained behind. Just before the caravan started off, Alf broke away from her and ran across the lawn to the buggies. Rose scurried after him, worried for his safety. Before she could reach him, he called out to the first buggy, "'Vinia, 'Vinia."

Rose looked on with astonishment as Alf approached her aunt, who stared down at him as if confounded by his presence. Rose caught up to him and gathered him in her arms. Squirming mightily, he said, as if in explanation, "I give it to 'Vinia." He held out one fisted hand toward the woman. Looking questioningly first from Rose and then to Caleb, Aunt Lavinia finally extended her open hand to the boy.

"'Vinia. Play with me one day, right?" Then he deposited an emerald-green marble in her palm.

Lavinia turned it over and over, then held it up to

her eye. Finally she slipped it into her pocket. "It is a very fine marble, boy. Thank you."

Then she nodded to Caleb, who flapped the reins for the horse to walk on.

Rose was left sputtering on the street. *Boy?* Hadn't the woman even remembered Alf's name? And *a very fine marble?* Indeed, the boy never let others remove a marble from his sight. What on earth had compelled him to give one of his precious possessions to the very woman who found him so lacking? For some reason, in his innocence and goodness, her boy had reached out to Aunt Lavinia in a way she herself had been unable to do.

The psalmist spoke of the spontaneous insight of children. *Out of the mouths of babes.* Today she had witnessed it in Alf's loving act. Perhaps it was a beginning.

Chapter Seven

A collective gasp followed by shocked silence fell over the congregation on Sunday when Lavinia Dupree, swathed in rustling royal purple taffeta, walked down the aisle of the church. Her gaze steadfastly fixed on the altar, she ignored the stir she was causing. Pausing to bow to the cross, not a custom of this community church, she settled in a pew beside Lily, Caleb and Mattie and withdrew her silk fan from her bag.

Rose gave a mental shake of her head. Aunt Lavinia's regal bearing would do nothing to endear herself to the residents of Cottonwood Falls. Yet even as she wanted to feel insulted on behalf of her friends seated in the church, she succumbed to a moment of doubt. Was there any possibility that Lavinia felt out of place? That her frosty demeanor might signal defensiveness? When the organ started wheezing out "There's a Wideness in God's Mercy," Rose had no more time to ponder the questions.

Throughout the sermon, Alf squirmed beside her, his attention alternately fixed on the circling bird that had flown in through the open window and the bushy hair of the man sitting in front of him. Mattie, on the other hand, sat quietly on her mother's lap, only occasionally sneaking a peak at her great-aunt. At one point, Aunt Lavinia handed Mattie her fan and helped her open it. Meanwhile, Alf began kicking the pew in front of them until Rose stilled his leg. Surely Aunt Lavinia would have little tolerance for a restless, curious little boy.

Displaced by Lavinia from their regular pew, Sophie, Seth and Andrew sat across the aisle from Rose. When the congregation stood for another hymn following the sermon, Seth reached across the aisle and pressed something into Rose's hand. Opening her fist, she saw a small wooden carving of a horse's head. She glanced up at Seth, who winked and nodded toward Alf. When the congregation sat again, Rose pressed the gift into Alf's tiny hand. He examined it, then looked up, his eyes wide with pleasure. "You?" he whispered.

She laid a finger to her mouth and mouthed, "Seth."

Ignoring her caution to silence, Alf erupted with a joyous, "Sett, thank you!"

Heads turned, and when Seth, red-faced, hushed Alf, his eyes were full of affectionate mischief. Rose heard little else of the service, her emotions churning as she reflected on Seth's devotion to Alf and his kindness in coming prepared with the carving. It was as if he was born to be someone's father. Rose's breath stopped, and for the first time ever, she wondered what it would be like to be married to such a man.

Rattled, she forced herself to focus on the closing prayer, but in vain. She couldn't look across the aisle. In the past few moments, Seth had become someone new to her. Could her father be right? In some way, did Seth's attentions to Alf have something to do with her? Breathless, she identified the strange feelings in the pit of her stomach—feelings she had not experienced since her early encounters with the handsome Fort Larned sergeant.

Panic and joy suffused her, rendering her oblivious to her surroundings until the final hymn erupted and folks around her stood. She noticed her father lingering in the pew to speak with Bess Stanton, who had been seated behind them. The words "diphtheria" and "new treatments" were all she could make out of their conversation.

Alf had jumped into Seth's arms, holding the carving aloft as if it were a laurel wreath. "My horse?"

"Your horse, little man." Shifting Alf onto one arm, Seth stepped aside to let Ezra and Rose precede him toward the door.

"Thank you," Rose murmured as she slipped by him.

"Anything for our boy," he said.

Our boy. For one crazy minute, Rose let herself contemplate what it would mean if Alf were, in truth, theirs. So wild were her thoughts, she decided she must be suffering from the heat. She was grateful to be pulled into the present by Aunt Lavinia's commanding voice. "Your minister delivers a surprisingly passable sermon."

Turning, Rose embraced her sister, then stood awkwardly before her aunt. "Pastor Dooley is a blessing to us all."

Caleb encircled the ladies with his outspread arms and suggested they move outside where the churchwomen had set up a refreshment table. The glare of the sun caused Rose to blink momentarily. "Where's Alf?" Lily asked, as Mattie tore from her grasp.

"There." Rose had spotted Seth standing a few yards away, laughing as he tossed Alf into the air. As they watched, Mattie captured Seth's legs in her arms. "Me, too," they heard her squeal.

"My brother-in-law seems to have quite a way with children."

"Alf adores him."

"As does Mattie. If Caleb didn't love his brother so much, he has said he might even be jealous." Lily smiled winsomely at her handsome husband.

"Seth needs a good woman," Caleb said, turning to Rose. "Know any, by chance?"

Rose willed the ground to swallow her lest her discombobulated state betray her. "Perhaps the Widow Spencer?" When laughter erupted, Rose reminded herself that what Seth claimed to need was a housekeeper, not a wife.

Lavinia wrinkled her nose. "What is the cause of this levity?" Lily tried tactfully to explain the widow's need for a husband and provider. Lavinia turned to Caleb. "Prudence, young man, prudence." The idea of Lavinia charging forth on Seth's behalf caused Rose a soundless giggle, and she felt her breath returning.

Lavinia scanned the crowd. "Now where is Mattie?"

In that moment, Rose's spirits deflated. Her aunt cared only for Mattie's whereabouts, not Alf's.

Lavinia would need time to embrace a boy not of her heritage, and Rose herself would need time to sort her ever more complicated feelings for Seth.

Just then the two children ran toward them, trailed by Seth. "Brudder got horse," Mattie shouted as she approached. "And me got a posy," she said, holding forth a carved daisy.

"Sett did it," Alf explained in an admiring voice.

Rose barely heard Lavinia's "How nice" before her eyes teared up when Alf put his arm around Mattie's shoulder and said matter-of-factly, "We love Sett."

The sun bore down, causing Rose to feel faint. *No, I can't let myself think about love. Not with Seth, not with any man. I couldn't bear the hurt again.*

Perspiration dripped from Rose's forehead and she wished nothing more than to step out of her stifling dress and sink into a cool bath. Laundry day in the Kansas summer came too often. Elbow deep in the steaming water, she scrubbed their clothes along the corrugated surface of the washboard, knowing, as she did so, that her roughened knuckles would tell the tale. She glanced up to check on Alf, who sat in the shade of the backyard elm tree playing with his blocks, which had lately become a stable for his new horse carving. Nearly finished, she wrung out the clothes and piled them in a basket.

"Alf, would you help me hang the wash?"

Trailed by Ulysses, he joined her where she stood beneath the clothesline, the laundry basket at her feet. "Your job is to give me these clothespins," she said, handing him a drawstring bag.

He extracted a handful, studied them, and said, "Sojers."

"Soldiers?" Rose laughed, already picturing him commandeering her clothespins to populate the fort he now would undoubtedly construct from his blocks. Then another thought came to her. "Alf," she asked cautiously, "where did you see soldiers?"

He shrugged, then handed her a clothespin. "E-nah and me."

Such a tiny clue. That and his "cage." What else did he hold in his little head that had no means of expression and how closely dared she question him? "Did you know a soldier?"

"Bad man." Alf sucked on the end of a clothespin.

"Here, give that to me." She took the damp pin and began hanging shirts on the line. "Is your horse lonesome?" she asked, knowing she couldn't delve any more deeply into his past at this moment and hoping to divert him.

The boy looked up at her, as if questioning her abrupt change of subject. "Lonesome? He's sleeping." He reached again into the clothespin bag, handing one to her. "Another sojer for you."

As they continued hanging the laundry, Rose wondered for the hundredth time where Alf had come from, who his parents were and why someone had so cruelly abandoned him. With the chore finally completed, Rose went to the pump and plunged her hands into the cold water, wiping her face and neck with a cool cloth. "Alf? Are you hot?"

Shaking his head, the boy gathered up his toys and followed her inside. She had just recombed her hair and gathered it into a bun when she heard a knock on the door. "A man is here," Alf called from the parlor. Straightening the collar of her plain dress, Rose hurried to the door, dismayed to see Sheriff Jensen standing there, his hat in his hand.

"Come in, please," Rose said, her mouth dry. "Let's go to the kitchen. Perhaps you could use a glass of lemonade."

Glancing in Alf's direction, the lawman took the hint. "That would be welcome." The boy looked up briefly, but then turned back to his marbles.

Rose poured two glasses of lemonade, not permitting her mind to go to the reason for the sheriff's visit. "You have news?" she finally mumbled.

He cupped the glass in his large, freckled hands. "Nothing but a clue. I thought you needed to know."

She sat, her lemonade untouched, as he told her of a report from a small town south of Fort Riley, home of the U.S. Cavalry, concerning an army deserter and the Pawnee woman he had been seen dragging about four years earlier. When the man left her to go into hiding, she scrabbled for work, performing the most menial of chores. Then as it became obvious she was pregnant, she, too, disappeared. Whether there was any possibility these were Alf's parents remained unclear, but at least it put the Indian woman in the Flint Hills territory.

Swigging down the last of his lemonade, the sheriff leaned forward. "Since we have identifications of these two, if either shows up nearby, the law will take them in. Of course, time has passed, and it's possible they've vamoosed. Or that they have nothing to do with this case." The man picked up his hat and stood. "I wish I had more definite news for you, but meanwhile, you are doing a splendid job with that boy."

Meanwhile? Alf was not a temporary charity project. She got to her feet and ushered Jensen out. "Thank you for coming," she managed before closing the door and sinking to the floor. In that moment, she had realized how desperately she didn't want to know Alf's history or have a parent reappear. He was hers.

As if sensing her distress, Alf left his playthings and settled in her lap. "Don't cry," he said, lifting his hand to her face.

Until then, she had been unaware that tears were standing on her cheeks. She sniffled and then gathered him even closer. "I'm crying because I love you so much."

As if that weren't enough for one day, later while Rose was taking the clothes off the line, she heard an unfamiliar female voice calling from the front porch. "Miss Kellogg, are you home?"

Sighing, Rose placed the folded trousers in the laundry basket, and stepped to the side fence gate. "We're in the backyard."

Hannah Foster, her face flushed, rounded the house and stood before Rose. "I knocked, but there was no answer."

Embarrassed to be found in her workaday gown by one who undoubtedly dressed her mistress in the finest of silks and satins, Rose folded her arms across her chest. "It's wash day," she said by way of explanation.

"In this heat?"

When else? Rose wondered. "We can't delay. The only relief from the heat is rain, and that won't do for laundering."

"Oh. I suppose not."

Rose figured Hannah would discover that sooner than later, unless, of course, Aunt Lavinia hired a washerwoman. "Would you like to come in?"

Hannah shook her head. "Thank you, but no. I merely came to give you this." She reached in her pocket and extended a note. "It's from Mrs. Dupree."

Then she bobbed a hint of a curtsy. "I'll be leaving now."

With the envelope in her hand, Rose watched the young woman walk away, and was loath to open the message. Finally she slit the envelope flap and withdrew the creamy notepaper embossed with the initials *LD*.

I should like to invite you to call upon me Friday at eleven.

If you wish, you may also bring the child.

Your loving Aunt Lavinia

Rose looked down at her shabby dress, contrasting it to what fine ladies undoubtedly wore when making social calls. Not only did Rose feel inferior, she resented being summoned. *Friday at eleven.* No room for accommodation there. And *If you wish, you may also bring the child.* The *child* had a name, for mercy's sake. Furthermore, how could the woman possibly presume she would leave Alf behind? Even as she raged, she knew she was being uncharitable. Taking a deep breath, she reminded herself, *There's a wideness in God's mercy, like the wideness of the sea.*

She couldn't wait for Papa to get home. She longed for the reassurance of his embrace and his soft voice soothing away the events of this troubling day.

"Rose?" Alf tugged at her skirt. "I'm hungry."

That, at least, was something she could address.

On Thursday, Rose prepared a blackberry cobbler with fresh cream to serve after Lily and Bess Stanton finished discussing midwifery procedures. Ezra had prevailed upon the nurse to assist him in the care of expectant mothers, and Bess had welcomed the opportunity. Now, while the two women bent over the books spread on the kitchen table, Rose sat quietly on the back porch with her darning, minding Alf's play. Overhearing occasional words like "afterbirth" and "breech presentation," she was vividly reminded of the time at Fort Larned when she was pressed into service to help with a delivery. Sadly the mother had died. The travail of childbirth was not to be taken lightly, yet it was an ordeal she would gladly have undergone if only... Disgusted with the direction of her thoughts, she picked up her papa's stocking and attacked a hole with fingers flying.

Watching Alf set his "sojers" on the blocks, Rose couldn't help recalling Sheriff Jensen's words. Could it be that Alf was the child of a former soldier and an Indian woman? Yet the trail was cold. Perhaps no more information would be forthcoming and she could formally adopt the boy. She prayed it would be so.

When Bess's lesson came to an end, Lily stuck her head out the door. "That cobbler smells mighty good."

Rose called Alf to come to the kitchen. After dishing up generous portions of the dessert, the women turned to community matters. "I think the Courthouse Ball will be the grandest occasion Chase County has ever experienced and a fitting way to celebrate the building's dedication," Bess said. "A small orchestra is coming from Topeka. There will be sumptuous refreshments, speeches and dancing. We must begin planning our gowns."

"How glorious!" Lily gushed.

Rose wished she could work up enthusiasm, but she couldn't imagine what she could wear or with whom she might dance. Her experience with such grand affairs had been limited and painful.

"The committee will soon be announcing plans in the newspaper," Bess added. "We are hoping everyone in the region will attend."

"Later in the summer, we have the county-wide camp meeting to look forward to. Brother Hampton Orbison will be coming all the way from Iowa to preach the word." Lily paused to take a bite of the cobbler. While the other two prattled on, Rose busied herself helping Alf spoon up the cobbler lest he stain his overalls. Finally there was a lull in the conversation, and Lily softly called her name.

Rose looked up, noting the perplexed expression on her sister's face. "You're awfully quiet today," Lily observed.

"I don't mean to be rude. I'm merely preoccupied."

"About tomorrow's time with Aunt Lavinia, perhaps?"

Rose sighed. "How did you hear about that?"

"Lavinia told Caleb when he came to town earlier in the week to help her with some house repairs."

Bess covered Rose's hand with her own. "Dear, do share your concerns."

Looking from Bess to Lily and noting the affection in their eyes, Rose decided to unburden herself. She told them about the sheriff's visit and her fears concerning Lavinia's reaction to her taking Alf in and to the reality of his parentage. She explained that it was difficult enough to feel socially awkward around her aunt without also running the risk of being morally judged.

When she finished, Bess patted her hand and said, "Best not to borrow trouble. Wait to see what your aunt wants. How she will react."

Lily leaned forward. "Aunt Lavinia can appear un-approachable, Rose, but I think she's searching for a new way to be. However, we can't expect her to change overnight. As hard as it is, I believe we are called to love her through her grief and transition."

Spontaneously, the haunting words of the hymn once again sprang to mind—"the wideness of God's mercy." Rose nodded her head, then addressed her friend and her sister. "Perhaps I have overly focused on my own problems and needs. Thank you for reminding me not to fear censure or to judge another prematurely."

Lily opened her mouth to say, "All things in—"

"—God's time," Rose finished, and the two broke into laughter, remembering the many occasions when they had invoked their mother's words.

Walking toward Lavinia's home the next morning, Rose felt her courage waning. She had scoured her wardrobe for a suitable dress, finally settling on a full gray skirt and white waist trimmed with lace. At her neck she wore her mother's cameo. This outfit would have to do. She'd dressed Alf in short breeches and a wide-collared white shirt. When they were two houses away from Lavinia's three-story limestone dwelling, Rose took hold of Alf's hands and reminded him once again to behave like a little gentleman. The boy nodded with a solemn air. "I will be good."

Hannah admitted them into the house, its high ceilings airy and the burnished wood floors gleaming, and led them into the parlor, furnished with stiff-backed chairs, marble-top tables, Oriental rugs and glass lamps. Noting the numerous gewgaws adorning every surface, Rose cringed, hoping Alf wouldn't break anything. The two of them perched on the edge of a horsehair settee awaiting Aunt Lavinia's entrance, a delay which Rose supposed was part of the social ritual.

After only a few minutes, Lavinia Dupree swept into the room, the short train of her rich blue dress trailing behind her. Lavinia extended her arms, and Rose stood to receive a formal embrace. When Lavinia sank into a nearby chair, Rose sat back down, pressing a restraining hand on Alf's knee.

After a perfunctory exchange of greetings, Lavinia rang a small bell to summon her maid. "I took the liberty of asking Hannah to prepare some cake for the boy, so she will take him to the kitchen while we visit."

It wasn't a question, it was a command. Rose felt prickles run down her spine. *Patience,* she urged herself. "I'm sure he would enjoy that."

After looking at Rose questioningly, Alf permitted himself to be led from the room.

"Children get bored easily," Lavinia remarked, "and I should so like to have a decent tête-à-tête with you. While I have had happy occasions to become acquainted with Lily, you remain something of a mystery. I should like to know what interests you, what ambitions you have for yourself."

Rose scrambled for the words to acquit herself favorably. "Of the two of us, Lily is the more social, and I, the more domestic. I should say housekeeping and cooking are my two talents. As for ambitions, mine are simple. I should like to be a helpful daughter to my father and a loving mother to my son."

Lavinia's eyebrows shot up. "Son? Son? Surely you can't mean that foundling boy."

Before she could even consider censoring herself, Rose retorted, "*Boy?* I most certainly do mean him. And may I take this opportunity to remind you he has a name. *Alf.* Please do me the courtesy in the future of referring to him by his given name." Rose sat back, limp with vexation.

Frowning, Lavinia fussed with the ruffles on her bodice and then, after a deep sigh, she spoke. "As you wish. Pray tell me how this boy, excuse me, this Alf came to be your concern."

In clipped phrases, Rose explained how Alf had come to live with her and her father. "He may not be of my own flesh, but he is a child in great need of love, and I have that love to give. Surely, God requires no less of me."

Lavinia sniffed. "Well, now that you bring God into it…"

"Jesus would have us care for 'the least of these.'"

"Of course the boy…*Alf* must be cared for. I'm sure he is a delightful little fellow. However, it surely has not escaped you that as an unmarried woman, it is unseemly for you to accept this burden. Especially given his—how shall I put it—dubious parentage."

"Alf is not a burden. He is a joy." Rose felt her cheeks flame. "He was left in my care. He is in need, and his origin matters not at all. I shall not turn my back. It is true I am not married, nor do I have any prospects of such a state, but others like Papa, Caleb and Seth are generously filling the paternal role."

"But what will people think?"

Rose had anticipated Lavinia would come to that and had prepared an answer in advance. "I pray people will think I am helping this boy to grow up knowing he is loved. I am fully aware that there are those who do not approve of my decision and are unsparing in their judgment. However, I hope you will not be among them. You are family, Aunt Lavinia, and I ask you to get to know Alf and come to regard him as a great-nephew. I understand that you will need to consider my request prayerfully and that it will take time for you to accept us as we are. Please do take that time."

Lavinia sat stock-still, seemingly lost in thought. When she finally spoke, Rose had to lean forward to hear her. "I had no children," the older woman began. "Nor am I accustomed to them. I shall not know how to act."

"On the contrary, Aunt Lavinia, you took the marble from Alf. He has not found you wanting."

"Oh, that reminds me." She rang a bell and when Hannah appeared, Lavinia asked her to bring Alf into the room.

As the boy edged forward, he smiled at Rose. "I 'member now." He pointed at the older woman. "She's the marble lady." He approached Aunt Lavinia and stopped in front of her. "Will you play marbles with me?"

For once, Aunt Lavinia looked unsure of herself. "Young man, perhaps one day soon."

"We should take our leave now." Rose stood. "Thank you for your interest in us."

"You are family," Lavinia said quietly. "And, Rose, I shall take the time to consider what you have told me about Alf."

Hearing his name, the boy looked up and said, "Marbles. You and me."

As if his words brought her out of a daze, Lavinia

started and then said, "Oh, dear, Alf, I nearly forgot. I have something for you." She put a hand in her pocket and drew out a gray, black and white agate, far larger than those in Alf's collection. "This is for you." She placed the stone in Alf's hand.

Alf beamed up at her. "Rose told me I would love you."

Lavinia patted the boy's shoulder and then, over his head, found Rose's eyes. "I'll try," she said softly before her expression hardened. "But it will be difficult."

On their way home, Rose reflected that trying was all she could ask of her aunt, but the gift of the marble showed promise.

Chapter Eight

Seth gnawed on a piece of beef jerky as he rode toward the far pasture. The mid-July heat had been blistering with nary a rain cloud in sight for days. The spring-fed ponds usually provided an adequate water supply for the herd, but some springs were now mere trickles. If the upper pond was low, he and Caleb would have to consider moving the cattle.

If that wasn't enough of a worry, they were short one hand. After the man's bout with pneumonia, he had opted to move back to Kansas City. Caleb credited Doc Kellogg with saving the fellow. Cottonwood Falls was lucky to have Ezra. Lately Seth had noticed the doctor was accompanied on some of his rounds by Bess Stanton. Well, folks could use all the medical help they could get. Thank God Alf's illness had passed and the lad was once again his lively self. Since his mother's death, Seth could not remember a time he had been more frightened than when he was praying at Alf's bedside. How Rose had pulled that prayer out of him was a mystery. But then, he admitted with a jolt, he could hardly deny Rose much of anything.

He liked thinking about her creamy skin, dusted with freckles, her reddish-blond hair that looked as if it would be soft to the touch and her blue eyes, as calm as a deep pool. Even though he dropped into bed each night sore and spent, he often lay awake picturing her and reflecting on the easy comfort he experienced in her presence. He found himself wondering what it would be like to be a real family—Rose, Alf and himself. Such wayward thoughts were dangerous. *Goliath, Goliath.* Why set himself up for rejection? It would be foolish to mistake Rose's mere kindness for something more.

After arriving at the pasture and assuring himself that a sufficient water supply existed, he turned Patches toward home, deciding at the last minute to detour by Lily and Caleb's to see little Mattie. She would have to be child enough for him.

"Seth, what a surprise!" Lily stood in the doorway, her rose-colored dress covered by a white apron that bore vestiges berry juice. "You look road weary. I have just the thing to perk you up."

Mattie rushed toward him, holding out her arms to be picked up. The sweetness of her chubby arms around his neck and her curls tickling his cheek filled him with delight. "We having a treat, Unca. You come."

Seth kissed her forehead, then set her down. She tucked her little hands in his and led him into the kitchen where she climbed onto her chair and began eating. Lily served him a slice of jelly roll and a tall glass of cold tea, then settled across from him.

"I'm glad you came by. We haven't seen you in a while."

"'Make hay while the sun shines' is my motto. I'm sure Caleb is just as busy as I am."

"Have you been to town recently?"

He suspected this wasn't an innocent question. "Not lately," he said before taking a bite of the warm jelly roll.

"I saw Rose and Lavinia last week at the Library Society meeting."

He wanted to ask about Rose but thought better of it. "How did that go?"

"It was quite interesting. Bess Stanton read a fine paper concerning British female novelists, and Dora Jensen brought Swedish krumkakes and berries for dessert. But the highlight—"

"Lavinia Dupree."

Lily threw back her head and laughed. "Why, Seth Montgomery, you're as wise as Solomon. Dressed to the nines, she sashayed in as if she owned the place. For the longest time, she sat like a queen surveying her subjects. It made for a bit of an uncomfortable afternoon until right toward the end when she finally spoke up. 'I declare, this was a most tolerable afternoon. Ladies, I shall make note of the date of our next meeting.'"

Seth grinned. "You do a fine Lavinia imitation."

Lily sobered. "I do wonder how difficult it must be for her to make such a dramatic transition. I know how I felt when I went to St. Louis. Everything was strange and unnerving. For all of Aunt Lavinia's outward show of confidence, I sense her usual customs and behaviors aren't serving her well here, and she knows it."

"Jelly good, Unca?" Mattie asked, her mouth smeared with raspberry jam.

"Very good, Miss Mattie." Momentarily diverted by

his niece, Seth returned to the discussion. "Rose was full of trepidation regarding Mrs. Dupree."

"She's concerned primarily on Alf's behalf."

"I know." Seth ground his teeth. "Alf has done nothing to the woman. Surely, she will come to see how important he is to Rose."

"I will tell you what I told Rose. Let's see how time may alter all of our opinions."

"Good advice."

"Speaking of Lavinia, she has asked a favor of you or Caleb. She would like one of you to take her for a tour of the surrounding countryside."

Seth recoiled, imagining himself escorting the intimidating Lavinia about the county. "Caleb already knows her. He can do it."

"Oh, no, my dear brother-in-law. That's exactly why you are the chosen one. You need to get better acquainted. You are already close to Rose and Alf. Lavinia needs to understand what a fine man you are."

Narrowing his eyes and suddenly feeling every bit the Goliath of his schoolboy days, he glared at his sister-in-law. "What do Rose and Alf have to do with anything?"

Maddeningly, Lily seemed about to erupt with laughter once again. "I'm surprised you can even ask such a question. You would be a dreadful poker player. Anyone can see you're a few weeks shy of a full-blown courtship with my sister."

A full-blown courtship! Seth fumbled for a way to divert Lily from such a preposterous notion. "I never play poker."

"Go ahead. Change the subject. You'll see. I'm right. And that's why," Lily leaned across the table to wipe

Mattie's face with her napkin, "you'll pick up Aunt Lavinia Saturday morning at ten."

"Caleb, you mean—"

"Not Caleb. You. It's already been arranged."

"And Caleb agreed?"

Mischief flashed in Lily's gaze. "Agreed? It was his idea."

Somehow Seth endured the next few minutes before he could excuse himself to find Caleb, wherever he was lurking about the place, and give him a colorful piece of his mind. A tour with Lavinia? He'd rather jump into a frozen pond!

Saturday morning Seth dressed in a clean shirt and his second-best trousers, slicked down his hair, slapped on a straw hat and headed for the barn, all the while thinking murderous thoughts. Squiring Lavinia Dupree around in a buggy? Making polite conversation? Beyond that, Lily's remarks implied that he was expected to make a favorable impression.

On his way to the Dupree home, Seth stopped by the sheriff's office. Caleb had asked him to report the signs of a campfire, several days old, that he had discovered on a rock outcropping near the stream.

"Thanks, Montgomery," the sheriff said as he stood with Seth outside the office. "So far we haven't seen any evidence that these wayfarers are up to no good, but it doesn't hurt to be vigilant."

Seth tried to keep the tremor from his voice as he asked the question so important to him. "Any news about Alf's people?"

"The only response from other lawmen involved an army deserter and his Indian woman, but that report is over four years old and in the Fort Riley area. I can't put much stock in it."

"Rose Kellogg is quite attached to the child. For her sake, I hope no parents show up to claim him."

"That's the way Doc feels, too." The sheriff moved his tobacco chaw to the other side of his mouth. "It's probably a cold trail."

Relieved, Seth headed for the Dupree house. Walking up to the door, he steeled himself for the coming encounter. Hannah answered and told him her mistress would be right out.

Sure enough here Lavinia Dupree came, dressed in a slate gray riding dress he was relatively sure had never seen the inside of a stable. "There you are, young man." She consulted a watch hanging from a gold necklace. "Punctual." She nodded with approval. "Let's be off."

As she swept down the walk, he hurried after her, arriving at the buggy just in time to assist her.

Starting along, he decided it was safer to seize the conversational initiative. "This is big country, Mrs. Dupree. What do you have in mind?"

"Naturally I saw the countryside to the north coming in from the depot. Now I want to inspect the land to the west or south. I realize we can't cover the ground all in one day, so you decide our route."

Dutifully he clucked to the horse and they passed the courthouse, going south. His passenger craned her neck to study the nearly completed building. "Imagine, such an imposing structure here in…" Seth was sure she was going to say "in the sticks," but then she caught herself. "Here in these hills."

"The courthouse is quite the talk." With an effort, he elaborated. "My sister Sophie is sweet on the chief stone mason, Charlie Devane, a fellow from Vermont who's supervising the laying of the stone. All quarried locally."

"Do tell." They rode in silence, leaving the town behind. "'Sweet,' you say. I suppose a fetching young man from the East is a welcome novelty for a young girl."

Seth clamped his mouth shut against the demeaning suggestion of his sister's sweetheart as merely a "welcome novelty." "And what about you? Are you sweet on anyone?"

Was the woman always so inquisitive? "No."

"'No'? Come now, Mr. Montgomery. It's high time you settled down with a wife and children. Isn't that how the West is to be populated?"

"I couldn't say." The woman's suggestion had turned his thoughts to Rose and Alf, and once there, they tended to abide. "I'm not the marrying sort."

He'd always held that opinion. Until recently. He kept such fantasies at bay by remembering his mother racked by the pain of childbirth and the heartbreak his father lived with every day. His current life was orderly, predictable. Why set himself up for possible disappointment?

Lavinia tapped him on the shoulder with her fan. "Nonsense. Surely there are some young women around here who require a mate."

Seth cringed. Lavinia's remark made him feel like an animal being paired off for breeding purposes. He seized upon a change of subject. "Tell me about your impressions of Cottonwood Falls."

As they started up a rutted path toward a low rise, silence fell between them until finally Lavinia spoke. "I must confess it is a very different place from what I had pictured. I had not expected to find culture here, but I was pleasantly surprised by the program at the Library Society. The town is more genteel than I had imagined. But the rugged, untamed terrain, while breathtaking, is strange in its openness and rawness. Yet I find it full of possibility." She paused as the buggy rumbled over the rocky roadbed near the top of the hill. "In St. Louis I have been unaccustomed to mingling with, well, just anybody. Here, there are few of the class distinctions with which I am familiar."

Seth stared straight ahead. On the one hand, she was a grand lady examining the place, while on the other, she appeared to be making a genuine attempt to articulate her impressions.

"In certain respects, frontier society seems more… democratic. It will take time to adjust and find my place here."

"Would you like to do that? Find your place?" Seth pulled the buggy to a stop facing a view of hills rolling away toward the horizon.

Instead of answering, Lavinia surveyed the panorama before her. Only an occasional farmhouse or clump of cedars marred the sweep of sky, rock and tall prairie grass. "Untouched," she murmured. "Beautiful in its own way."

He nodded, never having found words adequate to express his deep and abiding love for this land.

"So to answer your question, young man, I would like to claim a place." As if a sudden thought had occurred to her, she asked, "What is the price of land currently?"

Slowly making their way down the other side of the hill and into a small valley shaded by cottonwood trees,

Seth expounded on land prices, cattle and grain markets and the business opportunities for those who might settle in the area. Talking about such familiar subjects finally put him at ease with the woman, who stared straight ahead but seemed attentive. When he had exhausted the subject, they turned back toward town.

Then, she made a statement that reduced his newfound comfort to distress. "That boy is a half-breed."

"Alf?"

"Yes, Alf. Although he is an engaging chap, Rose and Ezra have made a mistake taking him in."

Seth controlled himself with great difficulty. "Is it ever a mistake to care for those in desperate need of it? He is only a child."

"One can give care without becoming emotionally attached. Rose thinks of the child as her son."

"She does. He gives her pleasure and seems to fill a void for her."

"But a half-breed?" Lavinia might as well have been talking about an aborigine.

Stopping the buggy abruptly, Seth speared Lavinia with the intensity of his gaze. "Alf is a child of God. His parentage is not our concern. His well-being is." He paused to stem his anger. "My apprehension in this matter is the heartbreak Rose may experience if Alf's parents come to claim him. I fear it would be her undoing."

Lavinia eyed him shrewdly. "You want to protect her from such heartbreak."

"Yes. And I want to protect Alf."

"You don't care what people say about Rose, serving as an unmarried mother and all?"

"What other people think matters little in God's eyes."

"You are fond of both Rose and Alf."

"Yes."

The buggy creaked along for some minutes before reaching Lavinia's street. Only when they pulled to a stop in front of her house did she speak again. "Thank you for the ride."

He shrugged acceptance of her gratitude. As he escorted her to her door, she walked head down, as if lost in thought. Just before she entered the house, she straightened and looked directly at him. "As for Rose and Alf, you have given me much to consider. She is my family. I don't want her hurt. Not by those who speak ill of her and not by the boy's missing family." Then in a firm voice she added, "And most certainly not by you, young man, should you ignore her affections for you."

All the way home, Seth reviewed the morning and Lavinia's puzzling attitudes. Surprisingly, he decided he might come to like her, but her last statement troubled him. Why would she think he had the power to hurt Rose? That was the last thing he would ever consider doing. But "affections"? What did she mean?

In the searing July heat, everything seemed to wilt—grass, flowers, trees and the residents of Cottonwood Falls. Few left home in the afternoon. Relief came only late at night and early in the morning. After the midday meal, Rose made a pallet on the cool parlor floor where she and Alf stretched out for storytelling and naps. He was especially charmed by her make-believe tale of Brave Alf who fought giants and saved fair maidens from danger with his magic marble. In addition to her regular chores, this morning, she had made dozens of cookies for this weekend's camp meeting. She hoped the heat would break before Brother Orbison's arrival. Anticipating the event was the one thing invigorating the townspeople. Although Rose wouldn't have said it aloud, she knew camp meetings provided entertainment as well as conversion opportunities.

She had just roused from a brief nap and was straightening her dress when she heard a knock at the back door. Leaving Alf sleeping on the floor and brushing a stray lock off her forehead, she slipped down the hall and into the kitchen. Seth waited on the porch, shifting his hat from hand to hand.

"Am I disturbing you? I know you weren't expecting me." His large frame filled her vision, and his expression was tentative, as if he feared being turned away.

"No, but Alf is sleeping." She let herself out the back door. "Perhaps we could visit out here. Please sit down," she said gesturing to a nearby bench.

He settled beside her, hunching forward, still fingering his hat. "Much obliged."

From his taciturn manner, she had no idea why he was here or what she was expected to say. "Are you and your family planning to come to the camp meeting this weekend? I understand Brother Orbison has a powerful delivery."

"We'll be there, but I don't hold much with a fire and brimstone God. A God who takes a young mother or orphans a helpless lad for what some folks would call sin is no God of mine."

"Who is your God?" she blurted out before she could stop herself.

He set his hat on the bench and leaned back against the house before replying. "My God is about doing right by everyone you meet no matter who they are. I would sorely like to question Him, though, about why folks have to suffer." He stared off into space as if resigning himself to the fact no such answer would be written on the horizon.

"I sometimes think we may go crazy with the questions," Rose said quietly. "Perhaps we are arrogant to want answers on this earth. Maybe we must accept the mystery of God's purpose." She seldom spoke of these things, yet it felt right to do so with Seth. He left silences between their words, and in those silences, she felt drawn to his soul just as she was attracted to him as a person. If ever she could bring herself to trust a man again, he would have to possess Seth's vulnerability as well as his honesty and strength of character.

"The mystery, huh?" He turned toward her and for the first time since they sat down, gazed into her eyes. "I'm used to working with my hands. Laying out a plan, getting the materials, doing the labor and coming up with a result. There's no mystery to that. But Alf?" He sighed and looked down. "The only way I can think about mystery is if it's a blessing. Alf is."

Rose fought the impulse to reach for his hand. This was no glib, shallow man. "Yes, Alf is both mystery and blessing. A genuine gift from God."

"I appreciate your letting me be his friend."

"He adores you, Seth." Unbidden came the thought, *As do I.* She stood up in the attempt to keep her confusing emotions at bay. "We can't know what kind of person his father was, but he couldn't ask for a better example of a man than you." Clasping her hands in front of her, she felt the nails digging into her palm, in a silent prayer that Seth wouldn't pick up on the deeper meaning behind her words.

"He's quite a little fellow. I enjoy him." Then he stood and took her hand, holding it clumsily between his. "I appreciate you letting me come by to see him on the spur of the moment."

Her heart sank. He had just said it. He had come to see Alf. How foolish she'd been to think his visits had anything to do with her. "We welcome you."

"Besides," he added, a smile breaking across his suntanned face, "I favor your cooking." As if he had just discovered he was holding her hand, he looked down. "And I can talk to you, Rose. Not to many would I say such things as we discuss." Then he disengaged his hands and, as if remembering the purpose of his visit, said, "I brought something for Alf. Will he be awake soon?"

Before Rose could answer, the back door opened and Alf, rosy-cheeked and tousled from sleep, ran toward Seth, who scooped the boy into his arms. "Sett, you wanna play with me?"

"That's exactly why I'm here. I have a surprise for you." He handed Alf to Rose. "You wait here with Rose while I get it out of the wagon."

"Surprise! He gots a surprise for me, Rose!" He wiggled in anticipation.

"What could it be, Alf?"

Alf shook his head sagely. "I 'spect a marble. Maybe like 'Vinia's."

"Or perhaps a spinning top?"

The sound of Seth's approaching footsteps caused them to turn. Rose set the boy down to scamper to meet the man, who pulled from behind his back a magnificent stick horse, painted with the same spots of Seth's horse Patches, complete with a mane of real horsehair and leather reins.

Alf's delighted, "Horse, my horse!" could've been heard by people streets away. Without instruction, he straddled the stick and went galloping around the back yard. "Faster, faster," he cried in a shrill voice.

Rose stood beside Seth watching the happy child cavort across the grass. "Did you make that?"

Seth shrugged. "Yep. He's too young yet for the real thing, but every boy needs a horse."

Standing on that back porch in the late afternoon sunlight, Rose gave no thought to the oppressive heat or the need to start supper. Only to the delighted boy and the generous man beside her.

Chapter Nine

Fortunately, the heat broke in the late afternoon of the first day of the camp meeting when a cooling breeze stirred the banners hanging from the large canopy tent erected near the river. As folks gathered, pious looks did little to conceal the undercurrent of anticipation. Such circuit evangelists were a novelty, and their oratory often had a mesmerizing effect on their audiences.

Rose had delivered her cookies to the refreshment table and, with Alf in tow, was making her way to the children's area where several of the church ladies would tend the little ones during Brother Orbison's preaching. Her father and Bess Stanton were saving her a seat while she settled Alf. No settling was needed, however, when he spotted Mattie running toward him. "Brudder, I play wif you, right?" The two children joined hands and ran toward their friends.

Trailing Mattie were her parents and Aunt Lavinia, who was doing little to conceal her distaste for the signs of religious fervor around her. "Mercy," she murmured to Rose, "I have no idea what I'm doing here."

She turned then to Lily. "You remember our church in St. Louis. One could count on dignified worship."

"Call this another frontier experience, Aunt Lavinia." Lily caught Rose's eye and an unexpressed giggle passed between them. "Camp meetings are a meaningful addition to worship for many people. You might even like it."

Lavinia sniffed, then spoke to Caleb. "Your wife is ever the optimist."

He smiled fondly, cradling Lily's elbow. "Indeed. After all, she came here and married me."

Lavinia looked around. "Where did my great-niece go?"

Lily pointed to the children's circle. "Over there."

"Isn't she precious, that one? And so precocious?"

A lump forming in her throat, Rose followed her aunt's gaze. There were two children there. Couldn't Lavinia see that? Yet in the time she had been in Cottonwood Falls, aside from the gift of the marble to Alf, her attention seemed focused solely on Mattie, as if Alf could be easily dismissed. Try as she might to rationalize that it was natural for Mattie, a blood relative, to be favored, Rose ached for Alf, who, happily, seemed oblivious to his inferior status.

As the group made their way to the revival tent, Rose glanced back over her shoulder to assure herself that the children had adequate adult supervision. Slipping into her place next to her father on the third-row bench, Rose sensed excitement building among the congregation. Folks had come from all over the county, and many expected to camp out or spend the night at friends' homes. Tapers on either side of the lectern illuminated the raised platform. Attached to the tent canvas was a large poster of Jesus holding a lamb beneath which were the words *Hear Brother Hampton Orbison's Christian message and be forever changed. To God be the glory.*

Bess leaned around Ezra and whispered, "Alf didn't put up a fuss?"

"Not after Mattie arrived. They're inseparable."

When Pastor Dooley walked down the aisle, smiling and nodding at his flock, a hush fell over the crowd. Arriving at the platform, he turned, spread his arms in welcome, and said, "Blessed are we who gather here this evening to open our hearts to the Spirit. May those who grieve be comforted, may those who are troubled find peace, and may any who doubt find faith in our Lord Jesus Christ."

Rose couldn't help thinking of Seth, who clung to faith even amid his deep and persistent questions. She turned her head slightly and scanned the crowd. She had thought he would be here, along with Sophie and Andrew. Although she was thus momentarily disconcerted, Brother Orbison's thundering voice returned her to the moment.

A large man with mutton-chop whiskers and a head of thick silver hair, the preacher had a stately presence, yet a gentle facial expression. He and Pastor Dooley invited everyone to pray the Lord's Prayer. Hardly had she murmured her *Amen* than Rose became aware of a stir at the back of the tent. Once again risking a glance, she saw that Seth, his father and sister had entered and taken seats in the last row. From then on, she was aware she was filtering Brother Orbison's message through Seth's possible reaction.

"Brothers and sisters, God did not promise us a life

of ease. Consider Job. God did not give us a world free of temptation. Remember Bathsheba." Brother Orbison rattled on, moderating his volume for effect and gesticulating when emphasizing a point, but Rose was lost in her own thoughts. Was it a sin to crave a child's love? To find her identity in the act of mothering Alf? To believe the boy was, in all ways, a gift from God?

Then with a collective intake of breath, the assemblage waited for the emotional conclusion. "But in all things and above all things, God is love. Brethren, we are to love one another. God is not the instrument of our pain, but of our comfort." Finally Rose relaxed, buoyed by the preacher's hopeful words. "It is He who forgives our sins and offers us redemption. It is He who bids us to love our neighbors even as we love ourselves. Whatever your burdens, give them to the Lord. Whatever your blessings, praise the Lord. And in every moment love your Lord even as He loves you, His beloved children. Amen."

A hush fell over the gathering, finally broken by scattered coughs and nervous foot shufflings. Then Pastor Dooley rose to announce the next afternoon's preaching to be followed by baptisms in the river and the concluding meal. In the darkness, folks left in family groups, heading for their overnight lodging. Bess whispered good-night and left, while Ezra and Rose walked toward the children's tent. "Daughter, what did you make of Brother Orbison's remarks?"

"I liked that he acknowledged we live with pain and uncertainty."

"Redeemed by love," her father said quietly. "If I didn't believe that, I could not have borne what I saw in the war or the loss of your dear mother."

Rose considered his words. She had never before reflected on the faith that had sustained him through such horrors and grief. It was a sobering and a welcome thought. She, too, would try to lean on her faith and pass it on to Alf.

"There she is." The hissed comment caused Rose to look to the side where Bertha and Chauncey Britten were strolling just ahead of them. Bertha continued, her words fading as she and her husband pulled farther ahead. "I wonder what Brother Orbison would make of that boy's situation with Rose Kellogg."

Rose tried to make allowances for Bertha's childlessness and her resulting unhappiness, but the woman's judgment hurt and had nothing to do with Brother Orbison's message of God's love.

Just then she felt a hand take her arm. "May I?" Seth had come alongside her. She nodded, and he joined them.

"What did you think of our preacher?" Ezra asked.

Rose's heart pounded in anticipation. Had Brother Orbison's words had any effect on Seth?

"He presented his message well."

Rose looked up at him. That was all he had to say? "And the message?" she prompted.

He walked slowly; his attention seemingly focused on what lay ahead. "Bears thinking about," he finally said.

When they reached the children's area, blankets had been spread on the grass and several of the younger ones were fast asleep, including Mattie and Alf. "Let me," Seth said, gathering Alf into his arms.

Ezra nodded. "I'll go on and tend to the animals if you'll accompany Rose and our boy home."

"Gladly."

As they retraced their steps heading for the Kellogg home, they passed Caleb, Lily, and Lavinia on their way to fetch Mattie. It was to Seth that Lavinia spoke. "Mind what I warned you about."

Seth studied the ground. "Yes, ma'am."

Rose was puzzled. A clear message had passed between the two. To deflect the awkwardness, she said, "What did you think of the camp meeting, Aunt Lavinia?"

"It was…different. A bit theatrical for my taste. A sound message, though."

Caleb winked as he put an arm around Lavinia. "I think it's safe to say, she won't be wading into the river tomorrow."

Rose noticed Lavinia attempting to conceal a smile. "Thank you very much, Caleb, but I have already been baptized, so you will not see this old lady creeping down a riverbank, although I pray blessings on all who do."

Seth chuckled as he steered Rose away from the group. "Could your aunt be developing a sense of humor? Caleb seems to bring out the best in her."

"You and she seem to have a connection, as well."

Alf stirred, and Caleb shifted him to his shoulder. "You probably heard I took Mrs. Dupree on a tour of the countryside. She was most interested in learning about her surroundings. She is quite perceptive."

Curiosity overcame discretion. Rose had to ask. "What did she warn you about?"

Seth didn't speak. Had he even heard her question? Rose, however, understood Seth's silences needed to be honored. So they walked on. Only on Rose's front porch several minutes later when he handed Alf to her did Seth reply. "Brother Orbison preached about love. Your aunt warned me of it." Then he wheeled around and disappeared into the night, leaving her with more questions than answers.

Sweat poured into Seth's eyes and his back ached, but still he wielded the pickax, determined to loosen the outcroppings of limestone. Sophie wanted to enlarge the garden, and the rocks had to go. The demanding physical labor was preferable to another trip to town to listen to Orbison's second day of preaching, endure Lavinia Dupree's scrutiny and evade the questions in Rose's trusting blue eyes. With each fissure in the soil, he felt an easing of the tension that had held him captive throughout the night. With her one comment, Lavinia had cast a pall over his time with Alf and Rose.

He didn't know whether to be angry or grateful. How was his relationship with Rose any of her business? The pick struck flint again and a spark glinted. What relationship? He couldn't even define it himself, more's the pity. But hurt her? Hurt Alf? He wouldn't. He couldn't. At least so long as he kept everything simple. So long as he didn't permit his fantasies of a family to alter his conduct.

"Seth, what are you doing, fella?" Deep in his thoughts, Seth had not noticed Caleb and Lily approaching in their wagon. He remembered then that Sophie was riding with them into town, since he and his father had opted to stay home.

With a sigh, he dropped the pickax, wiped his

shirtsleeve across his brow and walked toward them. "Clearing land for the garden."

Lily eyed him intently and then said, "What about the camp meeting? Aren't you going?"

"Nope. Last night was enough."

Caleb quirked his mouth into a smile. "Preacher too much for you?"

"I've heard worse. His message was tolerable."

"Tolerable?" Lily snorted. "Since when is God's love merely 'tolerable'?"

"I've got no quarrel with God's love. It's His punishment I question."

Frowning, Caleb studied his hands, clasped between his knees, and Seth knew he, too, was remembering their mother's death.

"Seth, bad things happen," Lily murmured. "It's part of being human."

Seth grimaced. Lily sounded just like her sister. Yet he knew in his heart that God was in this fertile, beautiful land and that He worked in people's lives for good. Take Alf, for instance. It couldn't be mere coincidence that led someone to leave the boy with a woman as kindhearted as Rose. It was just hard for him to balance the blessings with his questions. "I guess there's no getting around the human part," he said by way of answering Lily.

Before he could go on, Sophie bounded out of the house, holding her bonnet by its ribbons. "Sorry to keep you waiting," she called to Caleb.

"No problem. We were jawing with Seth the infidel, here. Hop on in."

Sophie stood on tiptoe to give Seth a kiss, and whispered in his ear, "Infidel? I don't think so. You're as pure as they come." Then she took Caleb's hand and pulled herself into the wagon.

"We'll miss you," Lily called as the wagon started down the road.

Seth watched them depart, aware of the sudden silence, broken only by the squawk of a nearby crow and the breeze sighing through the prairie grass. It had been his decision not to go with them. So how was he to account for the loneliness sweeping over him? As if he was not where he was supposed to be or doing what this day demanded of him. Was God love? He hoped so, because he could surely use a good dose about now. Then before he could stop himself, he looked skyward and mumbled, "Whoever it is I'm supposed to be, Lord, help me."

He stood rooted to the spot, hoping that like the hard Flint Hills limestone, his heart would crack open to God's purpose.

After sharing the bread, cheese and meat Sophie had left them for the midday meal, Seth and his father sat at the kitchen table poring over the ranch accounts. Seth found it difficult to concentrate on the ledger book before him. So much of the success of the cattle operation would depend on the fall market prices, but that uncertainty was part of being a rancher and didn't explain his agitation. Finally his father looked up and said, "You've got something on your mind, and it isn't the herd."

Seth pushed back from the table. "It's the heat."

"If breaking stone apart didn't fix you, accounts aren't going to. Not today. Take Patches and skedaddle and leave me to concentrate."

Maybe a good gallop was what he needed. "I don't want to let you down."

His father's eyes were kindly. "Son, you have never, ever done that. Go on, now. Get out of here."

Seth stopped at the well and poured a ladleful of cool water over his head, then clamped on his straw hat and headed for the barn. It was only later as he felt Patches moving rhythmically beneath him and the wind brushing his cheeks that his tension eased. Watching the land sweeping away beneath Patches's flying hooves and breathing in the air rich with the earthy scent of mown hay, Seth acknowledged the grace that had led his family to this place.

On top of a flat hill, he reined in his horse and paused to study the scene before him. In the distance, he could see the nearly finished cupola of the courthouse and the white steeple of the church. Most of his neighbors were still in Cottonwood Falls for the conclusion of the camp meeting. Pulling his watch out of his pocket, he reckoned the baptisms were nearly over and the ladies would be laying out the victuals. They might find God in Brother Orbison, but he found Him right here in the open, the Creator's hand evident in each blade of grass, rocky ledge and soaring hawk.

Turning back, he set Patches to a leisurely trot. The closer they came to the ranch house, the more unsettled Seth once again became. Something wasn't right, and he was supposed to fix it. Where that idea had come from he couldn't say, but the urgency of the message vanquished his peace of mind. Was it because his family hadn't yet returned from town? As if reading the tension of his rider, Patches wheeled and began cantering toward Cottonwood Falls. In his heart, Seth knew he was supposed to be there, but that certainty arose from an inexplicable fear rather than rational sense.

Seth spurred Patches to a gallop, his mind echoing the prayer his lips couldn't form. *Please, God, let everything be all right.*

Rose and Lily sat near the riverbank under a shady elm as the strains of "Shall We Gather at the River?" filled the air. Aunt Lavinia had chosen to remain at home. As she put it, "I shall observe the Sabbath with my prayer book." Pastor Dooley and Brother Orbison led those who wished to be baptized, now robed in white, to the river's edge. Then, as the singing continued, the two preachers dunked the newly converted and shouted out the words of initiation. "Amens" and "Hallelujahs" provided a counterpoint to the singing. Caleb and the sheriff, along with some other men, turned away from the river following the baptisms and formed a circle near the horses, talking and swapping stories.

Rose fanned herself, loath to leave the comfort of their shady spot to begin setting out the food. Alf and Mattie had joined a group of children playing in the school yard under the supervision of several of the older church ladies. "It's been a good meeting."

"I agree. Eight new souls brought to Christ." Lily yawned, and then stood up. "I swear I'll fall asleep if I don't move."

Reluctantly, Rose got to her feet. "It's been a joy, us all being together this weekend."

"As much as I love Caleb, this place would have been far bleaker had not you and Papa moved here." Then she leaned forward as if confiding a secret. "I think it's been a good move for Papa. Look." She tilted her head slightly in the direction of a small grove of trees.

Rose followed her sister's gaze and gasped at what she saw—her father standing quite close to Bess Stanton, holding her hands in his and saying something in what could only be described as an earnest and intimate fashion. "Lily!"

"I know." Lily giggled. "I've had my suspicions, but I do believe dear Bess is becoming very important to our father."

Rose pondered sister's remark. "They seem to work well together, but I thought that was all."

"You're too close to the situation. You see them every day, I, only on weekends." Lily took hold of Rose's shoulders. "Would you mind so very much?"

"Mind?" Rose wanted only good things for her father and for Bess, yet she had never considered a possible romantic connection. Was it selfish to wonder how that kind of relationship would affect Alf and her? "Honestly?" She hesitated, then plunged on. "I desire their happiness."

Lily took Rose's hand. "I didn't mean to upset you. Come, let's make our way to the church grounds to help with the supper."

The rest of the afternoon was a blur of conversation, food and the conclusion of the camp meeting—one of the few occasions where the entire county came together for fellowship. Periodically, Rose glanced toward the school grounds where the youngsters were playing tag. Remembering Alf's shyness when he had first come, she watched him now with pride and misty eyes—he was an outgoing, animated little chap, frolicking with the other children, with Mattie always following close behind. This time last summer Rose had been longing for a child, remote as that possibility seemed. And now…there was Alf, climbing aboard the seesaw. How richly he had blessed and changed her life.

She turned back to covering her leftover food and stowing it in the picnic basket. All around her, people were gathering their children and exchanging farewells. In the distance she saw Caleb tearing his sister away from a besotted Charlie Devane. Lily came up beside Rose with a sleepy Mattie holding her mother's hand. "Where's Alf? Have you picked him up?" her sister asked

Mattie rubbed her tired eyes. "Brudder, he gone wif a lady."

Rose's heart lurched. To reassure herself, she again looked toward the school yard—now empty. In the moment it took her to register the sight, she picked up her skirts and started running toward the school, knocking people aside, her attention riveted on the seesaw where she had last seen her boy. She stopped only when she came to the school ground, now eerily vacant. "Alf! Alf! Where are you?" she screamed. Her question reverberated off into the void. She searched the grounds in vain, then sprinted toward one of the women charged with tending the children. "Where's my boy?"

"Alf?" The woman looked dazed. "Why, isn't he with you?"

"With me? You were to watch him until I called for him." Panic surged in Rose. What lady had Mattie meant?

"I'm sorry, Miss Kellogg, but I thought you had come for him. When I left, there were no children remaining at the playground."

By now, Caleb, Lily, Mattie and Sophie had converged on her. Rose gripped Mattie by the shoulders. "What lady did you see, Mattie?"

The child buried her face in Lily's skirts. "Nobody."

Caleb supported Rose by the elbow, but she shook him off. "Alf's lost. We've got to find him." And on trembling legs, she began running about the area, shouting her son's name. Others joined the search and "Alf" resounded through the community. Some of the men ran toward the river. Rose couldn't let her mind follow them. Please, God, no! And yet, had the little tyke seen the white-robed figures entering the water in a kind of celebration?

It was not until her father appeared that Rose sank to the ground in despair, her chest heaving. "Oh, Papa, what has happened?"

Bess appeared then, wiping Rose's tears. "The sheriff has organized a search party, Rose. There's no more for you to do here. Let us take you home."

When the word *home* registered in her brain, Rose seized on a shred of hope. "Home. He must be there." She stood and started running the short distance toward the house, followed by Bess and Ezra. She tore open the back door and raced through the rooms shrieking Alf's name again and again. Silence was the only response.

She swooned against Bess who helped her to the sofa. "I have to do something. Think, think. Where could he be? Oh, God, please."

Her father entered the room, his face gaunt and drawn. He started to speak but had to clear his throat before he could choke out the words. "I found this in the barn. In exactly the same place we originally found Alf. Nothing else was disturbed."

Stooping in front of her, he pressed a piece of paper into her hand, then bowed his head as if awaiting the guillotine.

Rose looked down, studying the words on the paper, her eyes blearing with tears. She read. She read again. Then she howled as only a wounded animal would. The paper fluttered to the floor, the message visible to all: I KUM FER ALF. MY BOY AGIN.

Chapter Ten

Seth rode into a milling sea of his friends and neighbors, men shouting to their wives to herd the children into the church. In the growing dusk, it was difficult to distinguish the cause of such hubbub, yet the shrill cries and hoarse commands left little doubt that something was very wrong. He scanned the crowd for his family. Sophie was helping calm the children heading for the church. The sheriff was directing the men to gather by the schoolhouse, but Caleb, Lily and Mattie were nowhere to be seen. Nor were Ezra, Rose and Alf. He dismounted and hurried toward the group around the sheriff. "What's happened?" he rasped out, breathless.

"It's the half-breed brat," one of town idlers said, his sly look causing Seth to clench his fists. "Missing. Good riddance."

Before Seth could land a blow, Lars Jensen shoved through the crowd. "Montgomery, hold up." With a satisfied backward glance, the mean-spirited informant slunk away. "Here's the situation. When Miss Kellogg went to collect the boy after the supper, she couldn't find him. We've been unable to locate him so far. All we know is that your little niece mentioned seeing a woman with him." Seth reeled and the sheriff put a steadying hand around his shoulder. "I'm organizing a search party. We could use your help."

"But Rose?"

"She went to look for him at Doc's house. That's where your brother and his family are, too."

Seth shook off the sheriff. "I'll be back." He ran to Patches and headed for the Kelloggs' home, his mind unable to accept the sheriff's words. Alf, missing? How could that be? Rose was always so careful with him. How could he disappear in the midst of so many people?

His heart splintered with the admission he could only now permit into his consciousness. He should have been here. Not at the ranch indulging his doubts, not escaping into the land and not ignoring the hold Alf and Rose had on him. He stifled the sob catching in his throat. What kind of man turns his back? *God, forgive me, I should've been here.*

Without pausing to knock, he burst into the house, stopping at the parlor door, his mind nearly unable to take in the scene before him: Lily, crying softly, stood in a corner, pressing Mattie's face into her skirt; Caleb nestled Lily to him, his jaw working; and Doc slumped in a chair, his head in his hands. However, Seth scarcely registered any of them for the pathetic tableau of Rose, cradled in Bess Stanton's arms, her face mottled and streaked with tears.

"I came as soon as I could." His words mocked him with their impotence. He had never felt more the intruder than in this moment. Caleb moved toward him, while the others simply stared at him. "Is Alf here? Do you have any idea where—"

"Stop." His brother's quiet word was an imperative. "There is something you should know."

Rose averted her face as Caleb crossed the room to retrieve a soiled piece of paper. Doc looked up at Seth and merely shook his head in an unspoken message of sympathy. Caleb clapped an arm around his shoulder, as if to brace him for what was to come, and then, without a word, handed him the piece of paper. I KUM FER ALF. MY BOY AGIN.

Rage, helplessness, despair—an eddy of emotion swept over him, so powerful it threatened to send him to his knees. He had never before been so thankful for his brother's strong presence. Hardly able to process the crude message, he found himself crossing the room and kneeling in front of Rose. "I am so sorry."

As if his words had roused her from some faraway place, she lifted her face to stare at him as if she'd never seen him before. "My fault," she said in a monotone. "I should've kept him with me."

Ezra spoke then, his slumped shoulders squaring with resolve. "No, Rose, no. You can't blame yourself. All of us were there, too."

Seth hung his head. *Except for me, except for me.*

Ezra continued. "If Alf's mother—and we certainly hope it was his mother—was determined to snatch him away, she would've found an opportunity somehow. It will be important to learn if we're dealing with a parent or someone more sinister. All we can do now is depend on the search party and pray."

"No!" The force of Rose's one word set Seth back

on his heels. "No, I'm through praying. A God who could take Alf from me is too cruel."

Lily joined Seth in front of her sister. "Then we will do the praying for you. Grieve as you must, but don't lose hope. Don't ever lose hope."

Seth stood and backed away. "Rose, we will find him. I promise."

Even as he uttered that pledge, his heart sank. If Alf truly was with his mother, how could he—or anyone—wrest him away?

"I'll come along," Caleb said, then turned to Ezra and asked to borrow his horse.

Ezra rose and came to the two men, placing a hand on the shoulder of each. "God be with you," he whispered.

As he waited impatiently for Caleb to saddle his mount, Seth seethed. How could God be with them? It was pretty clear He was with whoever it was that skulked away in the night with the dearest of boys and not with Rose, whose whole being had been shattered by that act.

Even after midnight, he rode, although most of the others had given up the search. He combed the stream beds for footprints, looked for a swath of bent prairie grass, climbed the highest hill to search the horizon for movement—all in vain. As if the earth had swallowed him up, Alf was gone. Finally, drenched in sweat, Seth slumped over Patches's neck and gave in to despair.

Caleb, who had trailed him all the way, giving him the distance he needed, rode up beside him and laid a hand on his heaving back. He waited for Seth's paroxysm of grief to pass and then spoke. "You have always been full of love, brother. You set me the example.

Sometimes, though, like now, love hurts. And sometimes it even seems as if God has abandoned us." Caleb's voice trailed off, and Seth wondered if his brother was remembering the unmerciful conditions of his service in the Civil War and his participation in the Battle of the Washita River. "But I am here to tell you that God is with us in our struggles and pain. He is with you now. Don't ever forget it." Then Caleb turned his horse and galloped into the night, leaving Seth sitting astride Patches staring at the moonlit landscape stretching out endlessly before him. *I should've been there.*

"Ezra, leave everything to me." Lavinia's tone was one that brooked no argument. "I will be in charge."

Rose tried to swim up from the depths of the dark sea holding her in its grip. Her head felt heavy on the pillow. She couldn't imagine why Aunt Lavinia was in their house bossing her father around. A dream? She felt something beneath her fingers—the edge of a blanket? She struggled to open her eyes, but they refused her bidding. So sleepy. Wasn't she supposed to be doing something? But her consciousness, as if it existed in limbo, refused to consider the question. Then she was once more dragged into the depths.

A bird pecking at her window was the next sound she heard, followed by the sensation of a presence standing nearby. This time she succeeded in opening her eyes, nearly blinded now by the glare of the sun on her face. Quickly she closed them again, but in that instant of vision she thought she had seen a woman, a familiar woman. She tried to speak, but her throat was too dry to form the words.

"Rose, don't try to talk. I'll fetch you some water."

Had it been Bess? Lily? She couldn't tell. Why were her limbs useless? Her mind so bleary? She relaxed against the mattress and wished herself back into the blackness.

"Here, drink this." Rose felt someone raising her up and holding a cup to her lips. She took a sip, grateful for the coolness of the water, then took another and another. "Your father gave you a sleeping potion. That's why you're so thirsty."

It was Bess helping her drink. Rose licked her lips and croaked out, "Why?"

"You were distraught, my dear. Sleep knits up the raveled sleave of care, as Shakespeare tells us."

Distraught? Raveled sleave of care? Rose batted the cup away. There was something vital she must remember. She struggled to recall that something. Turning her head, she tried to focus her vision. Then she saw it. Alf's trundle. All made up. His stick horse lying across the blanket. Then she heard, as if from a great distance, her own voice keening in terrified recognition. "Alf!"

Immediately, she felt Bess lowering her into the down of the pillow and placing a cool cloth on her forehead. "Shh, there'll be time later for that. Sleep, Rose, sleep."

When she awoke again, Rose figured it was late afternoon because the east-facing room was in shadows. Once again she tried to focus her mind, to remember the reason she lay in her bed instead of preparing supper in the kitchen. She shoved herself to a sitting position and studied Alf's bed. Where was the boy? Was she sick? Is that why he wasn't cuddled next to her?

Then, as if lightning had sparked inside her skull, awareness returned. Alf, her beloved boy, was gone.

Someone had taken him. His mother? She struggled
from the bed, her hair streaming down her back, her
bare feet cold against the floor. She had to do something. She stumbled down the hallway into the kitchen.
Bess rushed to her side to support her. Her father sat
at the table and Aunt Lavinia stood commandingly by
the door. "Where is he?" Maybe they hadn't heard her,
so she shrieked her question again. "Where is he?"

Her father raised red-rimmed eyes to her and said
in a forlorn voice, "Oh, Rose."

Aunt Lavinia, however, marched right up to her.
"Rose, you must get hold of yourself. Your boy has
been kidnapped, probably by his mother. Do you remember?"

Moaning, Rose sank against Bess. The note. *I kum
fer Alf. My boy agin.* She shook her head frantically.
"No, no!"

Lavinia was unyielding. "Denial will serve no purpose, my dear. Now that you've slept, you must eat
something and let us care for you. Grief has its own
manner and time, and we will respect that. If there is
anything to be done to ascertain Alf's whereabouts,
rest assured, it will be done."

As if moving under the hand of a master puppeteer,
Rose allowed herself to be ushered back to the bedroom, where Bess washed her face, dressed her in a
clean shift and coiled her hair into a bun. "Live, Rose.
Live. That's what we must do, with God's help."

Rose only briefly reflected on Bess's widowhood
and her presence at the side of so many dying soldiers,
before she whispered the only words she had left. "I
don't know how to live without Alf, and as for God's
help, where is He now?"

Bess looked at her with sad, knowing eyes. "With you, dearest, with you. And with your precious Alf."

Rose felt the emptiness gnawing at her. "If only I could believe that were so." It would be all she could do to put one foot in front of the other and endure the passing of the minutes, hours and days ahead, much less turn to the God who had abandoned her.

When Seth finally rode into the ranch barnyard after a sleepless night on the prairie, he found no comfort in the smells of hay and horseflesh or in the sturdy lime-stone house he had helped build. It was as if a permanent gray cloud had settled over all he had worked so hard to create. It was said one could find solace in hard work. He doubted it, but toil was all that could keep him from rash actions he might come to regret. Murder would be too good for whoever had crushed Rose's spirit and had stolen Alf away from the home in which he was thriving.

He stabled Patches and stomped toward the house, pausing to strip to the waist and wash up before going into Sophie's kitchen, where, no doubt, he would have to endure her reaction to the events of the previous evening.

The aroma of fried potatoes and salt pork drew him inside where Sophie stood, her back to him, stirring the contents of the skillet. His father was noticeably absent. "Where's Pa?"

Sophie turned to face him, her eyes soft with concern. "Out looking for you. He knows how much you care for Alf."

Seth slumped into a seat at the table. "Sorry if I worried you or Pa."

"We understand. You needed to be part of the search." Then as if she already knew the answer, she asked, "Any leads?"

He shook his head. *Leads?* The boy had vanished, simple as that.

Sophie poured him a cup of coffee and then dished up the potatoes. "You must be starved. Eat while it's hot."

He had thought he wouldn't be able to swallow a bite, but hunger took over and he plowed into the food set before him.

"Do you want to talk about it, or are you going to stifle your feelings as usual?" Sophie poured herself a cup of coffee and sat down across from him. "It's not unmanly to grieve. Discussing your thoughts can help."

Irritated at her intrusion, he said, "Nothing to discuss."

"Balderdash! I'm your sister and you're not fooling me for one moment with that strong, silent type pose. You're hurting, Seth. I know I can't change things for you, but I listen. Go on, what's eating at you besides the fact that Alf is gone?"

He picked up his cup and drank deeply, all the time eyeing Sophie over the rim. He didn't want to admit his guilt in front of another human being, even one as close as his sister. Yet, setting down the cup, he knew the confession was too corrosive to contain within himself. He couldn't look at Sophie, didn't deserve the compassion pooling in her eyes. "I should've been there," he mumbled, staring down at the plate of congealing potatoes. "God help me, I should've been there."

Sophie studied him, letting several moments pass. "Perhaps. Hindsight tends to cause us all to question our actions. In truth, would your presence have made any difference? The children were being well cared for. Rose checked on the boy throughout the day. He and Mattie seemed to be having a great time. Would your vigilance have been any greater than that of all the rest of us? The abduction undoubtedly occurred in the blink of an eye. Perhaps Alf recognized his captor and didn't cry out. It happened, Seth. Now it's up to the sheriff to resolve the situation."

"How can I possibly sit by and let time pass?"

"Because you have to. Just like you had to go on each day taking care of Baby Sophie and becoming a parent to Caleb at an age when you should have been carefree. We go on, Seth, doing what we can, what is needed."

He moved the now-soggy potatoes around on his plate. "I love that boy."

Sophie smiled with sadness. "We all know that. We saw it in your actions."

A fly buzzed inside the window, and in the distance, one of the ranch dogs barked. "I guess I'm not meant to have children, even if they're not mine."

"Nonsense. You have Mattie who adores you. And one day you will marry and have some of your own. For right now, though, there's one thing you can do."

He raised his head. "And what would that be?"

"You can be a comfort and a support for Rose, who must be devastated. If you're feeling guilty for not being at the camp meeting, think what a burden she must be assuming? You may be the only person with whom she might be able to share that burden."

Seth's immediate reaction was rejection of Sophie's advice. How could he bare his soul to Rose and incur her blame for his absence from the camp meeting? Yet, the last thing he wanted was for her to shoulder the responsibility. They had all failed, everyone who should have been watching and who should have realistically been on guard against someone reclaiming Alf.

Sophie rose from the table, ran her hands through her unruly curls and broke four eggs into another skillet. "I'll reheat the potatoes and have eggs ready for you in bit. You can't be effective if you're starving."

He watched her preparations, trying to relax into the normalcy of the scene, but he couldn't. Sophie had given him not only breakfast, but food for thought. One thing about his sister, she never hesitated to speak her mind.

When she piled the food on his plate, he was once more able to eat. He was sopping up egg yolks with a piece of bread when Sophie delivered her ultimatum. "Get some rest today, clean yourself up and ride into town first thing in the morning. You and Rose should talk, sooner rather than later."

He shied away from the thought, but in his heart he knew that as a man, it was what needed to happen. Anything else was hiding, and that he wouldn't do.

Walking out to the barn after breakfast, he met his father riding in from his search. Andrew dismounted, patted his horse and turned to Seth. "I'm glad you're home, son. I was worried when I couldn't locate you."

"I needed some time after the chase to think."

"You're mighty partial to that little boy."

Seth shrugged. There were no words for his sense of loss.

"While I was out looking for you, I saw the sheriff, already at his office early this morning. He is questioning Mattie and the other children and sending out a telegraph to the authorities in surrounding counties. Maybe we'll at least learn of the boy's whereabouts and well-being."

"I suppose that's all anyone can do."

His father eyed him sharply. "It's not like you to be so hangdog, son. I'm going to say this once and only once, but I want you to heed my words. You are not responsible for the child's disappearance."

Seth raised his eyes to his father's. "Be that as it may, I will do everything in my power to get Alf back."

"Everything legal, son. You cannot take the law into your own hands."

"Agreed." While every instinct screamed that he would like to do exactly that, as a man of conscience, he knew he could not. But he would not rest until he had done everything possible to find the boy and comfort Rose.

"That's settled, then," his father said as he took his horse by the reins and led him toward the barn.

The second morning after Alf was taken, Rose forced herself to dress only because she had seen in his whole demeanor the degree of her papa's worry about her. She longed to feel her mother's arms around her in a comforting embrace, and that impossibility widened the void in her heart. Perhaps some would see her loss as vastly more insignificant than her father's, but who could measure the depths of anyone's suffering? Despite her own pain, she would not inflict further distress on her dear papa.

She stared at Alf's little trundle bed, at the stick horse Seth had so lovingly made for him. Visible from beneath an edge of the pillow was Alf's marble bag. Succumbing to a wave of nostalgia, she sat on his bed and opened the bag, fingering the marbles as if they were talismans that would suddenly restore her boy to her. Then she spilled them across the counterpane, noting how they sparkled in the sunlight pouring through the window. All but one. She frantically searched the bag again. The agate Aunt Lavinia had given him was missing. He often carried it in his pocket. She prayed he'd had it with him Sunday. Maybe it would remind him of this home and the people here who loved him.

With a start, she realized that was the first prayer she'd offered since Alf had been taken—how spontaneously it had poured from her. Yet how could she still be trusting in a God who had given and then cruelly taken away? With a heavy heart, she gathered the marbles and one by one dropped them back into the bag, pulling the drawstring tighter and replacing it under the pillow.

Breakfast consisted of a warm coffee cake Hannah had delivered at Lavinia's request and a tin of stewed peaches. She and her father sat at the table, each lost in thought. Finally Papa spoke. "Bess will be coming over to keep you company today."

Rose's first instinct was to rebel. She did not need a keeper. Or did she? She was aware she wasn't always thinking straight. Memory played tricks on her. One moment she would be poised to call out for Alf, and in the next, she would be light-headed with the awareness of his absence. If only she knew he was being cared for. That he was safe—and loved. "Bess? She needn't come."

"She wants to, my dear. She's quite fond of you."

She couldn't look into her father's eyes and read the

anguish written there, so she dished up a forkful of the coffee cake she had no appetite to eat. "Very well."

Bess arrived shortly and insisted on washing up the dishes. While she and Papa went out on the porch to discuss some patients, Rose retrieved the bag of marbles from the bedroom. For some reason, having them close made the pain slightly more bearable. She sat in a rocker in the parlor, holding the marbles. Ulysses curled up beside her, his head resting on her knee. She ran her hand over the cat's sleek back. How Alf had loved "our cat." She couldn't have said how long she sat there, as if in a trance, rocking back and forth, back and forth. Once Bess stepped in the room and asked if she would like her company, but Rose just shook her head, replaying in her mind all her happy times with the boy who had seemed a gift from God, the boy who would assure her future happiness.

Abruptly she stopped both her reverie and her rocking. Pacing around the room, she came to a hurtful but practical insight. Never again would she put herself in a position to be hurt for love's sake. It was too painful to bear. Plenty of people lived without love. Take Aunt Lavinia, for instance. Childless. Years spent in a loveless marriage. Yet she survived and functioned. Lily and Caleb used to be her models of happiness in life. For her, such happiness was a mirage. Somehow she would endure, but her life would never be the same.

That settled, Rose went back into the bedroom and packed away in a trunk all vestiges of Alf's presence. She could not be tortured at every turn by reminders of the boy she might never see again. Bess came and stood in the door watching her. "Do you think it's too early for this? Might Alf still be recovered?"

"The best chance of finding him was night before last. The more time that elapses, the colder the trail. Besides, what claim do I have over him?" Rose wrapped her arms around her waist in the attempt to keep from flying into pieces. "I was simply a temporary custodian." Even as she spoke, she was aware of the flint in her voice.

Bess crossed the room and gathered Rose in her arms. "Oh, lovie, don't succumb to bitterness. Never lose sight of the joy he brought and may one day bring again." Rose felt Bess's strong hand rubbing her back, easing the coiled muscles bunched beneath her gown. "Come, now, Rose. The morning is yet cool. Let's sit on the front porch with a glass of lemonade and watch the passing scene. Small as it is, Cottonwood Falls is a bustling place."

Rose allowed herself to be led to the porch. Zinnias bloomed in a riot of color along the picket fence and the shaded porch brought a measure of relief to her troubled soul. Ulysses trailed them and stretched out atop a porch railing. Along with the lemonade, Bess had brought out the latest issue of *Peterson's Magazine*. Rather than talking, she began reading one of the stories aloud. Although Rose made no effort to follow the intricacies of plot and character, she relaxed to the melodious sound of Bess's voice. Soon her eyes drifted shut, although she remained aware of the soft breeze caressing her face and the light floral fragrance of Bess's *eau de cologne*. Would she ever be more than a sleepwalker drifting through her remaining days?

She was startled out of her reverie when Bess abruptly stopped reading and stood. "Seth is here," she said. "Good morning. What brings you to town?"

Rose watched the big man come up the walk, where he paused at the base of the porch steps and spoke to Bess. "Begging your pardon, ma'am, but I need to talk with Rose."

Rose shrank in her chair. What could they possibly have to say to one another now that Alf, who had drawn them into company with one another, was gone? More than that, seeing Seth threatened the emotional defenses she had so carefully put in place. "I couldn't impose upon your time or your duties here in town," she heard herself saying in a stilted tone.

"You are my duty in town. Please, hear me out."

Bess gathered her book. "I must begin preparations for the midday meal. Please excuse me." Before Rose could protest, her friend was gone.

"May I?" Seth asked, nodding to the chair Bess had just vacated.

"I suppose. After all, you're here."

Seth placed his hat on the porch railing and drew his chair closer. "I have come to apologize."

"Whatever for?"

"I didn't come to the camp meeting." He voice was scratchy, as if he needed to clear his throat. "I should've been there. Perhaps," he shrugged helplessly, "I could have helped watch over Alf or seen something to prevent what happened."

"The blame is mine," Rose said. "Alf lived with me, I considered him my boy, and his welfare was my responsibility."

"No, Rose, no. Many of us loved Alf. Perhaps most of all, the two of us. I had come to regard him as the son I will never have. You cannot accept more than your share of this burden. I forbid it."

Rose couldn't help it. A sardonic laugh escaped her. "Who are you to forbid me anything or to forgive me my sin of neglect?"

Seth ran a hand through his curly hair in frustration. "Who is any of us to forgive? Are you going to forgive me?"

"Forgiveness lies with God."

"So I've been told." He shook his head doubtfully, and she waited for him to continue. "I'm having trouble with that God about now."

"So am I." Even as she spoke the words, she was aware of the poison of a creeping bitterness. "Where is the gentle, compassionate Father?"

Seth sighed as if from the depths of his chest. "My hope is that He is with Alf."

For a long while, they remained awkwardly silent. Seth showed no signs of leaving, yet she had nothing further to say to him. Conversation that used to flow between them had simply dried up.

Then Seth turned to her and picked up her hands, caressing her fingers with his callused thumbs. "Rose, I'm not good with words, so this is hard for me to say. It's not only Alf I will miss. I also enjoy your company."

Rose sat dumbly, her only sensations that of his warm hands and his choked voice.

"I failed you the other night when you needed me. I never want to fail you again."

Something in his words and the sincerity evident in his eyes cracked the ice encasing her heart. "Seth, I know you would never hurt me. You are a kind man. Perhaps more than anyone else, you are able to empathize with my pain. On the one hand, you are a reminder of happier times. On the other, I see my grief mirrored in you."

Seth seemed to be considering her words. "Then, please, Rose, let us be friends who can help each other through this situation. Our faith has been shaken. Maybe through each other, we can find it once more. And best of all, find our Alf."

Our Alf. If only. "Friends, then."

He stood, drawing her to her feet. He cupped her face, studying it as if he'd never really looked at her until this moment. "Lean on me, Rose. Lean on me. And forgive me."

Then he picked up his hat and walked away, leaving her far less stoic. In fact, leaving her in a confused state, more peaceful than bitter.

Chapter Eleven

Ten days passed, although for Rose, one day brought the same emptiness as the next, and the passage of time served only to remind her how long it had been since she had seen Alf. Bess, Aunt Lavinia and Hannah alternated caring for her. In her mind she knew she was not an invalid and that they were helping to assuage her father's anguish, but she could not rouse herself to resume her duties. Sunday, they had all encouraged her to go to church. She refused. There was nothing there for her any longer. Her only solace was the loyalty of her beloved Ulysses, whose purrs and soft paws kneading her chest reminded her that beneath her stony exterior, she was still capable of affection.

Her father sent her doleful looks, Bess offered tender ministrations and Aunt Lavinia seemed poised for the moment when she could effect some change in Rose's self-protective isolation. The sheriff had told Ezra that a couple of townspeople had reported seeing a shadowy figure lurking in back alleys the night before Alf disappeared, but neither was able to give a clear description. It was only the children who had mentioned seeing a woman. Rose couldn't let herself consider the possibility that Alf had been taken by some unscrupulous opportunist. Much as she recoiled from the scrawled note that had sealed Alf's fate, she clung to the hope that only a parent would love a child enough to leave him for a time in better conditions and then reclaim him.

Today was the meeting of the Library Society, to be held at Lavinia's. Rose couldn't imagine attending and facing the pity on some faces and the satisfaction on others like Bertha Britten's. How the undertaker's wife must be gloating over her comeuppance. As usual, Rose sat on the porch with Ulysses rocking away the morning, carefully controlling her emotions.

When a carriage pulled up in front of the house, Rose was startled to see Aunt Lavinia and Lily emerge, dressed in their Sunday finest. They marched up the walk and stood in front of Rose. Lily leaned over and whispered in her ear, "Get up, sister. We're here to dress you for this afternoon's meeting."

Rose recoiled. "I can't."

Lavinia took hold of her arm and pulled her to her feet. "'I can't' is no longer part of your vocabulary. You've languished long enough, and we've respected your need to do so. Now it's time for you to return to the land of the living. The evening meal will be the last prepared by any of us. For today, you will get dressed and accompany us to my home in time for the arrival of my guests."

Unnamed emotions roiled within Rose, but mutely she permitted herself to be led to her bedroom, where Lily proceeded to select a gown and Aunt Lavinia supervised her toilette. When it came time to leave,

Rose stood stock-still in the bedroom door. "I can't face them."

"Who?" Lily asked. "Your friends who care about you, sympathize with you and miss you? You mean, those terrible women?"

"There are some who—"

"Pooh!" Aunt Lavinia exploded. "Are you referring to the sanctimonious few? Neither Lily nor I will permit you to cower here, avoiding the likes of such folks. You have done nothing except provide a loving home for an abandoned waif. You will not, nor will any who love you, make apologies for that exercise of compassion. Now, then, hold that head high and come along." Brooking no opposition, Lavinia escorted her to the carriage, trailed by Lily who grabbed Rose's bonnet as she left the house.

While they waited at Lavinia's for the arrival of the other women, Lily placed the tea sandwiches Hannah had left for them on a glass platter, and Lavinia sliced the pound cake into pieces, removed them to china dessert plates and poured strawberry sauce over each serving.

As the guests filed in, it was soon obvious that they were more enthralled with examining Lavinia's lavish furnishings than with scrutinizing Rose. One or two of the women sought her out and murmured their sympathy. When Bess arrived, she came straight over and embraced her. "I'm so glad you're here. Come sit with me." She led Rose to a horsehair settee with a view of a magnificent oil portrait of Lavinia as a younger woman. "She was a beauty," Bess whispered.

"I can see my mother in her," Rose replied, with a stab of longing.

At the bang of a gavel, Willa Stone opened the meeting. Rose sat still, as if looking down upon herself from a cloud, listening to words which failed to penetrate. *Book selection committee. Next month's paper on King Arthur. Courthouse Ball.*

When Bess stood up, with an effort Rose refocused her attention.

"Ladies, plans for the grand celebration for the dedication of our new courthouse are taking form. It will be both exciting and elegant, especially the ball to be held on the premises." With a sparkling smile, she added, "It's not too early to engage your dressmaker to create a new frock for the event."

An excited murmur circulated through the room as Bess sat back down and squeezed Rose's hand. "This will give you something to look forward to."

An icy chill ran through Rose. A celebration? She was hardly in the mood. And a dance? That was Lily's forte. She herself was clumsy. Besides, one needed a partner. She wasn't inclined to attend.

She sat back, giving scant attention to the presentation of today's paper, a lengthy, uninspiring ramble on the Cavalier poets. At last came a reprieve. Adjournment and refreshments. Rose followed Bess to the intricately carved mahogany dining room table and picked up her plate, intending to retreat to a corner of the parlor. To her chagrin, Bertha Britten sidled up and waylaid her in conversation. After meaningless small talk, Bertha got to the point Rose suspected she'd had in mind all along. "So sad about your orphan boy. But I imagine it's all for the best, don't you? He belongs with his people." Rose gritted her teeth at the way the woman uttered *his people*.

Relentlessly, Bertha continued. "You were, of course, a saint to take him in without regard for tarnishing your reputation, but we all know that such abandoned children are not of our class. You may someday expect children of your own, and then you will, no doubt, understand my meaning."

Rose was speechless with outrage. How dare Bertha Britten so demean both her and Alf. Just then Aunt Lavinia swept up, apparently having overheard Bertha. "Madam, class has nothing to do with one's origins, but rather with one's behavior in society." Lavinia pinned Bertha with a haughty stare. "You, my dear, have some things to learn on that account."

Bertha's jaw flapped helplessly as she scrambled for a riposte, but all she managed was "Some people!" before hurrying off to join a group on the far side of the room.

Lavinia moved close to Rose and spoke softly. "That woman is unworthy of your attention or concern. I myself am proud that I have a niece who puts others before herself."

Then Lavinia moved off to circulate among her guests. With a start, Rose realized that this recent exchange had left her more alive than she'd felt in days. If Aunt Lavinia, of all people, could fight for her, she certainly should do all she could to stand up for herself and for Alf.

Lily approached, a secretive smile gracing her features. Rose knew that look. "What?" she said.

"Look at you, sister. I do believe you now have one foot in Lavinia's land of the living."

Rose blushed. "I have been a bit of a recluse, haven't I? I'm sorry if I've caused all of you concern. I need to grieve, but that doesn't mean I must remain passive." Then she, too, managed a grin. "Who would've believed that Bertha Britten and Aunt Lavinia would be the agents of my restoration?"

"God works in mysterious ways."

There it was. God again. Had she been wrong to dismiss Him? Was there still room for Him in her life? Her mother had always counseled giving God time to work, and so often she had been right. Perhaps this was one of those times. Yet waiting was excruciating. "Perhaps." That was all the answer she was prepared to give.

Lily put an arm around Rose and nestled her close. "Today was a start, dear. I'm proud of you. I realize it was an effort to come. We know life is not the same for you now, but better days will come."

Rose shrugged with doubt. "Promise?"

"I promise." Lily hugged her again. "Just you wait and see."

On his way back to the ranch from picking up supplies in town, Seth paused the team on the hill above Caleb's house. Fattened cattle grazed in the distance. The open range stretched out before him, offering the promise of bountiful pastureland. Meat prices were on the rise, so the fall roundup and sale stood to bring a handsome profit to the Montgomerys. However, rustlers were always a threat. As a result, he and Caleb had posted outriders. Seth had read about the introduction of barbed wire fencing in some areas, but he hoped it wouldn't come to that in the Flint Hills. Surely gentlemen's agreements regarding the open range would be sufficient.

Back at the barn, Seth escaped into the manual labor of unloading the supplies. Work was all that kept him from going crazy wondering about Alf. The more sweat, the better. He knew he should have stopped to see Rose while he was in Cottonwood Falls today, but he was too cowardly to do it. Her ravaged face had pierced his heart. And what more would they have found to say to one another?

Just as Seth finished unloading the wagon, Caleb rode up. "I know you planned to see Sheriff Jensen while you were in town. Any news?"

Seth perched on a nearby hay bale. "No. Every day it's all I can do not to ride out to hunt for Alf, but where would I go?"

Caleb dismounted and sat down beside him. "I don't know which is worse—taking ill-conceived action or waiting. That same dilemma faced us in the war."

Seth figured his brother had a heap of experience with both. "I should be able to shake this off. Come to grips with the fact that Alf is with a parent. But I can't. I have a bad feeling about what's happening with him." He studied his hands, clasping his knees in frustration. "It's hard to know where God is in this situation. I try to hang on to my faith, but Alf's kidnapping is too much."

"I know that feeling." Caleb went silent, seemingly lost in his memories. "Trying to find God on a battlefield…" He did not finish the thought.

"You seldom talk about your army experiences."

"They're not pretty. You can't watch men being blown to smithereens or running through a rain of bullets in unfamiliar territory, without questioning the sanity of the human race."

"So how did you reconcile God with all of that?"

"Seth, you cannot believe the acts of courage and compassion I witnessed. Individual men can be astonishing in the face of chaos. I knew I would drive myself crazy if I thought God was the source of all that pain and destruction. The only way I made it through the war was to focus on the good I saw amid the terror and to honor the many selfless acts performed by men on both sides. There is infinite good in humanity just as there is greed for power, money or position." Caleb sat quietly, his jaw working. Seth knew he had more to say. His brother cleared his throat before continuing. "Seth, Lily is the only other person who knows what I'm going to tell you. At the Battle of the Washita River out in Indian Territory after the war, Custer led us into an unnecessary and bloody massacre, one I was helpless to prevent but which has wounded my soul. For a time after that, I thought I was unworthy of love, unworthy of God's forgiveness."

Stunned, Seth was at a loss for words. He'd known his brother carried battle scars, both physical and emotional, but hearing this now, he could feel the immediacy of Caleb's pain.

"I don't tell you this for you to pity me or think less of me. I speak because I have learned there is forgiveness. Redemption." Caleb laid a hand on Seth's shoulder. "I want that for you."

"How did you...?"

"Lily, for starters. She helped me to understand that God isn't the cause of the bad things that happen. Human beings are. She also helped me learn the patience of waiting for God, of understanding His timing. It was His timing, not ours, that finally brought Lily and me together. Her steadfast love has healed me, to the extent that is possible."

The two men fell silent. "If only I could know Alf is safe," Seth said.

"Turn him over to God, brother."

"It's hard."

"God knows what Alf needs. He can do more for him than we have any idea. Pray for the boy."

"I try."

"You're expecting immediate answers. Remember, all things in God's good time."

His brother had given him much to ponder. Seth rose to his feet and, looking down at Caleb, said, "One way I hold out hope that there is a caring God is you. Thanks for being a fine brother."

Caleb stood and the two embraced awkwardly. Just before they broke apart, Seth heard his brother mutter, "And don't forget that God sent you Rose."

Late in August, Lily persuaded Rose to spend a couple of weeks at the ranch. "The change of scene should do you good," her sister had said by way of persuasion, and, truth to tell, while the daily routine at the Kellogg house kept Rose busy, the surroundings constantly reminded her of her missing child. Lavinia was once again sparing Hannah to prepare meals for Ezra, and Bess also had agreed to stop by to check on him and feed Ulysses, so there was really no reason not to accept Lily's invitation. Rose figured one place was as good as another to grieve.

Yet when she arrived at Caleb and Lily's, there was one factor she had failed to consider. Mattie. She loved her niece and couldn't find it in her heart to resent her. Yet, holding her, smelling the lemon-sweet scent of her washed hair and feeling her niece's tiny hand clasped in her own, brought memories that ripped Rose apart. Once when Mattie looked up at her and questioned, "Brudder?" Lily shushed her, but not before Rose teared up with the bittersweetness of it. Watching Lily and Caleb with their daughter dredged up the very pain that Rose was trying to come to grips with. Yet she found comfort in cuddling Mattie and sharing in her giggles over the fuzzy caterpillar they found on the porch.

Happily, the ranch house was situated on a hill and was blessed by breezes that never reached the house in town. Daytimes, the heat was relentless, but almost every evening, it cooled off. After supper the four of them would often sit on the porch. Sometimes Lily read poems aloud or Caleb told a Bible story for Mattie's benefit. One night they sang familiar hymns, with Caleb's rich baritone leading the way. Being witness to such contentment, Rose found herself relaxing into the ebb and flow of their family life.

Toward the end of her stay, Rose and Lily lingered on the porch one evening to enjoy the full moon while Caleb and Mattie went on to bed. The prairie was aglow with moonlight, and myriad stars blanketed the heavens. The creak of their rockers and the baying of far-off coyotes provided accompaniment to the silence between them. In that moment, Rose felt especially blessed to have such a sister. No words were necessary. Lily's acts of kindness and common sense were proof enough of her love. How strange, Rose reflected, that Lily's ambition to live in a cosmopolitan city had, instead, brought her here—brought her to a love worth the sacrifice.

"You can have other children, you know," Lily whispered into the dark.

Rose startled. She had long ago given up that hope. "No, I can't."

Lily turned toward her, her face highlighted in the moonglow. "I know there will never be another Alf, but, dear, you may very well marry and bear children."

"I know you're trying to help," Rose said, "but that will never happen."

Lily continued to study her, to the point Rose finally had to look down. "There's something you're not telling me, isn't there?"

Her throat filling with bile, she shut her eyes against painful memories.

"Rose?" Lily moved her chair closer. "Please. I hope we can confide anything to one another."

As she brushed away the traitorous tears streaking her cheeks, Rose looked at her sister. "Before Papa and I left Fort Larned, I'd decided marriage was not for me."

"Why ever not? You would make some man a delightful helpmate."

Rose strangled on bitterness. "Men are not to be trusted."

"Who could you possibly mean? Papa? Caleb?" Then as if clouds had suddenly obliterated the moon, Lily's mouth fell open and she gripped her sister's hand. "What man, Rose? Tell me. It must've been after I went to St. Louis."

As if a raging flood had surged against an earthen dam and breached it, Rose could no longer withhold the brutal details of her sergeant's betrayal. "I thought he loved me, Lily, truly I did. He made me feel…oh, dear…lovely. Desirable." Then she laughed scoffingly. "Me? Rose Kellogg, desirable? What a ninny I was to believe one word that came out of that man's mouth! How pathetic to be so giddy and vulnerable."

Lily, apparently sensing her sister's need to purge herself of the venom of betrayal, let her ramble on.

"It is one thing to enter upon a private dalliance, but some at Fort Larned, though not Papa, knew the sergeant was courting me. And how many of them, do you suppose, also knew he was married? What a joke on me, they must've thought. More fool I."

"He was very wrong to so mislead you, Rose. However, that doesn't mean he didn't have feelings for you or was being untruthful about your charms. You are an appealing woman, especially, I imagine, to someone who is lonely and far from home."

"Don't excuse him. That only makes me feel all the more naive." Rose stewed with the effort to get her sister to understand. "For once, I truly thought a man would cherish me. That I, homely Rose Kellogg, could have a home of my own and children. Well, you can forget about that."

"That cad hurt you to the core." Lily's eyes now shone with tears. "He's lucky I can't get hold of him. But, Rose, you mustn't tar all men with the same brush."

"Intellectually, I understand that and have evidence of that in Papa, Caleb and others."

"Seth?"

Rose groaned inwardly. Her sister would have to bring him up. "Seth and I are friends. That is all we will ever be to one another. Evidence suggests that he is a fine man. But hear me now. I will never again put myself in the position of making a fool of myself for a man nor allow a man to have power over me or inflict hurt upon me. Not if I can prevent it."

"Oh, Rose," Lily said. "I am sorry for your pain and puzzled as to how to help you understand that one man's perfidy is no cause to reject another."

Rose relented. "I know you mean well, Lily. I've held in this episode with the sergeant for so long that while it is a relief to talk about it, I am sorry it has caused you distress. More than anything, I hope it will help you see why I am resigned to living as a spinster and why Alf's loss has so injured me."

"That's enough," Lily said, her voice charged with purpose. "We will not speak of this again, nor will I permit you to indulge your poor opinion of yourself. I heard you, now you hear me. You are a lovely, talented, caring woman who deserves all that God has in store. Trust me, His eye is every bit as much on you as on the sparrow. Good things are in your future, Rose, so pay attention and don't let the past blind you to what awaits. There," she said, rising to her feet, "that's enough for one evening. Pray take your rest and consider the one thing I know for certain. God is not finished with Rose Kellogg."

Seth and his father sat at the kitchen table devouring the pork chops, biscuits and gravy Sophie had prepared. "Sit down, Sophie," Andrew said. "I reckon you've piled us up enough food to stave off starvation."

Sophie eased into her chair and helped herself to a dainty serving. "I surely wouldn't want you menfolk to be deprived of nourishment this close to the roundup."

With so innocent a look that Seth was immediately put on the defensive, she added. "I guess I'll soon have to start bulking up a bit more myself."

Andrew eyed her as he ladled a spoonful toward his mouth. "And why might that be?"

"So I can keep up with you."

Seth sputtered. "Keep up with us? Tell me you're not saying what I think you are."

Smiling, Sophie wiped her mouth with her napkin. "Brother dear, if you conclude I'm riding with you on the roundup, well, then, go to the head of the class."

Seth turned to his father. "Pa, do you know about this?"

"Well, we are short a man," he admitted with a sheepish grin.

"Have you looked lately? Sophie is no man." The mere thought of his sister riding the range with a bunch of ill-mannered rubes sent his temperature soaring.

"No, son, she isn't. But she's a darned good hand and she can ride better than most of our cowpokes."

"Who'll protect her?"

Sophie shoved back her plate. "Who needs protecting? I can outride and outshoot any of those fellas."

"You can outtalk them, too," Seth muttered, glaring at his father. "Now I'll have to keep one eye on you and one eye on the steers."

"Since when did you get so all-fired protective of me? Seems like I did everything you boys did when we were growing up."

"But…" Seth sought the words he needed "…you're a lady now. You're even being courted. Maybe it's time to grow up. Do womanly things."

Sophie's laughter eased the tension. "Seth, you are

a dear to concern yourself, but I can be both—a tomboy and a flirt."

Seth once again appealed to his father. "Pa?"

Andrew shrugged. "Son, when have we ever bested this one in a debate? Not likely to start now. She'll come with us."

Defeated, Seth slumped in his chair, moving his spoon through the gravy on his plate. Sophie was, indeed, one of a kind, yet he'd no more let Rose go on a roundup than fly. Shoot. Where had that thought come from? The woman had taken up residence in his brain and wouldn't budge. Friends, that's all they were. Rose had made that quite clear. He had no claim on her, so persisting with anything further would lead only to awkwardness and hurt.

Sophie leaned over and caressed his forearm. "See? It's all settled. I appreciate your concern, Seth, but it's time you understood that I'm my own woman now. You no longer have to take care of me."

As if. He would always take care of her, however she needed him to. "We'll see, sister, we'll see."

Later that night after they'd all gone to bed, Seth tossed restlessly, thinking about the way life changes. Sophie, once a little firecracker of a girl, was now a woman in love. Alf, who'd been given a loving home, was lost in the wilds of Kansas. It was as if there wasn't a thing a man could count on. He knew what Caleb and Lily would say to that. He could count on God, they would remind him. Reflecting on his recent talk with Caleb, it was obvious how God had played a role in his and Lily's lives. It wasn't so obvious with others. Were some just lucky? Favored by the deity? Or in ways still lost to him, were all people under God's care and direction?

Sometime after ten, he fell into a deep sleep only to be aroused by a clatter from the henhouse, followed by the howling of the ranch dogs. Jumping out of bed, he ran barefooted to the front porch. It was then he made out a figure on horseback approaching the ranch.

"Hush," he said, motioning the dogs to be still. In a moment he was joined by his father, also having been rousted by the racket.

"Who's that?"

"Can't tell yet," Seth answered, straining his eyes to identify the rider.

"Can't be good news, coming like this in the middle of the night."

Then they were joined by Sophie, her shoulders covered by a shawl. "Mercy, what's happening?"

"Seth, I believe it's the sheriff," Andrew said.

Seth sighed. "Hope that doesn't mean rustlers."

"Or worse," Sophie whispered, shivering against Seth.

They waited for what seemed an interminable time for Jensen to cover the ground separating them. Finally the man rode up to the porch, dismounted and tied his mount to the post. Eyeing the threesome clad in nightclothes, the sheriff apologized for disturbing them before saying, "I have some news about the boy the Kelloggs took in."

Seth held his breath, his chest expanding with both dread and hope.

"I've already talked with Doc and I'm on the way to your brother's place to visit Rose, but since you're on the way, I thought I'd stop here and tell you what I know."

"We thank you, Sheriff," Andrew said. "Go ahead."

Sophie slipped her hand into Seth's, as if to steady him, as Jensen began to speak. "Up Council Grove way, there's been an unfortunate circumstance. Indian woman who worked at the saloon was killed last night. Murdered, it appears, by her drunken white husband, a fella who, it turns out, is an army deserter, wanted all over the territory. Perhaps the same man we heard about earlier, up Fort Riley way."

Seth strained with impatience. *Get on with it. What does this have to do with Alf?*

"Seems the woman was living in a lean-to behind the saloon with her son. Little half-breed boy about three or four years old."

"Alf?" Seth's knees nearly buckled.

"Don't know yet, Montgomery, but it could be. The authorities in Morris County have incarcerated the alleged killer, and the sheriff's wife there has taken the youngster in, pending identification by someone from here. Sorry to bother you, but I thought you'd want to know."

Rose. Dear God, let it be Alf. Seth felt as if his chest would explode any minute.

"Indeed, we do—" Andrew started his reply, but Seth was long gone into the house throwing on his clothes and boots and gathering up his hat. He ran back onto the porch. "I'm going with you, Sheriff," he said as he raced past the group on his way to saddle Patches. All he knew was that he had to get to Rose. Now.

Chapter Twelve

Despite the sweltering heat, Rose and Lily had had a busy day, canning the last of the season's tomatoes and baking the stollen Ezra favored. In the upstairs bedroom she shared with Mattie, Rose packed her valise in preparation for her morning return to Cottonwood Falls. She took down her hair and slipped into a lightweight nightgown, grateful for the cooler September nights. Before she climbed into bed, she stood observing Mattie, one little fist tucked under her chin, her long eyelashes closed in slumber. Rose wrapped her arms around her waist to hold in an involuntary sob. How often she had stood just so over Alf's trundle bed, glorying in the sight of her dear boy? Although this time with Lily's family had been therapeutic, it had not for one moment assuaged her sense of loss. Life would go on. Somehow it always did. But nothing would ever be the same.

Lying on her back in bed, unable to sleep, Rose fixed her gaze on the moon, wondering if somewhere that same moon shone down on Alf. Although she'd turned her back on the church, there was still one prayer she uttered every night before sleep took over. Tonight was no exception. *Dear God, wherever Alf is and whomever he is with, bestow on him the gift of love. May he always know that a woman in Cotton-wood Falls loves him very much.*

Finally, caressed by the night breezes and spent from the day's labors, she succumbed to sleep. Dreams flitted in and out of her awareness. In one, a happy boy trotted around the lawn on a stick horse while a big man and a smaller woman looked on with pride and joy. In another, though, a woman with unkempt long hair and talonlike nails grabbed a child from her arms, cackling with triumph. As if grappling with a restless spirit, Rose woke up, her heart pounding with the knowledge she was powerless. Gradually, she adjusted her eyes to the darkness. Everything was normal. Mattie was still sound asleep, the house was quiet and the gentle breeze brought comfort. Rose felt consumed by restlessness.

Gathering a light robe around her, she tiptoed down the stairs, eased open the front door and curled up in one of the rockers. The night was luminescent and laden with the fragrances of growing things. Ordinarily she would have had every reason to be at peace in these surroundings. Peace…the illusive balm that never came. She sat there a long time, caught up in the night sounds and her own wayward thoughts. The Creator who made this beautiful world would surely never turn His back on a child He had also created.

A shift in wind direction brought with it a new sound, inconsistent with the night's tranquility. A rhythmic clopping noise, far away and yet drawing closer with each breath she took. Horses. Voices. She rose to her feet, aware that night riders were either outlaws or harbingers of ill tidings. Papa? Had some accident befallen him? Behind her she heard the clatter of footsteps, and Caleb burst onto the porch, a rifle clutched in his hands, trailed by Lily, tying the sash of her wrapper. "Shh," Caleb whispered. "Get inside and lock yourselves in."

Lily grabbed her arm, drew her inside and latched the door. The two women huddled together, fearing the worst and hoping for the best. Caleb remained silent as the hoofbeats grew louder and louder. After what seemed an eternity, Caleb rapped on the door and said, "Come on out. It's Seth and Sheriff Jensen." Simultaneously the women expelled the sighs they'd been holding in. They crept back onto the porch, knowing that the two men, though familiar, could still be the bearers of unpleasant news.

Seth waved his hat before he dismounted, and after hitching their mounts to fence posts, the two walked rapidly toward the house. "The sheriff has possible news of Alf," Seth shouted.

Rose sagged against her sister, unable to read Seth's expression. Could this be the good news they'd been praying for or something sinister? Caleb ushered the group into the house. The men remained standing, but Lily and Rose sank onto the love seat. Rose dared a peek at Seth, willing him to give her a shred of hope. He nodded briefly, but his expression conveyed nothing. Nearly overcome with anxiety, she clenched her fists and waited for the sheriff to speak.

After what seemed an eternity, he looked straight at her and said quietly, "We have reason to believe we have found your Alf."

A hundred rampaging questions flooded her mind:

Was he alive? Was he safe? Who had taken him? Could he be returned to her?

"Currently he is being well cared for by the sheriff's wife up in Council Grove. That's the good news. However, he has witnessed a heinous crime."

Taut with anticipation, Rose listened with the others while the sheriff told of the strangulation death of the Indian woman who claimed to be Alf's mother at the hands of an army deserter who admitted to fathering the boy. Faint with relief and concern for Alf, Rose saw spots swimming before her eyes and lowered her head to her knees. Quickly, Lily knelt beside her. "Take a deep breath, Rose." Caleb got her a glass of water. "Drink," Lily murmured.

Finally regaining her senses, Rose sat up, limp with emotion. Then in that deep voice she recognized so well, Seth said, "I believe this is good news, Rose. When you are able, I propose we go to Council Grove to make a positive identification."

Unbidden, a rush of fear clouded Rose's thinking. "I'm afraid to hope." She rose to her feet and faced the sheriff. "How can we know this is our Alf and not some other boy?"

"You are right, Miss Kellogg, to exercise caution, lest your hopes be dashed. We cannot know with certainty until we see the boy. That is why I hope you can make the trip."

"I would cross any ocean to be with Alf."

"As would I," Seth added.

The sheriff clapped his hat back on his head. "Well, that's settled. I propose we leave as early in the morning as you two can get to my office. It will be best to travel in the cool of the day."

Seth moved to Rose and took her hands in his. "I will bring the buggy shortly after dawn."

Rose looked up into Seth's warm hazel eyes, reading there his love for the boy. "I will be ready."

The sheriff started toward the door, then turned back to face them. "Oh, one other thing. Do you know anything about a large agate? The Morris County sheriff says the boy has the marble with him constantly."

Rose fell against Seth's broad chest, laughing and crying all at the same time. "Lavinia's agate! Oh, Seth, it has to be Alf, doesn't it?"

Lily approached the two. "It's a very good sign, Rose. Thanks be to God." Then, easing Rose from Seth's protective embrace, Lily led her from the room. "You must rest. The journey tomorrow demands it."

Rose allowed herself to be escorted upstairs and tucked into bed by her sister. Before Lily leaned over to kiss her forehead, Rose heard her whisper. "You see, all things in God's good time."

Long after Lily had left the room, Rose lay smiling, marveling that so much could change in one day's time. Then a more unsettling thought surfaced. In that moment of happy revelation it was to Seth she had turned, not Lily. And it was there she had, at last, found strength.

The next morning, holding the reins loosely in his hands, Seth watched the twenty-two miles of countryside to Council Grove roll by at what seemed a snail's pace. Sheriff Jensen, mounted, led the way and the buggy horse followed docilely along. Beside Seth, Rose sat, her fingers intertwined, staring resolutely ahead. Neither of them had gotten much sleep, but so electrified by possibility were they, that dozing to the lulling rhythm of the buggy ride was unthinkable.

"What if it's not Lavinia's agate?"

Seth stewed. Rose had just asked the question plaguing him as well. Any number of other explanations occurred to him. Agates were not uncommon, so any boy might have one similar to Alf's. Or have found the marble at some random place. Yet there remained the fact of the dual parentage the sheriff had described. Shuddering at the thought of the crime that had been committed, Seth laid a hand over Rose's balled fists to reassure her. "Time will tell. For now, let's keep the faith."

"I'm trying." They rode for several minutes, and then Rose moved one cold hand to cover his warm one. "Faith. I wonder. We've been pretty hard on God, haven't we?" She looked up with a wistful smile. "Especially if our prayer for Alf's safety has been answered."

"We've talked about God's timing. Patience is a lesson I'd rather have learned some other way."

"Even if the boy is Alf, how do I know the Morris County sheriff will release him to me?"

Uncannily, she was voicing yet another of his concerns. "I can't believe that fellow and his wife will want to keep the boy indefinitely. And if it is Alf, he will take one look at you, and no one will question where he belongs."

Rose nodded, then withdrew into herself for a mile or two. Later, out of the blue, she said, "I want to adopt him legally."

Seth grinned. "Why is that no surprise? It's prudent, as well. For all intents and purposes, especially if his father is convicted of murder, the boy is an orphan. No one who has seen the two of you together would question the appropriateness of such an adoption."

She nearly bounced on the seat beside him. "Can't this wagon move any faster?"

"Old Nellie's doing her best."

Rose pulled a couple of ham sandwiches from her bag and handed him one. "I don't know if I can swallow, but I suppose it's best to take nourishment."

Seth took a generous bite, realizing his stomach had been growling for quite some time. In his haste to get away this morning, he'd grabbed only a couple of biscuits and headed to the barn. "Mighty tasty," he said. "But what else would I expect from a cook like you?"

Unable to finish hers, Rose wrapped the crusts back up and stashed them in her bag. "It's still a puzzlement where to find God in the bad things that happen."

Seth didn't know whether he should reveal his conversation with Caleb, but surely he could convey the essence of it. "I've been stewing about that question. Maybe we're not supposed to be able to justify things like my mother's untimely death, the devastation of war or the abduction of a child. Perhaps there's no accounting for the fact that we're human beings, subject to everything that entails. You know, Caleb helped me with my questions."

Rose glanced up, her posture one of attention. "How?"

"We're all eager to thank God for the blessings in our lives, but too hasty in our helplessness to place blame. Caleb spoke of the horrors he witnessed in battle—atrocities that challenged his faith. But he also spoke of the valor and compassion he observed in the most desperate of circumstances that proved to him that God is with us. Quite simply, He is with us through the kind and courageous acts of our fellows."

Rose took his hand in hers, studying it as if thereon commandments had been inscribed. "Seth Montgomery, I do believe that's the longest and most eloquent speech I've ever heard from you."

Seth could feel the flush rising from his neck to his face.

She patted his hand and withdrew hers into her lap. "It's also the most helpful. Thank you."

Engaged in their deep conversation, they had failed to notice clustered farmhouses and, in the distance, the spire of a church.

Sheriff Jensen wheeled his horse and came alongside the buggy. "Won't be too long now. We'll go straight to the sheriff's office and then on to his home for the identification." Before he retook the lead, he doffed his hat to Rose. "Miss Kellogg, I'm praying for you and your boy."

Seth swallowed the lump in his throat. "See, Rose? That's the sort of kindness that shows us we're not alone. God sometimes speaks to us through others— through folks like Jensen."

"I need his prayers," Rose said softly. "And yours."

"They are the least I can give to you." He found himself unable to speak from that point on, his heart too full of concern for this woman and hope for her future.

The afternoon sun bore down unmercifully, and Rose was grateful for the bonnet that shaded her eyes. Ordinarily she would've taken in the scene of the famous Council Oak that gave the town its name, but all her attention was focused on the sign in front of a clapboard structure on a corner of the main street: *Sheriff's Office, Morris County, Kansas.*

Wilting with heat and expectation, she took Seth's hand when he helped her from the buggy and led her into the small, sparse office adjacent to the annex housing jail cells. A tall man wearing a cowboy hat and sporting a bushy red beard came out from behind his desk, the silver of the star on his chest glinting in a shaft of sunlight. "I'm Sheriff Riley. You must be Miss Kellogg," he said, extending his hand.

"I am, and this is my friend Seth Montgomery, and of course you know Lars Jensen."

"Have a seat, miss, and we'll get right to business." He reclaimed his desk chair after directing the others to the three available wooden chairs.

Dizzy with expectation, Rose clutched her bag, willing the sheriff to act with expediency.

"We understand that you found a half-breed boy in your barn several months ago and took him into your home."

"Yes." She cleared her throat. "Yes. Alf. There was a note with him." She repeated the note's brief contents. "I took it as a sign that I was to care for him."

"Could you please describe the boy?"

She did the best she could to draw a mental portrait for the man. When she finished, he did not look up but studied several papers in front of him.

"Why would someone leave him with you? Have you any suspicions about who would do such a thing?"

"I have no idea who was involved. However, the note left after he was taken from the camp meeting would suggest it was one of his parents. As for why he would've been left with me, the only reason I can deduce is the fact my father is a doctor. Perhaps that seemed a sign the boy would be in good hands."

"Possibly," Sheriff Riley muttered. "Did the child take to you and your father?"

Seth interjected himself. "She and Dr. Kellogg could not have been more welcoming or done more for the boy. He is devoted to them both."

"Thank you," Riley said without looking up. He shuffled his paper work. "Are you willing to take over temporary care of the boy?"

"Not only that, I plan to adopt him."

The sheriff's head snapped up. "Adopt him?"

"I know what you're thinking. The fact that the boy is a half-breed is immaterial, as is the fact that I am unmarried. He is bright, engaging and in need of a loving home. Not only is it my God-given duty to care for him, it will be the great blessing of my life."

"Could you describe the marble the boy refuses to relinquish?"

"It is a black, white and gray agate given to him by his great-aunt Lavinia Dupree. He treasures it."

Riley turned to Sheriff Jensen. "Do you have anything to add, Jensen?"

"I think the specifics of Miss Kellogg's involvement with the boy are clear. I would add that I, as well as other folks in Cottonwood Falls, have observed her devotion to the boy and the way he has thrived in her care."

"Well, then," Riley rose to his feet, "all that remains is to take you to my home where Polly, my wife, has been tending to him. However, I must warn you, that the boy undoubtedly witnessed his mother's death and you may find him perhaps different from the child you remember. His mother had been working as a kitchen maid at a local saloon, living in a shack behind the premises. The owner and patrons often noticed a ragged-looking little boy with jet black hair trailing her about. On the evening in question, a drunken man burst into the tavern demanding to know the whereabouts of his wife and child, describing them accurately. When the proprietor tried to eject him, he created a scene, grabbed a bottle of whiskey sitting on the bar and lurched out into the night cursing God and everyone else. Apparently in the wee hours after consuming even more liquor, he found the woman and child in their lodgings and in a rage, strangled her."

With every nerve in her body, Rose longed to clap her hands over her ears and blot out the sheriff's voice.

"We found her body the next morning after one of the local residents noticed the boy wandering down the street crying and calling for someone named E-nah. Later we found the father in an alley near the livery stable, passed out cold. He is currently in custody and has been indicted for murder. As you can well understand, the child has undergone a horrific experience. I apologize for having to give you these sordid details, but if, as I expect, the boy at my house is your Alf, I felt you needed the background."

Rose stood then, more determined than ever to get to Alf. "I appreciate your candor. No matter into what state my Alf has fallen, I hope to restore his confidence in those who love him." Seth took her arm and escorted her to the buggy. On the short drive to the Rileys' home, he said only three words. "Good for you."

Despite the rapid beating of her heart as they walked up to the house, Rose felt enveloped by a God-given calm. A tiny woman with frizzy gray hair opened the door, her simple navy dress adorned only by a gold cross hanging from her neck. "Welcome. I'm Polly Riley. I pray we may be the agents of good news for you." She stood aside for them to enter and then led them into the kitchen.

Laying two hands on Rose's shoulder, she turned her toward the far corner. There hunkered on the floor, his back to them, was her Alf, moving wooden blocks in helter-skelter fashion.

With tear-laden eyes, she looked at Mrs. Riley, who, with a compassionate smile, nodded permission. With the men crowded silently in the doorway, Rose made her way to the boy, praying with every step. Reaching him, she knelt down and placed a gentle hand on his shoulder. "Alf?"

The child did not turn his head. Once more she said his name. As if rousing from a trance, he let the block in his hand fall to the floor and slowly turned to face her, his eyes at first blank and then suddenly filled with life. "Rose?"

"Yes, darling."

"Rose," he shouted, throwing himself into her arms. "My Rose?" Then he took her face in his small hands and ran his fingers down her tear-stained cheeks. "I seed you in a dream. Are you a dream?"

Rose held him close, enveloped by the sweet-salty little boyness of him. "No dream, Alf. I'm here."

Then without warning, he shoved her away. "You left me."

Rose crumpled. How could she never once have

thought he might blame her for his disappearance? She grasped him by the shoulders. "I would never leave, Alf. I promise."

The little fellow merely shrugged. "Maybe."

To Rose, it seemed as if the two of them were lost in their own private world. Then in the corner of her vision, she glimpsed boots crossing the floor. Seth. "Look who else is here, Alf."

The boy shrugged again, but finally turned around. As if the sun had burst forth after a tempest, the boy's eyes grew large with amazement, and he covered his mouth with one hand, as if unable to believe the evidence of his senses. He looked at her questioningly. "Sett?"

"Yes, dear, Seth."

By that time, Seth had reached Alf and swung him up into his arms. "Big!" the boy squealed.

Seth lowered him between his knees. "Little." He laughed before again tossing the boy toward the ceiling.

Rose clutched her heart. Never had she heard more welcome sounds or witnessed more spontaneous love.

Quietly Mrs. Riley moved around the kitchen preparing glasses of milk to go with a large platter of ginger snaps and sugar cookies. When they all sat down at the table, Alf between Seth and her, Rose noticed the boy had quieted down, intent upon fingering something in his hands.

"Alf, what is that? Can you show me?"

He sent her a distrustful look, but when she took his hands in hers, he slowly unfisted them and there in all its agate splendor was Aunt Lavinia's marble. As soon as she'd seen it, he quickly closed his fingers around it. "Mine," he said. "All mine."

Seth leaned closer and placed a hand on the boy's head. "Indeed, it is."

After supper, Seth went with Lars to engage rooms at the local hotel. Polly, however, had insisted Rose stay with Alf. Tucked together in a soft bed covered with a warm quilt, Rose cuddled the child near, shushing him when he yelled out from apparent nightmares. He seemed less trusting, more withdrawn. Given what had happened to him, that was to be expected. Yet she could never doubt the love he'd exhibited, if only briefly, when he'd recognized her and then Seth.

The next day Sheriff Riley intended to question Alf's father more closely, especially in regard to any claim he might have over the boy. Seth had tried to assure her that such a man had little concern for or interest in his son. Certainly he had no way to care for him from behind bars. Still, Rose would never feel confident until she had adopted Alf in a court of law. That day couldn't come too soon.

Laying a soothing hand on his little shoulder, she drifted off, soothed by memories of the kind man who had brought her to this moment and of the sleeping boy who fulfilled her every prayer.

Chapter Thirteen

The next morning Rose snuggled Alf close on the buggy ride home, grateful that Seth had taken time away from the ranch to accompany her. The trip home seemed shorter than the one to Council Grove, maybe because her apprehension had subsided. Total peace of mind would remain elusive, though, until she could formally adopt her boy.

Alf, who in the past had been curious and alert, seemed disinterested in the passing landscape. Rose realized recent events had been beyond a child's capacity to handle, and she wondered, too, what his life had been like in these many weeks with his mother. At the very least, his living conditions had been dismal. Could he be restored to his previous happier state?

After his initial joy—or relief—at seeing Seth and her, she had seen little evidence of enthusiasm, only resignation. He acted as if their rescue of him was simply another of the detours in his young life, one to be endured rather than embraced. This morning when Seth had come to pick them up, the two of them had conferred and decided to let Alf set the pace of his recovery. Too much love too soon might be smothering or interfere with his need to grieve his mother.

When they crossed the bridge over the Cottonwood River, Alf perked up, his head pivoting as if taking in everything at once. When he mumbled something, Rose leaned over and asked him to repeat himself. "I 'member this." In his hand, he clutched the agate, as he had during the duration of the trip.

When they pulled up in front of the Kellogg home, Alf seemed to shrink. "We're home, dear," Rose said in a reassuring tone.

The boy shook his head. "No home. I got no home."

Rose struggled for composure. "This will be your home if you want it to be. I want it to be. Seth wants it to be."

Alf stuck out his chin in defiance. "I'm scared here. Not safe."

Pulling him into a tight embrace, Rose blinked away the onset of tears. "I promise we will keep you safe and loved."

Seth, who had overheard everything, stood waiting to lift Alf out of the buggy. He enfolded the boy in one arm and gave his hand to Rose. When their eyes met, Rose recognized her concern mirrored in his. How could they protect Alf from his memories and create a stable life for him?

When Rose started up the walk, she saw her beloved family waiting on the porch—Papa, Aunt Lavinia, Caleb, Lily and Mattie. Alf buried his head in Seth's shoulder as he carried him toward them and then sat down on the top porch step, cradling the boy close. Something in Alf's demeanor signaled the others that this was not an ecstatic celebration, but a delicate situation to be handled with care. "Here you are, Alf, with all the people who love you."

Alf lifted his head, eyeing them one by one, as if they were laboratory specimens...until he came to Mattie, peeking out from behind Lily's skirt. "I see you," he said, the first grin enlivening his features.

"Brudder," she cried, escaping from her mother to join Alf in Seth's lap. "You gone. I cried," she confided, addressing Alf as if the rest of them were invisible. The little girl then took the boy's hand in hers. "Wanna play wif me?"

Alf smiled again, and the two of them slipped from Seth's lap and disappeared into the house. Caleb and Seth followed the children while Rose briefly explained to the rest what they had learned in Council Grove.

"Despicable," Aunt Lavinia intoned.

"He bears scars that will take time to heal," Ezra said.

Lily embraced Rose. "You are the one God has sent to his aid. We will all help in any way we can. We are grateful he has been removed from such an unsavory situation."

Inside, the two children were at the kitchen table eating slices of the apple cake Bess Stanton had prepared for the occasion. Rose looked around, then turned to her father. "Papa, where's Bess? I thought she'd be here."

"She felt the homecoming should be family only."

"But Bess seems like family." As soon as the words were out of her mouth, she realized the effect of her statement. If her papa had ever blushed, this was the moment. Perhaps Lily was right—something was brewing between her father and Bess Stanton.

After they had all celebrated over cake, Caleb, Lily and Mattie took their leave in order to get home before dark. Seth, too, bowed out. Alf clung to Mattie until the last moment, then dashed back into the house and sought refuge in the corner to which Rose had restored his marbles, blocks and other toys, oblivious to the three adults left sitting at the table. Papa seemed overcome with relief. "The boy has been through so much. We must take heart, though. Never underestimate the healing power of love."

"This is one time I wish I had experience with children." Lavinia studied the boy from afar. "Even in the midst of those who care about him, he seems lonely."

Rose wondered if her aunt was speaking as much about herself as about Alf. "We will probably never know exactly what he has endured. What he witnessed with his mother and father is beyond our imagining." She faced her aunt. "I understand that you had reservations about my taking Alf into this home. Reputation matters, but in my view, it is trumped by love and compassion. I hope you can accept this precious, damaged child into our family and support me in my decision to adopt him legally."

Aunt Lavinia drew in a sharp breath, averted her glance to study Alf, lost in his make-believe world, and then slowly turned back to Rose. For a long time she said nothing, a play of emotions altering her expression. Rose waited for her aunt's response. But no words came.

Her aunt slid back her chair and stood, her lips pursed as if in deliberation. Then, with a determined swish of her skirts, she turned away, walked over to Alf and dropped to the floor beside him.

Rose looked quickly at her father, whose eyes were wide with wonder.

"What is that in your hand?" they heard Lavinia ask.

Alf looked up at her rather like a baby bird. "'Vinia?"

"Yes?"

"I got it." He slowly opened his fist. Lavinia leaned forward to admire his treasure. "'Vinia's marble. Mine."

Aunt Lavinia picked up the marble bag lying close by. "And these?"

"Mine, too. Marbles." He grabbed the bag from her and poured the contents on the floor. He watched warily as Lavinia scooped them toward him.

"There. Now you can play with them."

Gently he set down the large agate in the midst of the colored marbles. Then he nodded his head, as if satisfied with the arrangement.

"You." He touched Lavinia's lace-covered wrist. "Please, 'Vinia, play with me."

"I would be honored," the woman said, brushing a finger briefly under her eyes. "You, sir, you begin."

Rose and her father exchanged smiles of the kind prompted only by God's wondrous and mysterious action in the lives of His people. As if to put "Amen" to the scene, Ulysses came out from under the sofa where he had been hiding from the crowd and curled up in Alf's lap. "'Vinia, look. Our cat."

In the next few weeks, Rose puzzled about the nature of the bond between Aunt Lavinia and Alf, but from the moment he had returned to Cottonwood Falls, the two had "played" often. Lavinia had taught Alf a marbles game, taken him for a picnic at the falls and updated his wardrobe at the mercantile. In truth, Lavinia was receiving more of his affection than Rose was, due in part to the fact that the boy still harbored insecurity about her care of him, almost as if he blamed her for his being taken at the camp meeting. It wasn't that he actively shoved her away, but his responses to her were guarded. While that hurt, Rose was determined to be patient with him.

Just this morning at breakfast, he'd looked at her accusingly and asked, "Where's Sett?"

"He wishes he could be with you, Alf, but he has gone on the cattle drive."

"Cows?"

"Yes, he, Caleb and others are herding the cattle to the railroad."

"Why?"

"So they can ride on a train to the market. Seth will sell the cattle to make money and then buy some more cows to feed. He's a rancher. That's what they do."

"Rancher? I like horses and cows. I wanna be a rancher. Like Sett."

"Someday perhaps, love."

Later in the morning a tall, blond peddler with scraggly hair and bloodshot eyes came to the door. Alf took one look at the man, shrieked, "Go away," and ran to his toy corner, where he curled up in a ball and covered his eyes.

Rose hastily dismissed the peddler and hurried to Alf. "Dear boy, whatever is the matter?"

"Bad man," he mumbled into his hands.

With care, she pulled him into her lap, folding his hands in hers, sick with the realization of the connection he must've made between the peddler and his father. "The peddler wouldn't hurt you." She paused before plunging on. "Did he remind you of someone?"

By way of answer, Alf slipped from her lap and picked up the rag doll inside the house of blocks he'd made for her. Then with childlike rage, he put his hands around the neck of the doll and shook her. "Kill you. Bad man. E-nah. He killed her." Then he gently placed the doll on the floor, carefully arranging the yarn hair. "Gone," he said in a forlorn tone that tore at Rose's whole being.

Her heart racing, Rose prayed for the words to ease the little boy's pain. "You loved your E-nah."

He nodded solemnly, tracing the face of the doll with his fingers.

"Alf, listen to me very closely. I am sorry this happened to you, but I am glad you loved your mother. She must've loved you, too, to come here and take you with her." The boy looked up, his attention fixed on her. "You are safe here. The bad man is in jail. He can't hurt you."

"In jail? Locked up? You promise?" He climbed back into her lap, clutching the doll.

What fears had been at work in this small child? "Yes, locked up for a very long time." With those words, he rested his head against her shoulder. While she waited for his body to relax, she had an idea, one that could only have come from God. She caressed his doll. "Alf, why don't we dig a little hole in the ground next to the beautiful rose bushes you like and bury your E-nah there. She would rest comfortably in the peaceful out-of-doors. We could wrap her in one of my pretty silk scarves, say some prayers and sing a song or two. Maybe your favorite, 'All Things Bright and Beautiful.' What do you say?"

He trailed his fingers down her arm while his little mind worked over her suggestion. At last, he turned to her, his face just inches from hers. "E-nah's gone. I'm sad. You—you bury her."

That evening, she, Papa and Alf gathered around the tiny grave site. Alf cradled the doll in his arms, crooning something that sounded like an Indian chant. Then Papa said several prayers, ending with the commendation of the body. Rose led the boy to the hole and knelt beside him as he laid the doll to rest. Then he picked up a thimbleful of dirt and sprinkled it over the representation of his mother. "Be at peace," Rose said. Then she took him by the hand and they stood. In a soft voice, she began singing, "All things bright and beautiful, / All creatures great and small, / All things wise and wonderful, / The Lord God made them all."

"Made them all," Alf echoed. "E-nah, Rose, Papa, Sett and 'Vinia. And Mattie, too."

The rest of the evening Rose and her father could hardly believe the change in the boy, as if he had exorcised the memories plaguing him. Tentative smiles replaced his grim expression. In his voice was a lilt Rose had not heard since he was taken.

Lying awake long after Alf was asleep, Rose thanked God for the inspiration. Perhaps even more important, she prayed for His forgiveness for her lack of faith in Him, in questioning His purpose. Then she added Seth to her petition. He, too, had questioned. Soon, she promised herself, she would seek out Pastor Dooley and confess her recent anger at God. Seth was right. God often worked in and through other people. Those people were to be found in community, and she had cut herself off from them for too long. Despite her doubts, miracles had occurred—Alf's deliverance once again into her care, Lavinia's acceptance of the boy and Seth's faithful concern for the child. Yes, all manner of things would be well.

In early October, a week after she, Caleb, Seth and Andrew returned from the cattle drive, Sophie prepared a family feast to celebrate the success of the sale of their livestock. The high prices assured both a good profit and a large reserve for the coming year. Spread on the table were beef roast, green beans with salt pork, cucumber and onion salad, pickled beets, hot rolls, honey, and freshly churned butter. Conversation was lively and full of stories from the trail. Over the dessert of blueberry pie, Sophie shocked Seth to the delight of the others. "Tonight is the night, brother dear, for you to perfect your dancing."

"Dancing? You know I don't dance."

"Well," said his determined sister, "I do know that. As of now, that condition ends." She grinned at her father. "Pa, is your fiddle tuned up?"

Andrew grinned. "Sure is."

Seth frowned, convinced his father and sister were in cahoots.

"It's not hard," Lily said by way of reassurance.

"If I can do it," Caleb added, "you can."

Fuming, Seth set his jaw. "The rest of you can have a merry time. I will not dance." He shook his head. "A clumsy oaf like me? I'd be the laughing stock."

Sophie came over to him and draped an arm around his shoulder. He knew what she was thinking. In most things he yielded to her. Not this time. He was a Goliath with snowshoes for feet. "My, my, you must've forgotten about the Courthouse Ball. All of Chase County will turn out, and all Montgomerys will do the occasion proud. And I do mean *all*." Her cajoling tone set his teeth on edge. "And that includes dancing. Pa?"

Before Seth could flee, his traitor of a father had pulled out his fiddle, Lily had placed her arm in his, and Caleb stood covering the grin he couldn't conceal. "Don't look at them," Lily said, "just concentrate on me. We'll start with a simple reel."

A cavorting chimpanzee would have been more graceful than he. At one point, Lily stepped away so she and Caleb could once again demonstrate the steps he'd ignored in their past attempts to instruct him. Then Sophie got into the act, swinging through his outstretched arm and grabbing him by the shoulder. All the while, Pa was sending contagious tunes through the air. Seth felt helpless in their hands. As the lesson wore on, he reluctantly admitted that the music was energizing. The others seemed to be having great fun, but they were experts. He was an embarrassment.

After a time, they wound down the hilarity and told him he was doing a passable job. He glared at them. "Can't make a silk purse out of this sow's ear," he said.

They all settled around the table for the hot cider that had been simmering on the stove. "Really, Seth," Lily commented, "you were doing well."

"And we have plenty of time in the next few days to practice," Sophie assured him.

"Son, the ladies will expect partners at the ball."

"Jolly for them. I'm sure others will more than fill the bill."

Sophie got that impish glint in her eye that he knew meant trouble. "You surely wouldn't disappoint a lady."

"Not just any lady," his brother added with an amused smirk.

"One lady," his sister-in-law said, her voice rising hopefully. "One particular lady."

"I will not dance with that Widow Spencer. No." He shook his head vigorously.

"Of course you won't," Lily agreed.

"What in tarnation are you talking about, then?" He looked accusingly at his family so clearly aligned against him.

Caleb stepped in. "I love you, brother, but sometimes you're as brainless as a tumbleweed. You are very fond of this lady."

"We mean Rose," Sophie said, reaching for his hand. "Surely you will not disappoint her on this glorious occasion."

Disappoint Rose? Never. But dance? "She wouldn't want to dance with me."

"Why ever not? Just like you, my sister hasn't had a wealth of experience with balls. It would mean so much to me if you would help make this one special for her."

Lily knew he couldn't refuse her, not when she'd put it in the form of a favor. He scanned their faces. "You won't laugh?"

With mock seriousness, they all held up their right hands as if giving testimony. "We promise."

"We'll see," he said shoving back his chair and stomping out into the night. Standing in the crisp autumn air amid the pleasant smell of wood smoke, he studied the stars. Who had ordained that human beings should dance? Why, he'd make a fool of himself. Then he thought about Rose, ever so patient, her love for Alf so enduring. She was the finest of women, but no flibbertigibbet. She probably wouldn't even want to dance.

Laughter from within taunted him. He was making excuses. He was thinking only of his own discomfort and humiliation. The longer he stood there, though, the more appealing the idea of dancing with Rose became. He could picture her eyes shining with delight, eyes he hoped would be only for him.

He raked a hand through his hair. Dreamer. What was happening to him? Did Rose regard him as someone special? Or as one who had failed her when Alf was abducted. They were friends, of course, but was his family right? Was there more? He had interpreted her kindness as simply that—kindness. But could it signal deeper feelings? Foolishly, he found himself grinning. With Rose as his dance partner, maybe he would no longer be a clumsy Goliath.

A week later, Bess, Rose and Alf drove out to visit Lily and Mattie. They had invited Aunt Lavinia, but she was unable to go, she said, because of some pressing business. Business? Here in Cottonwood Falls? Surely all of her financial matters were being handled in St. Louis. With Lavinia, though, there was no accounting for her actions. One day she'd looked down her nose at Alf and now they were nearly inseparable.

"Isn't this a beautiful day?" Bess said as they rode along. "The foliage is stunning. Not quite New England, but lovely in its own way."

"Lovely." Rose patted the valise at her feet. "Lily is quite a seamstress. She will transform our dresses into ball gowns. Growing up, I only attempted Pa's shirts, but she worked wonders with our frocks."

"My dress needs to remain somewhat plain, as befits a widow."

"Nonsense. Your loss was many years ago. It's time you blossomed again." Rose slanted her eyes to watch Bess's expression.

"The girl in me wants to do just that, but I'm past my prime."

"Papa doesn't seem to think so," Rose said with an air of affected innocence.

Bess nearly dropped the reins. "I declare, Rose, I have no idea what you're talking about."

Rose was relentless. "Then why are you blushing?" Only with difficulty did she stifle her giggles. "Bess, Lily and I are so fond of you and have already come to regard you as one of the family. We see the way Papa looks at you. Why, his eyes follow you whenever you're in the same room. I don't know about your feelings, but if you and Papa were ever to come to an agreement, Lily and I would not only approve, we would welcome you with our whole hearts."

Bess bowed her head. "You honor me. 'Tis true, I am quite fond of Ezra, and I believe he is of me. But no words have passed between us concerning anything other than friendship."

"But if he spoke of deeper feelings…?"

Bess turned to Rose, with the loveliest of smiles and said, "I would be blessed."

Rose nodded in satisfaction. "Good."

Alf had been dozing alongside her, but stirred now. "Are we there yet?"

"Not quite, dear boy. Soon."

That afternoon while the children played in the garden, Lily worked her magic on the gowns, adding lace to the sleeves of one, winding gold braid through the neckline of another and performing such alterations as were necessary. Rose's gown was a royal-blue taffeta that made her eyes come alive, while Bess's was a lilac shade complementing her silver hair.

"All right, then," Lily said, standing up. "I've done all the hemming that's needed. It's time for a fashion show worthy of *Godey's Lady's Book*. Go now and try them on."

The two retired to the bedroom and ultimately returned arrayed in their finery. Lily adjusted the parlor mirror so they could catch their reflections.

Bess clapped her hands delightedly. "I never imagined the dress that's been buried in my trunk for months could look like this." She twirled around and hugged Lily. "Thank you, thank you."

Then it was Rose's turn. In the mirror she saw a beautiful ball gown that failed to transform her plain normal self. How Rose wished she could glow with pleasure as Bess had done.

"What's the matter?" Lily stood beside her studying their reflection.

"The dress is fine. Really lovely. But—" Rose bit her lip "—it's not me. I'm most comfortable in gingham."

Bess moved to Rose's other side. "Beauty is in the mind, dear. If you tell yourself you're not pretty, it will show." She quirked her head to study Rose. "I have an idea. Lily, fetch me some combs."

The next thing Rose knew, Lily had led her into the bedroom and plopped her down at the dressing table and Bess was arranging her hair on top of her head in a coil. Lily gave her a pair of pearl earrings and then re-arranged the neckline to show off her shoulders. "Now then," her sister said, "come back into the living room."

Reluctantly, she shuffled into the next room where Bess turned her to face the mirror once more. "See? You're a swan, not an ugly duckling. Believe it."

Rose studied her transformation. With the coiffure of a high society lady, she looked like a stranger. Could she really be the woman reflected in the mirror?

The children burst into the room, and Alf stopped in his tracks "Rose? I never seed you like that." His eyes shone with wonder. "You look like a fairy princess."

"Fairy princess," Mattie echoed, dancing up and down.

Rose slowly turned. "Do you really think so?"

"We do, we do," the children shouted.

"And so do we." Seth and Caleb stood in the door, grinning in brotherly agreement.

Alf ran to Seth. "Sett. You see her? She's boo-ti-ful."

Rose longed for a hiding place, but she had no re-course other than to bear herself with dignity in the face of such unaccustomed compliments. "Lily and Bess have undoubtedly worked an improvement. But princess? I think not."

Seth picked Alf up in his arms. "What do you say, boy? I say princess."

Alf nodded vigorously. "Sett, my Rose is a·prin-cess."

Rose forced a smile and made herself look straight at Seth. "There's no accounting for some fellows."

Caleb stepped forward. "If you want an objective outsider's opinion, here's what I say." He draped his arm around his brother. "It's unanimous. A princess."

When Seth winked at her, she felt light-headed. "See, we told you so."

Caleb pounced. "She'll make quite a suitable dance partner at the ball, don't you think, Seth?"

It was Seth's turn to blush and he jabbed an elbow into Caleb's side. "We'll see," he said. "I imagine Miss Rose will have a full dance card."

Lily came to the rescue. "Shoo, the lot of you. We ladies have to change and pack away the gowns."

In the bedroom, Rose crumpled onto the bed. "I've never been so embarrassed in my life."

"That's because you've never dressed so beautifully," Bess said. "And you lit up when Seth came into the room."

"Certainly not!"

Both Lily and Bess shrugged, as smug as if they'd uncovered a hidden gem. "It seems it's one thing for you to comment on a man in my life," Bess said, "and quite another for us to turn the tables on you."

Rose jerked to her feet and began tearing the combs out of her hair. "Please stop. Lily knows how I feel, but I'll remind her again and say this also to you. I once thought I had a man in my life who would love and cherish me. I was very wrong. I will not go down that path again. Never." And before they could say anything more, she pulled the dress over her head, unable to see her friend and her sister shake their heads with the folly of it all.

Chapter Fourteen

Although she had once again started attending church services, Rose knew she still needed to see Pastor Dooley and set things right with her soul. The Sunday before the Courthouse Ball she prevailed upon her father to take Alf home. She loitered, waiting for the minister to finish greeting the other churchgoers. She knew she would not be light of spirit until she had confessed to doubting God. Her despair following Alf's abduction had rendered her self-absorbed and faithless. And yet…a miracle had occurred, but one with sad consequences for others. How could she exult when a woman lay dead at the hands of an abusive drunk?

Happily, through the efforts of the entire family, Alf seemed to be emerging from the trauma he'd experienced. Although at times he withdrew, by and large he was much more nearly his old self. His nightmares were infrequent now, and he would allow Rose to cuddle him and soothe him back to sleep. Rose knew, though, that there would always be a deep place in his soul where memories of evil could torment. Her job was to see that pleasant times crowded out such thoughts.

Finally Pastor Dooley saw her waiting and with a gesture invited her into the church, where they settled into a back pew. As if sensing her discomfort, he said, "Please be at ease.

"I have sinned." Rose expected the minister to flinch in shock, but he just kept looking at her with compassion. Then she poured out her confession. Finally, with a mournful sigh, she came to the end of her story. "How can I exult in Alf's return when his mother lies dead? As you've just heard, I've judged and I've doubted. Where was my God in all of this?"

"You are not the first, nor will you be the last to judge or doubt God, Rose. It is my belief that such dark moments test us and, with God's grace, ultimately bring us to a place of healing and forgiveness." He nodded toward the altar. "Consider that on the cross Jesus himself asked the Father why he had been forsaken."

Rose eased back in the pew. "What do I do to obtain forgiveness? To atone for my lapse of faith?"

"You've already confessed your anger and questioning of God's plan. Now, child, let me lay my hands upon you and commend you to God's grace."

The pastor leaned forward to place his hands on her head. Warmth and strength emanated from his touch and, as he prayed over her, she felt a peace in both body and soul. "Forgive and restore Your servant Rose to soundness of mind, bodily health and wellness of soul that she may go forth to love and serve others in Your blessed name."

The two then sat in companionable silence while Rose took deep, cleansing breaths. "You are a fine woman, Rose, who has much love to give. Alf has not been put in your care by accident."

"About Alf. I should very much like for him to be baptized. Could you do that?"

"It would be a privilege. However, your father told me you plan to adopt the boy."

"Yes, I've retained Lawyer Yarnell to act on my behalf with the court."

"When might you have a hearing?"

"Soon, I believe. Mr. Yarnell thinks it may be one of the first cases to be heard in the new courthouse."

"In that event, I propose we schedule the baptism for a time after the hearing, so that Alf's name will be both ecclesiastically and legally recorded." He stood and held out his hand to assist Rose to her feet. "I shall be praying for a satisfactory resolution concerning the court hearing. Meanwhile, if I can assist you in any pastoral concerns, my door is always open."

Rose clasped his hand and struggled for the words to express her gratitude. "I am most grateful for your counsel and your prayers. Indeed, I shall face this day and those that follow with a more open and faith-filled heart, thanks to you."

All the way home, Rose felt as if her stress, like a colorful balloon, had soared into the sky. She appreciated the way Pastor Dooley had assured her that her flaws were not uncommon and, more importantly, had been forgiven. For whatever reasons, God had restored Alf to her and she would love him always. As she passed Bertha and Chauncey Britten's home, her reverie was shattered by Bertha's shrill voice. "Rose, can it possibly be true?"

With a groan, she stopped in her tracks and turned

to face Bertha, who sat in a wicker chair on her front porch. Rose vowed not to take one step toward the woman. She needn't have worried, Bertha levered herself out of her chair and came to the edge of her porch. "Well, is it true?"

"Bertha, to what, may I ask, are you referring?"

"My dear Rose, it's all over town that you are actually planning to adopt that boy. You, an unmarried person!"

Rose sighed. Bertha was making her out to be some sort of scarlet woman. "Not that it's any of your concern, but, yes, I am petitioning the court to adopt Alf."

Bertha folded her arms across her ample bosom and shook her head. Rose was too far away to hear the *tsk-tsk* she imagined the woman was verbalizing. "The nerve," Bertha finally said. "That boy needs a good home with both a father and a mother."

And just where would you propose I get a father? "You are entitled to your opinion, Bertha, but now I must be on my way. Good day."

Rose made herself stroll normally when all she wanted to do was put distance between herself and that sanctimonious woman. The walk, however, gave her time to think, and by the time she reached home, she had calmed down. Bertha's behavior was disappointing but human. Pastor Dooley's message was to love and serve others. That wasn't always easy, she realized. The Berthas of the world tried souls, but that didn't mean such folks should be deprived of love. If God could love Bertha, Rose could at least tolerate her.

Excitement concerning the completion of the new Chase County Courthouse reached a peak on Friday,

October 17, the day of the Courthouse Ball. Wagons and buggies full of folks from distant parts of the county crowded the streets and that didn't take into account the many who arrived on horseback. Bess was bustling about attending to last minute details of the celebration, and Rose had outdone herself preparing fried chicken, mounds of potato salad and three apple pies. Finally it was time to bathe and dress. When Rose emerged from the bedroom in her blue dress with her red-gold hair heaped high on her head, Alf called to Ezra, "Look, Papa, it's the princess!"

Ezra came out of the kitchen, then stopped in the parlor doorway. Grinning, he made a show of checking his glasses. "Could this possibly be our Rose, Alf? Look at her. Why, she's not just a princess, she's a beauty."

Although she didn't believe a word, she basked in the approval that made her feel somewhat more confident in her femininity. "Are we ready, then?" Papa said, giving her his arm.

The gray limestone courthouse gleamed in the rays of the setting sun. The edifice literally took Rose's breath away—it looked exactly like a French Renaissance castle, something she'd seen before only in an etching. "Remember this day," Ezra said. "Something grand and unexpected has happened here. This building will last far into the future." He, too, seemed awed by the scope of the architectural achievement.

Entering the courthouse, they stopped in amazement. A wooden spiral staircase mounted three stories. Upon closer examination, Rose noticed it had no center support. A massive black walnut balustrade, hand-cut, so they'd been told, from trees growing beside the Cottonwood River was beautiful beyond description. The building was a beehive of activity with folks darting from room to room, exclaiming excitedly about the architectural features—the clock tower, the jail and living quarters for the sheriff and his family and the recessed oval window overlooking Broadway. Rose could hardly take it all in.

Aunt Lavinia approached, jewels sparkling from her heavy, ornate necklace. Her full-skirted gold brocade dress was a seamstress's vision. "Think of it, my dears. Having such a courthouse in this town defies the imagination. No matter how precise my powers of description, no one in St. Louis will believe such a European-inspired structure can exist on the wilds of the prairie. Of course, we'd already seen the exterior, but coming inside? I am stunned into speechlessness."

Rose curbed a giggle. She couldn't recall a time when Lavinia had been at a loss for words. "Would you join Papa, Alf and me for the dinner? It's spread out in the jail—enough food to feed a small country."

The four proceeded to the jail quarters where tables had been set up in every nook and cranny. Just after they'd served themselves, Lily, Caleb and Mattie arrived, trailed by Seth and Andrew. Exchanging excited greetings, the others filled their plates and joined the Kelloggs, Mattie insisting that she sit next to "brudder." Lily, in a full-sleeved claret gown, nipped at the waist and then swirling to the floor, sat down beside Rose. "Where's Sophie?" Ezra asked.

Lily laughed. "One guess. She hasn't left Charlie's side since we arrived. I think she's enjoying all of the congratulations due him for his stonework."

After comparing notes about the unusual features

of the building, at the sound of instruments tuning in the second-floor courtroom, the group dispersed. As Rose and Alf mounted the coiling stairs, Papa lagged behind. Looking over the railing, she saw what—or rather who—had detained him. Bess stood gracefully, her lilac dress the perfect hue to highlight her hair and complexion, receiving Ezra's kiss on the cheek. Rose paused, lost in the wonder of the two of them together, deserving souls who had blessedly found one another.

"Rose, c'mon. I hear music!"

Rose entered the courtroom where the ball was being held, awed by the craftsmanship of the high ceiling covered by embossed tin and the burnished wooden judge's bench. Beyond that, in celebration, the walls were draped with bunting, and chrysanthemums and bittersweet overflowed from strategically placed vases. When Ezra and Bess entered the room, Rose gushed to Bess, "What wonderful work you and your committee have done. This night is the stuff of storybooks."

"Bess's efforts have produced magnificent results." Ezra's doting look said it all. When the musicians struck up the first number, Rose led Alf to a row of chairs lining the walls. "We'll sit here and take in the fun."

"You. Dance."

"I think not, Alf. I've not had much practice."

"Let's try. You and me." He jumped up and before she could protest, led her to a corner, where he took her hands and pranced about in a ring-around-the-rosy manner. "See. We're dancing." Rose couldn't deny him this pleasure and found herself caught up in his enthusiasm. Behind them, couples cut figures on the varnished wooden floor, vibrating with the activity. When the music stopped, Alf bowed and Rose curtsied.

"You're quite the dancer, Alf. Maybe you could teach me." The deep masculine voice caused them both to turn around.

"Sett. You seed us? Rose and me?" The boy glowed with pleasure. "Now, you dance." He took Seth's large hand and placed it in Rose's.

"I, uh…"

"That's all right, Seth. I'm quite ready to sit."

"No! You and Sett. Dance." Then Alf's stubborn expression melted into an impish grin. "I did it, Sett. You can do it. You and Rose."

Rose looked up helplessly and read in Seth's expression his discomfort. He placed a forefinger between his neck and collar, as if unaccustomed to being so constricted. "Uh, Lily and Sophie tried to teach me."

"Well, then, you've had the benefit of lessons. I have not."

"Dance!" came the insistent voice of their boy.

Seth looked around the crowded ballroom. "Perhaps if we stay in the corner—"

"No one will see us?" Rose laughed then. "Are we being a bit silly? Who cares how we dance? Look there." She nodded toward the floor. "I see that farmer from over Strong City way lumbering around. Surely we can best that."

With a deep sigh, Seth placed a tentative hand on her back. When she put her hand into his, he straightened up and began guiding her in wide circles. At first her feet refused to cooperate, but then as she relaxed and he gained confidence, they were able to move more or less gracefully, not daring to look at one another for concentrating on the steps.

"See? I told you. You're dancing." Alf was jittery with excitement.

"We've made at least one person happy," Rose commented, nodding toward the boy.

Seth didn't immediately answer. Then squeezing her hand gently and drawing her a bit closer, he said, "Maybe two, or dare I hope, three?"

Her heart fluttered out of all proportion to the words he'd spoken, words she wasn't sure how to interpret. Caught up in the spell of the moment, she couldn't think how to answer him.

Just as the music ceased, she heard him mumble, "Well, two anyway." Then in an abrupt change of mood, he lifted Alf onto his shoulders. "What do you say we fellas go for some of that ice cream downstairs?" He faced her. "It is all right with you?"

She nodded, then watched them leave, suddenly feeling quite alone. As she moved toward a vacant seat, the next dance began. Observing the twirling couples, one thing was clear. Neither Sophie and Charlie nor her father and Bess were having difficulty with the intricacies of dancing. Nor, from the looks of it, with courtship.

She bowed her head. On a night when she should have been overflowing with happiness, melancholy blanketed her. Until Alf was legally hers, she could not celebrate.

When Seth and Alf returned, Rose took out a handkerchief and wiped the remnant of ice cream from the boy's mouth. "Was it good?"

The boy held his arms up to form a circle. "Sett and me had a big bowl."

"But not enough to give anyone a tummy ache," Seth added.

Just then Alf spied Mattie across the room. "I see Mattie. We can dance, us two," and he ran off to the little girl. As Seth and Rose watched, he took Mattie by the hand and began leaping about.

"Quite a lad," Seth said, sitting down beside her.

Rose merely nodded. Dancing with Seth had been unsettling. From the fact that he said nothing more and stared intently at the dancers, Rose sensed her failure to answer his earlier question had put him off. Did he make her happy? After all the humiliation she'd been through at the fort, might she risk making him happy? Or was he merely looking for a friend? Or, worse yet, a housekeeper?

Before dwelling further on those thoughts, she clamped them off. Once she had actually believed her happiness lay with a man. Foolishness! True, Seth was nothing like the sergeant to whom she'd lost her heart, but no good could come of entertaining anything beyond their friendship.

Seth fidgeted beside her, tugging at his cuffs and staring alternately between the ceiling and the floor. If he was that uncomfortable, why did he continue to sit beside her? She had to say something to break the ice. "Perhaps you would like to dance with Sophie or Lily?"

"No, thanks."

She couldn't imagine what was going through his head. Just then her father appeared before her. "May I have this next dance with my lovely daughter?" Papa whisked her away, but over his shoulder she spied Seth, standing with his back turned, gazing out of one of the large courtroom windows.

Seth stared into the night, neither the moon nor the twinkling lights of the town below registering with him. He was in a fix. For one brief moment, dancing with Rose while Alf clapped his approval, he'd entertained a vision of the three of them as a family, but the happiness he'd experienced was fleeting. Rose didn't think of him in that way. Her behavior made it obvious that they were friends…only. Women were puzzling. He'd thought he and Rose had drawn closer. Yet something held her back. Had he misread their relationship? Was it foolish to risk his heart when he had no assurance of a happy outcome? When the music died, the mayor climbed in front of the judge's bench and called for attention. "Ladies and gentlemen, please gather around to honor the architects and builders who have made our courthouse a reality."

Reluctantly, Seth moved to the fringe of the crowd, listening as the mayor expounded on the prodigious feats and financial generosity which had made the courthouse construction possible. Spontaneous applause broke out at several junctures and cries of "Hear, hear!" echoed throughout the room. Seth scanned the crowd. Squirming with delight, Mattie and Alf were with Lily and Caleb. Doc Kellogg stood close beside Bess Stanton, but much as Seth craned his neck, he could not spot Rose.

At the conclusion of the laudatory remarks, the mayor held up his hand. "Charlie Devane has asked to make an announcement. Come on up, Charlie."

The dark-headed young man, blushing from being

center stage, stood before them, his brown eyes twinkling. "As you know, I hail from New England, but you've made me welcome here. Cottonwood Falls has not only given me a home, but another priceless gift. I am proud to say that after speaking with Andrew Montgomery, Sophie has agreed to be my wife." He drew Sophie to him. "We will marry in a few months after I finish a job at the college in Manhattan."

Seth felt as if he had turned into a block of wood, incapable of either feeling or movement. He shouldn't be surprised; indeed, he should be elated for his sister. Instead, a wave of loneliness inundated him. His sister, resplendent in an aquamarine gown, at this moment was no longer the tomboy of his youth, but a radiant young woman with eyes only for her betrothed. Congratulations rang throughout the room. Then unexpectedly, he felt a small, warm hand slip into his and give an encouraging squeeze. "Seth, dear."

Where Rose had come from, he didn't know, but she, of all people, understood how difficult this moment was for him. Perhaps fearing his reaction, it was no wonder Sophie hadn't told him in advance. "You knew?"

"Lily told me earlier this evening. Sophie wanted to surprise everyone else." She looked up at him, her eyes troubled. "Will you be all right?"

He shrugged. "I'll have to be. How can I possibly begrudge my sister happiness? Devane is a good man, but it will be difficult to see her go."

"Your friends and family will help fill the void."

He stared down into her trusting blue eyes. "Are you my friend?"

"Always," she replied.

The moment was broken by yet another announcement. "To conclude this evening," the mayor called out, "please give your attention to Mrs. Lavinia Dupree."

Rose grasped Seth's hand. "What in the world?" she said, turning her attention to the judge's bench where her aunt was being escorted like a queen by the perspiring mayor.

Lavinia drew herself up and then studied the assemblage until, amid shushes, they quieted. "Good evening." Her voice rang out clear and commanding. "As you know, my home is in St. Louis, and I have experienced all the advantages a cosmopolitan city can afford its residents. So you may wonder what brought me to Cottonwood Falls. Family, of course. But what keeps me here beyond those bonds? I will tell you. The cooperative spirit of this community, which has now taken tangible form in this splendid courthouse. And now," Lavinia's voice soared, "I want to express my appreciation to you by making a sizeable donation toward the building of a library. My nieces will tell you I am not much of a reader, but I see great value in providing a place of learning for others, both now and in the years to come."

A buzz circulated through the crowd and Willa Stone rushed to Lavinia's side. "Mrs. Dupree, we are flabbergasted and delighted. Your generosity will indeed provide a worthy legacy." At her signal everyone joined in enthusiastic applause.

"One more thing," Lavinia said when the clapping died away. "I intend to invest not only my money to the betterment of this county, but also my energy and presence. I have purchased land in the area, and with young Mr. Devane's able assistance, am building a summer home here in Kansas."

Seth's hand tightened on Rose's. "Are you all right?"

She leaned against him. "I'm undone. In her generosity and openness, I see so much of my mother in Aunt Lavinia. Either she has changed or I've misjudged her."

"It's you and Alf, Lily, Caleb and Mattie—all of you. She loves you very much."

"I see that now, and I'm delighted she feels comfortable and welcome here."

"The people of Chase County are special."

"And you are one of them," she whispered before she started toward her aunt.

He watched her dodge around their neighbors to reach and embrace Lavinia Dupree. *Special*. He shook his head. Whatever that meant. Then he dutifully embarked on the errand of congratulating Sophie and Charlie.

Chapter Fifteen

The evening after the ball Ezra and Rose invited Lavinia to dinner, eager to hear more about her surprising announcement. Rose carefully removed her mother's good china from the cupboard and arranged the table just so, complete with a centerpiece of pumpkins and brightly colored gourds. A roast surrounded by onions, potatoes and carrots simmered in the Dutch oven and a Sally Lunn cake was cooling on the sideboard. Surveying the situation, she hoped she had not overlooked anything. She so wanted to approach Aunt Lavinia's exacting standards.

"Something smells mighty good," her father said, walking in the door. "I was afraid I'd be late. Jake Witherspoon's mule kicked him and broke his leg." Glancing at the set table, he hung his hat on the peg. "I'll go wash up before Lavinia gets here."

Alf grabbed Rose's hand. "Come. Watch for 'Vinia with me." Passing by the hall mirror, Rose checked her reflection. Even though she sometimes still felt inadequate around her aunt, Lavinia seemed to be warming to her. Not only that, Lavinia's interactions with Alf had gone a long way to soften Rose's opinion.

Alf straddled the porch rail, cowboy-style. "Know what, Rose? 'Vinia said when I'm a big boy, she'll buy me a pony."

"But for now you have the horse Seth made you."

"Yeah, Spot. He's a good horse, but—" the boy leaned toward Rose and spoke confidentially "—he's not real, you know."

Reflecting on the attention both Seth and Lavinia lavished on the boy, Rose smiled. So many wanted to make up to him for the tragedy of his mother's death. Pray God the court would favor her adoption petition.

Papa joined them. "Looks as if we're ready. If I know my sister-in-law, she'll make a grand entrance. Before she gets here, though, you need to know I saw David Yarnell today."

At the mention of the lawyer's name, Rose held her breath. "And?"

"Your hearing is on the docket for this coming Friday." He reached over and patted her hand. "Come what may, you'll have an answer soon."

"I don't know if I can survive the uncertainty till then."

"Be thankful. The hearing could have been in weeks, not mere days."

She watched Alf, caught up in the pretense that the porch rail was a mighty steed. For him, she could endure anything.

"'Vinia! I spy 'Vinia!"

Sure enough, Lavinia was drawing up in her buggy, driven by the hired man she'd recently engaged. She emerged, a fur stole over her black bombazine dress.

When Ezra went to the buggy to escort her up the walk, he was nearly bowled over by Alf who beat him to her side and grabbed Lavinia's hand. "Rose made roast beef. Come eat with me."

Preoccupied by Papa's news, Rose had difficulty following the dinner conversation until Seth's name popped up. "Seth?"

"Yes, dear, that young man was kind enough to give me a tour of the territory and point out the business potential of the Flint Hills. My husband rarely included me in his dealings, but I'm discovering I have a head for finances. When Lily was in St. Louis, she showed me that women are capable of being decision makers, and that is exactly what I intend to be."

"We're happy for you and will look forward to your upcoming ventures," Ezra said, wiping his mouth with his linen napkin.

"I'm particularly excited about the house I'm building."

"House?" Alf said. "Building like blocks?"

"Exactly. That fine Charlie Devane has helped me design a home made of your native limestone. It's tucked against a hill with a glorious southeastern exposure."

"It sounds lovely."

"And, Rose, I need your help."

"Mine?" Rose couldn't imagine what expertise she would have to offer.

"Who is the best cook in the county? You, my dear. Of course, I will engage my own cook in my new home, but I want an efficient, modern kitchen design. So... sometime soon I want you to accompany me to the building site to make suggestions. Will you help?"

"I'll enjoy the challenge."

Papa smiled from one woman to the next. "That's settled, then. Now all we need is to get the matter of our young man concluded."

Lavinia's eyebrows arched inquisitively. "What matter, Ezra?"

He lowered his voice, "Rose's court hearing. Friday next."

"What's a *court?*"

Not for the first time, Rose reflected on the truth of little pitchers having big ears. "Alf, it's what happens in the beautiful building with the clock tower. Grown-up business."

"How are you feeling about the prospect, Rose?"

"Oh, Aunt Lavinia, I'm both eager for it to come about and, at the same time, terrified. What if—" Rose found she couldn't finish the thought.

"Nonsense. You will not be alone in that courtroom. I will personally rally the family and the women of the Library Society as character witnesses. There is no question what justice demands in this case. Don't fret, my dear niece. All will be well."

All will be well. All manner of things shall be well. Rose smiled by way of thanks. In an odd way it was fitting to hear Lavinia mouth the same comforting words Rose had heard so often from her own mother. She studied Alf, his little hands now moving excitedly as he described for her aunt the kind of pony he would prefer. Rose knew she had done what she could for the boy. The rest lay with God.

The Friday morning of Rose's two o'clock hearing at the courthouse, rain beat incessantly against the kitchen windows and strewed the yard with dead leaves. Alf, oblivious to the high drama about to occur on his behalf, played happily in the parlor with the set of tin soldiers Lavinia had ordered him from New York. Papa had left to call on two ailing patients, leaving Rose incapable of doing anything, but pacing the floor and praying.

In a few short hours her future would either be ruined or made whole. She marched off to the kitchen to make bread. At least sifting and kneading might calm her runaway nerves.

Bess arrived at one o'clock, shaking raindrops off her umbrella. "It's still pouring out there and now the wind is coming up." She held her hands out to the stove. "How are you?"

Rose sighed. "Beside myself. I haven't been able to sleep or eat much lately. Bess, I simply can't imagine my life without Alf."

Bess turned and embraced her friend. "Oh, child, any judge with eyes in his head will see the bond you have with the boy. Does Alf understand what is happening this afternoon?"

"Papa and I tried to prepare him. We told him this was a formality so that perhaps he could be my son forever and ever."

"What did he say to that?"

"He broke my heart. He said since his E-nah was dead, he needed a mother and asked if after the hearing, he could call me Mama."

"He's a dear child, and you and your family are to be commended for the sensitive way you've helped him recover from the horror of his mother's death."

Rose offered Bess a cup of tea, and then the two sat

drinking in a silence for which Rose was grateful. The time for platitudes or reassurance was long past. After a few minutes, Ezra burst through the door, leaving at his feet a puddle. "Noah had nothing on us. Much more of this and I'm commissioning an ark."

Rose hurried to the stove to get her father some hot tea. "Here, sit and join us."

"Alf?"

"He's playing in the parlor. I pray nothing happens to threaten his well-being."

"Buck up, dear. It will all be over soon."

Then, before she knew it, she was climbing into her father's buggy next to Bess, with Alf perched on her lap. She wished the rat-a-tat of the rain on the roof didn't sound quite so much like nails in a coffin.

To her surprise, the courthouse was full of onlookers, most of them familiar—folks from church, patients of her father's, ladies from the Library Society and others she didn't recognize. Aunt Lavinia, with Hannah at her side, had established her territory in the first row and with a wave of her hand, summoned them forward to join her. "What are all these people doing here?" Rose whispered to her father.

Ezra leaned in close. "Supporting you mainly, although I suppose for some, there's an element of curiosity."

Rose gathered Alf close, sat down and looked around. No longer was this space a colorful, festive ballroom. Now it seemed austere and forbidding.

"All rise. The Honorable Titus Cornett presiding." A tall, rangy man with a shock of black hair and stern facial features entered in a black robe. From the first tap of his gavel until the sentencing of a thief, Rose could hardly focus for the heavy weight in her chest. Beside her, Alf yawned and fingered his agate. It was his nap time. Perhaps he could sleep through the proceedings.

Then as if time had accelerated beyond her notice, the bailiff called their case. Her lawyer approached the bench. "Your Honor, I am appearing on behalf of Miss Rose Kellogg of this city to ask the court to execute an order to give her legal custody of the minor Alf, full name unknown."

The minute Alf heard his name, he roused and tugged Rose's sleeve. "That's me, Alf."

"Yes, my love."

Then Yarnell summarized Alf's abandonment in the Kellogg barn, producing the original note left with him, the subsequent care Rose and her father had taken of the boy and finally, the circumstances of his having been taken back, presumably by his Indian mother.

The judge interrupted. "What of the boy's natural parents?"

Yarnell paced before the judge, outlining the unfortunate and savage murder of the Pawnee woman. "The boy's father signed the affidavit before you, attesting to the boy's birth date and relinquishing all further legal claims to the child. With that act, we believe he has cleared any impediments to Miss Kellogg's suit."

Rose sagged in relief. She had known nothing of the affidavit until now.

The judge harrumphed, then muttered, "I suppose you have witnesses who can testify to Miss Kellogg's fitness for motherhood."

"I have, Your Honor."

First Lily and then Bess took the stand to describe Alf's living conditions and Rose's loving care. The final witness was Pastor Dooley, who portrayed her as a faithful and prayerful churchgoer.

As the minister returned to his seat, he paused briefly to settle a calming hand on her shoulder. Rose was starting to breathe a bit easier. Her case had been made. Surely the judge would find in her favor.

Yarnell again approached the bench. "Your Honor, we ask that Miss Kellogg's petition be granted forthwith.

It will end now, praise God. Rose clutched the folds of her dress and waited for the Honorable Titus Cornett to fulfill her fondest wish.

"Before I pass judgment on this matter, are there others in the court who wish to be heard at this time?"

Others? What others? An ominous silence, broken only by a distant clap of thunder, hung over the court. Then, just as Rose was sure the judge would proceed, a shrill voice erupted from a back row. "Your Honor, I rise to speak in response to your question and to object to Rose Kellogg's petition."

Rose buried her head in her father's shoulder, her hopes fading. She would know that voice anywhere. Bertha Britten.

Lily's restraining hand on his knee was all that kept Seth from bolting from his seat. He couldn't believe the Britten woman. Everything had been proceeding smoothly, so smoothly, in fact, that he had been giving premature thanks to God for giving Rose custody of Alf. He should've learned not to count on anything. With an act of will, he turned his head to look at Bertha Britten, her holier-than-thou demeanor and grating voice setting his teeth on edge.

"It seems to me, Judge Cornett, that we, as a community must accept both physical and moral responsibility for this poor orphan. While Rose Kellogg may be a fine person, as others have testified, she lacks the single most important quality of Christian motherhood."

The judge slouched back in his seat, fixing his eyes on the complainant. "Pray tell, Mrs..."

"Britten." Bertha quivered with indignation.

"...Britten, what is this quality of which you speak?"

"Why, it should be obvious to anyone. I'm surprised it wasn't to Pastor Dooley, but be that as it may, Rose Kellogg is not married, sir. A child needs to be brought up in a Christian home with both a mother and a father. I would submit this is especially true for a male child."

A few spontaneous murmurs of agreement could be heard. Seth clenched his fists, longing to carry the woman bodily from the courtroom. How dare she so malign Rose, who had never done anything but love Alf?

Yarnell leaped to his feet and implored the judge, "Your Honor, what is relevant here is the nature of care this boy is receiving, not Miss Kellogg's marital status." He turned and pointed at Rose and Alf, huddled together under the onslaught of criticism. "See the evidence for yourself. The boy regards my client as his port in the storm, as the one person in the world upon whom he can count. Would the court sever that bond simply because Miss Kellogg has never married? How many children have been raised by maiden aunts or widowed grandmothers? I fail to see how this situation is any different."

Bertha stood her ground. "There are many of us *lawfully* wed, childless persons who would gladly undertake the rearing of this boy, persons who could provide both a father and a mother in a Christian environment. Marriage and parenthood are sacred, Your Honor, and I defy the court to deem otherwise by handing this child over to Miss Kellogg. There. I've had my say." With that, she abruptly sat down.

Beside him, Seth saw Lily wiping away a tear, and Caleb's jaw was as clenched as if chewing rawhide. Seth couldn't believe his own ears. The Brittens? Parents to Alf? Something had to be done. The judge leaned forward, folding his hands on top of the bench. An uncomfortable silence awaited his next words. Finally he spoke. "What is at stake here is Alf's welfare and his future. It would be presumptuous to act hastily in this matter. I declare a twenty minute recess, after which time, I will render my decision." With that, the judge swept toward his chambers.

Seth could see Lavinia, Ezra and Bess gathered around Rose, whose pale, stricken face leveled him like a powerful blow. Across the way, Bertha Britten sat beside her milquetoast of a husband, arms folded across her chest, her head held high, as if daring any present to fault her position. Pastor Dooley had removed himself and stood at a window, his head bowed as if in prayer. "I have to stand up," Seth muttered to Lily, who was rooted to the spot in shock. Not presuming to intrude upon Rose's family group, Seth pushed through the crowd and down the stairs. He needed air. Outside, racked with worry, he paced in the rain, now a gentle shower, wondering how Bertha Britten could so willfully jeopardize Rose's chances. Such pettiness defied description.

He brushed off those who tried to engage him in

conversation and prayed for a strategy to forestall the Britten woman's influence on the judge. Maybe he, too, could speak to the court. He could talk about Rose's cooking, her attention to the boy's manners and dress, the way the two played together and took walks and… He kicked the unyielding trunk of an oak. He was no orator. But surely everyone in town could see how Rose loved the boy and how he, in turn, doted upon her. The very idea of anyone…*anyone* hurting Rose in such a callous, self-righteous manner made his blood boil. But what was he to do? *Please God, if You're listening, find me a way to help Rose and Alf.*

He straggled in behind the last few folks returning to the courtroom and slumped down next to Lily. "How are you?" he asked.

"Oh, Seth, I'm so afraid. This is not looking good. I've overheard several here in the courtroom seriously questioning Rose's unmarried state. During the recess I went to Rose. She's terrified."

"All rise."

To Seth's ear, no words had ever sounded so much like the trumpet of doom. Before resuming his seat, the judge paused and beckoned to Alf. "Come here, boy."

Alf looked inquiringly at Rose, who gave a slight nod. Embarrassed by the crowd, Alf approached the judge with his head bowed. The man took hold of his arm and knelt beside him. Whatever Cornett was saying or asking of Alf was inaudible. The spectators watched as the boy nodded his head a couple of times and then whispered something into the judge's ear. Then the judge stood and shooed Alf back to his seat. Seth would give a great deal to know what had transpired in that brief conversation.

Cornett returned to the bench and with a sigh began his pronouncement. "Rearing children is a sacred obligation bestowed by God. Therefore, it behooves parents to exercise discipline, patience, perseverance and love to nurture in a child all those gifts and talents that God has given him or her. Sometimes that can be an onerous and frustrating parental obligation. In a case where two parents are involved, perhaps one can exercise love when the other has reached the end of the tether. Mrs. Britten's objections are ones I cannot overlook. On the other hand, evidence suggests that Miss Kellogg is devoted to the boy Alf and, thus far, has taken seriously her parental responsibility. Now the court would have no difficulty adjudicating this matter if Miss Kellogg, in fact, had a husband, but—

The powers of heaven could not have kept Seth in his seat. "Go no further, Your Honor. What if Miss Kellogg were married? Would that make a difference?"

"You are out of order, young man. Besides, your question is merely hypothetical."

"Rose," Seth shouted as he hurried across the room, "Rose, will you marry me?" The onlookers gasped and then chattered excitedly among themselves.

Oblivious to the hubbub Seth's proposal had generated, Rose stood and slowly turned to face him, her fair skin mottled with red. "Seth, oh, Seth, don't do this." She shook her head in sadness.

He knelt in the aisle by her chair and took her hands in his. "Please, Rose. Be my wife. Let me be a father to Alf."

"I can't let you sacrifice yourself in this manner."

"Sett?" Alf wedged his way between them. "You

marry Rose and then you'll be my papa, my very own papa!"

Seth caught Rose's eye. "Be very careful now, my dear. We can make this work. It's God's answer to us, to Alf."

In a moment customarily filled with joy, Rose hesitated for long seconds before raising their clasped hands to her lips and choking out her answer. "Yes."

The judge banged his gavel. "Order in the court, order in the court." Seth took Alf on his lap and settled next to Rose. "This is highly unusual." Cornett glared at Seth. "I will not have you make a mockery of this court with your spontaneous outburst."

Seth set Alf aside and stood. "It is not my intention to make a mockery, Your Honor. Rose and I have been good friends for many months, and to some degree, we have participated together in the care of Alf, whom we both love dearly." He faced Rose. "I would be honored to share my life with this woman and her son, if it please this court."

The judge took Seth's measure for what seemed several minutes, then he said, "Sit down, sir." He turned his gaze to the boy. "Alf, would you come forward now, please."

Alf again wandered over to the judge, who lifted him into his lap. "You told me your Rose is a good mother, is that right?"

Alf nodded vigorously.

"Remember when I asked you if you would like a father, too? What did you say?"

"I know, I know. I said Sett!"

"You certainly did, son." The judge picked up his gavel and said, "In the matter of Miss Rose Kellogg's petition for adoption of this young man, petition granted." Then he banged his gavel and the courtroom exploded.

Instead of entering his chambers, The Honorable Titus Cornett descended from the bench and approached Seth, clapped an arm on his shoulder and looked him in the eye. "Do right by these two."

"I will," Seth replied, suddenly humbled by the manner in which God had answered his prayer. Before he could say anything further, Alf jumped into his arms. "Papa, Papa, Papa. I can call you Papa."

Rose had not moved, but stood studying the two of them. "Oh, Seth, what have we done?"

As the courtroom cleared, Seth could say nothing, drained of words and emotionally spent. He was a reasonable man who stewed over decisions, certainly not one prone to spontaneous outbursts such as his proposal. Yet looking at Alf's smile, how could he have done otherwise? Rose remained motionless, her expression unreadable.

Their marriage, while solving the immediate problem of Alf's adoption, would be unconventional, to put it mildly. Without Alf, would a wonderful woman like Rose ever have considered him? And there was always the danger that the more he invested of himself in these two, the greater his risk of getting hurt. Rarely had he allowed himself to consider marriage, but if it was to happen, no woman other than Rose had the potential to make him happy.

"Seth, you rascal, you!" His brother approached and gave him a bear hug. Seth managed a smile. What was done was done, and he'd make the best of it.

Amid their families' questions and congratulations,

Seth and Rose had no opportunity to speak to one another. Ezra looked mildly concerned, Lily cradled her sister's face and nodded her approval, Lavinia stood to one side, not so much shocked as smug, and Sophie had thrust her arm through Seth's with a "Good for you, brother." Mixed reactions. What else could he expect, particularly when he, too, was experiencing a storm of contradictory feelings?

Pastor Dooley sidled up to him. "Seth, might I have a word with you?" The minister drew him aside. "That was a brave and compassionate thing you did, son. Yet I am concerned that yours was an intemperate decision. I would be reluctant to marry you and Rose unless I am convinced this is what you both want and that you will commit to a godly partnership as man and wife."

"I am a man of my word, sir. I believe God has led me to this moment, and while it may not have come about in the usual manner, my proposal was heartfelt. I shall do my best to provide for Rose and Alf and to create a wholesome Christian family."

"Good man. Before we proceed with the wedding, I will need to obtain those same assurances from Rose."

"I understand."

Seth stood apart, watching as the pastor sought out Rose and led her over to a window where they stood talking. Rose listened to what the minister was saying to her, all the time with her head bent and her fingers working the fabric of her skirt. She mumbled something and nodded her head twice. Seth could stand it no longer. He strode across the room and joined them, searching Rose's face for a clue. Did she have serious doubts?

"Seth, Rose has pledged herself to a marriage dis-

tinguished by mutual affection and respect. One with
Christ at its center," said the pastor.

Seth let out a sigh of relief. He took Rose's hands
in his. "This marriage cannot be only about Alf. Rose,
you are a fine woman who deserves to be treated with
decency and affection. We have a friendship. That
should serve us well. I'm ready to go forth if you are."

Although the depths of her blue eyes betrayed some
reservation, her words rang firm and resolute. "I would
be honored to be your wife."

So it was that only two days later in the afternoon
following the regular Sunday church service, Rose
waited in the parsonage while Aunt Lavinia, Bess and
Lily clustered around her oohing and aahing. In one
day, Lily had made over her own wedding gown, adding gussets of lace and lined pleats, to be more flat-
tering to Rose. Studying herself in the mirror, Rose
had little reaction. She had long ago ceased imagining
herself as a bride and never as a loveless one. What
was she was undertaking? A marriage of convenience?
Certainly there had been no protestations of undying
love. This was an arrangement, pure and simple. She
should never have agreed to Seth's proposal. How could
she ask him to sacrifice himself in such a manner?
Yet, how could she not? She and Seth were united in
their love of Alf, but was that sufficient grounds for
marriage? She would do anything to avoid Alf's being
turned over to the likes of a couple such as the Brittens, to a home where his lively, loving spirit might be
repressed. Seth, too, wanted to protect the boy from
such an eventuality.

Lily put the final touches on Rose's hair and stood back to admire the effect. "You are beautiful, sister."

"I've peeked at the groom," Bess said. "He is looking quite handsome."

Nausea threatened to overcome Rose.

Lavinia approached and took up Rose's hand. "But it's Alf who wins the day. He is beside himself with excitement. Be happy for him."

"I am. I truly am." In that moment, a look of recognition passed between the two women as if Aunt Lavinia was conveying her understanding of why Rose had agreed to marry Seth. She, too, had married for reasons other than love. Seth was a good man, a caring friend and would undoubtedly be a faithful husband. Was Rose selfish to wish for more? For romance? Passion? Yet the truth was that she was guilty of using Seth in order to ensure she could keep Alf, just as Seth, too, was protecting the boy.

The time came to walk to the church. As she studied the cross atop the steeple, she nearly lost the will to put one foot in front of the other. The most important question of all tore at her conscience: Were she and Seth defying God's plan in marrying for any reason other than love?

Her father met her at the church door. Lavinia, Lily and Bess scurried inside to gather with Seth's father, Caleb, Sophie and Charlie for the small family wedding. Mattie and Alf, who stood proudly at the back in their functions as flower girl and ring bearer, jumped up and down when they spotted Rose. "Mama, you're my mama and you're even better than a princess!"

The organist began playing "Blessed Be the Tie That Binds," a hymn dear to Lily and Caleb and especially fitting for the occasion. The children started down the aisle. Rose had not yet been able to look at Seth, nor to entertain the joy that the sacrament demanded. Ezra tucked her arm through his. "Remember what your mama always said, Rose. I truly believe in this case she is right. All really will be well."

Then he began slowly walking her toward Pastor Dooley and her groom. It was only then that she finally looked at her husband-to-be. He stood tall, his broad shoulders filling out a new suit coat and his sun-bronzed hair curling just below the collar. But it was his eyes that arrested her. In them she read only warmth. And when he smiled at her as he took her hand, she melted. *If only...* In that moment, Rose knew Seth was and always had been more than a friend. No one else had treated her so kindly or made her heart race with a rare kind of excitement.

She could hardly speak her vows for the shock of her sudden realization. She was in love with this dear man. But how could she ever tell him? He had long proclaimed his desire to remain a bachelor. Now he was simply accommodating Alf. That was all. It would be up to her to govern her emotions and let him take the lead in determining the nature of their marriage.

As if in a trance, she went through the motions of receiving her ring, exchanging vows and praying. Only Seth's steadying hand kept her from being overcome both by her new insight and by the sacredness of their promises to one another.

Too soon, the pastor's voice called her into the present. "I now pronounce Rose and Seth, man and wife. Those whom God hath joined together let no man put asunder." Seth offered her his arm. A wife. She was a wife. And, thanks to the court, a mother. But none of it had happened as she had once dreamed it. "And now, Seth, you may kiss your bride."

Rose blushed to the roots of her hair. She had not foreseen this awkward moment. How could this happen? And in front of everyone? Seth studied her face, then caressed her shoulders, drawing her near. "Mrs. Montgomery," he whispered and then she felt his lips on hers and a traitorous tingle zinged from the top of her head to the tips of her toes.

"Seth," she breathed as the kiss ended. "Oh, my."

"Kissing. Papa's kissing! Look, Mattie. He's kissing Mama!"

Alf's outburst shattered any decorum on the part of the witnesses, and one by one, the people she loved came forward to press their congratulations on the two of them. The last to approach her was Andrew. The grizzled old man took her hands in his, holding them tightly. With glazed eyes, Seth's father spoke softly for her ears only. "I love my son, Rose. He has little thought for himself, only for others. It has been thus since he was a boy forced to take on the care of his brother and sister. He will be good to Alf and to you." He paused, swallowing several times. "Someday he will admit to you what we all know already. My son loves you with all his being. Be patient, my dear."

Thunderstruck, Rose was at a loss for words. Could it be? Was Seth as fearful of rejection as she? She wanted to believe Andrew, but did she dare?

Seth, carrying Alf, came to her and picked up her hand. "Shall we go? The banquet awaits at Aunt Lavinia's and this little fella is hungry."

"C'mon to 'Vinia's," Alf urged, looking between

the two adults. "Now you're my mama and Sett's my papa. We're a fambly!"

Please, God, let it be so.

Chapter Sixteen

Lavinia had spared no expense for the wedding dinner. "Why, I swear I'm back in St. Louis," Lily cooed over the cream of squash soup.

Rose and Seth sat together at one end of the long table with Ezra and Lavinia at the other. Alf sat to Seth's right, carefully studying and emulating his new papa's table manners. Bess Stanton sat on the opposite corner next to Ezra. From her vantage point, Rose was able to watch the loving looks the two exchanged. She envied them the certainty of their feelings. She glanced surreptitiously at Seth. Would she ever find that degree of contentment?

Within this family, she felt protected, unlike her experience at the regular church service earlier this morning. Beneath the brims of their hats and bonnets, several of the women had looked down their noses at her, and she had overheard one of Bertha Britten's friends confide to her husband, "'Marry in haste, repent in leisure.' Rose Kellogg and Seth Montgomery? Imagine." She and Seth had shocked the community.

Who knew how long it would take until their marriage was tolerated, if never fully accepted?

"Was the soup satisfactory, Mrs. Montgomery?"

Hannah startled her out of her reverie. *Mrs. Montgomery.* How strange that sounded. Rose examined her nearly full bowl. "Quite, thank you. I'm just not very hungry."

"Very well," Hannah said, removing the soup.

Caleb, who sat on her left, reached over and placed a hand on her arm. "The past three days have no doubt been exhausting for you." He looked beyond her to determine that Seth was engaged with Alf. "Rose, I know my brother. He's a fine man."

Rose nodded, not daring to look up lest Caleb notice the tears pooling in her eyes.

"He will never give you cause for concern. Besides," her brother-in-law grinned and winked, "he's always been mighty partial to you."

That would have to do for a start. There was always the chance, though, that *mighty partial* was all she would ever know.

When the beef tenderloin and steaming sweet potatoes were served, Rose did her best to take nourishment, but every morsel stuck in her throat. Seth seemed to be having no such problem. He liked good food, and she took comfort from the fact he was complimentary of her cooking. Between the main course and the dessert, Seth leaned close. "You're mighty quiet."

"It's been a big day," she murmured.

Then, as if seeing her for the first time since the wedding, he reached under the table and took her hand. "One we will never forget." Then his face reddened. "Or one I, at least, will not soon forget."

She could tell he was trying to put her at ease. Surely she owed him some sort of positive response. "I'm not sorry for our decision. I hope you're not."

"Sorry? Never." He nodded in Alf's direction. Her gaze followed. Alf was chatting with Andrew about "'Vinia's marbles." With a start, Rose realized that in this one day, Andrew had become Alf's grandfather. "We are starting something good, Rose. Look at our boy."

"Our son," Rose whispered wonderingly.

Hannah returned with a crystal trifle bowl, filled to the brim with pound cake, whipped cream and tinned fruit.

"My dear," Aunt Lavinia called from her end of the table, "I hope this will do in lieu of a wedding cake."

"It's lovely," Rose said.

"Looks delicious," Seth added.

"Mama, I gets the cherry?" Then Alf glanced down the table. "Oh, I mean Mattie and me. Cherries."

"Anyone else for cherries?" Ezra asked. Amused silence greeted his question. "Well, then, young man, cherries it is for you and Mattie."

Spooning the rich dessert into her mouth, Rose took a moment to glance around the table, thankful for the gracious way their families interacted with one another. The Bertha Brittens of the world might throw their proverbial sticks and stones, but secure within this circle of love, Rose vowed to be unmoved by petty criticism from outsiders.

After dinner, Rose and Seth stood awkwardly in the parlor bidding good evening to the family. Because of the rapidity of the arrangements, they had realized they had no place to call home. Andrew and Seth planned to add a room onto the ranch house, but that would take weeks. Until then, Ezra and Caleb had moved Alf's trundle bed into Ezra's room, leaving the double bed in Rose's room for her and Seth, although most weekdays he would have to stay at the ranch to work.

Lavinia swooped down on them. "Now for my surprise, dears." Standing between them, she linked her arms through theirs. "I couldn't come up with a honeymoon trip on such short notice, so here's what we'll do. Ezra has agreed to take Alf on home, but you two will be staying in my lovely third-floor guest room tonight. You'll have plenty of privacy there."

A flush suffused Rose. She had counted on Alf's presence to help get her through this night. "Aunt Lavinia, that's a lovely gesture, but—"

"We accept your kind offer," Seth blurted out.

Rose leaned around Lavinia to glare at Seth, but he was ignoring her. "Really, Lavinia, that's more than kind, but—"

"Your things are already here. Lily helped pack."

Lily! Was everyone conspiring against her?

Ezra approached, carrying Alf. "We came to say good-night, didn't we, little man? You and I will slip on home and leave your Mama and Papa to celebrate. We'll see them in the morning, remember?"

Alf nodded vigorously. "I 'member. Morning time is when I see Mama and Papa Sett."

Knowing she'd been bested, Rose held out her arms to give Alf a hug. "I love you, dear boy."

"I know," he said, his eyes sparkling. "Sett loves me, too."

Seth leaned over and kissed the boy's forehead. "Indeed I do. Sleep tight, son."

Son. Rose took comfort from that single syllable.

"Shoo, now, everybody," Lavinia ushered Alf and Ezra, the last of the visitors, to the front door. Rose watched them, wildly speculating how she and Seth could possibly stay the night here. Somehow she had assumed he would return to the ranch. Of course, she had known that eventually they would share a bed, but the immediacy was both embarrassing and daunting.

"Up you go," Aunt Lavinia chirped as she returned to the parlor. "Sweet dreams."

Seth turned to Rose, looking every bit as uncomfortable as she felt. He held out his hand, giving hers an encouraging squeeze. "Come, Rose."

She had no choice but to follow.

Seth had never seen such an ornate room. The large four-poster canopied bed stood at least two and a half feet off the floor. The windows were draped with heavy velvet and the fragrance of patchouli perfumed the air. Watercolors and oil paintings bedecked the walls, and beneath his feet was a thick Persian rug. Rose clutched his hand as they surveyed the room's accoutrements. He could feel her shivering beside him. "Are you cold? I can stoke the fire."

"It's nerves," she said in a low voice. "I don't know what I expected, but not this elegant room."

He knew all about nerves. He was miles out of his element. A gentleman would put a lady at ease, but everything he thought to say sounded weak. Finally, he took the plunge. "Rose, dear, what if we turn down the covers, take off our shoes and talk? We really haven't had much time, just the two of us, to figure out how we proceed with this marriage."

At last a flicker of a smile from his bride. "That would be a good place to start, I believe. We need to think about how we will live, how we want to raise Alf, what will become of Papa and—"

"Shh." He placed a finger on her lips. "One thing at a time." He spanned her waist with his hands. "Now, up with you," and he lifted her and sat her against the heap of pillows at the head of the bed and then gently removed her shoes. He shrugged out of his wedding coat, tugged off his own shoes and joined her, being sure to keep an appropriate distance between them. "First, let's talk about today. We will only have one wedding day, so I want to fix it in our memories." He put his hands behind his head and sighed more contentedly than he had thought possible just a few short minutes ago. "You looked so lovely coming down the aisle."

"Thanks to Lily," Rose confessed. "She worked wonders on the dress."

He turned to look at her. "I wasn't talking about the dress."

"But—"

"You don't think much of yourself, do you?"

"Lily has always been the beauty."

"And so she is in her own way, and in your own way, so are you. You can't help what your eyes reveal." He stared at the ceiling. "And how about Mattie and Alf coming down the aisle? Oh, that's right, you were behind them. How I wish you could have seen Alf's beaming face. I'm smiling just thinking about it."

"And Aunt Lavinia's dinner? Magnificent."

He relaxed. She was starting to get into the reminiscences. As she recalled each course of the sumptuous meal, he gently laced his fingers through hers. By the time the clock struck ten, they had talked for over an hour. Strange. He was a solitary fellow. This was more conversation than he'd had at one sitting in…well, maybe ever. Surprisingly, he decided it felt good—this having someone with whom to discuss the day's events.

He turned to gaze at Rose and couldn't conceal a smile. She was fast asleep, one hand crossed over her chest. Carefully, so as to avoid waking her, he slipped off the bed and walked around to her side. In the dim light of the oil lamp, he studied her features. Creamy skin, faint freckles, pale long lashes, red-blond hair splayed across the pillow and lush red lips. Kissable lips. He groaned silently and forced himself to return to the duty at hand. He picked up the cashmere throw at the foot of the bed and wrapped it around her. Around…his wife.

Then he extinguished the lamp and returned to his own side of the bed where sleep eluded him. He was married. Rose had required a husband and he had obliged. He wondered if she would ever need him for anything more. He didn't want a sham marriage. They had both promised before God to create a loving home. For that to happen, though, they would need to be honest with one another. He thought he could do that… wanted to do that. But how did a friendship move toward something more?

He rolled over onto his side. His life had always been uncomplicated. He'd liked it that way. But now? Rose was a woman, and he'd never had the remotest notion how to deal with women. What had possessed him to think he could begin now?

In the next few days, Rose settled into her new routine. In some ways weekdays were the same as before, occupied with cooking, laundry, cleaning, making calls and tending to Alf. On the weekend when Seth was due, she redoubled her cooking efforts. She took extra care with her appearance, even though she couldn't tell if he noticed. Thanks to the balmy Indian summer weather, the Saturday after the wedding they had been able to take a picnic to the river. Seth was teaching Alf to fish, an experience more comical than productive. Sunday, they had gone to church and paid calls. In the evenings, Bess often joined the two of them and Ezra to read aloud or play word games.

As she worked extracting the pulp from a pumpkin and kept an eye on Alf playing in the yard, Rose reflected that she need not have worried about their temporary living arrangements. Seth treated her with great courtesy, but she was gradually concluding that friendship was all there might ever be between them. While theirs was an easy relationship, undemanding and comfortable, Rose knew she wanted more. The revelation at her wedding that she was in love with this man she called *husband* had caused her to mine their every exchange for some nugget that would indicate he returned her feelings. That very effort, in turn, caused her to question her reaction to his words and gestures. Was she reading more into them than he intended? *I wasn't talking about the dress.* Bother. She needed to guard against wishful thinking and, instead, weigh the reality. Yet the dilemma remained. How could she let him know of her love without risking humiliation and rejection?

Whenever Seth came into the room, her breath caught. No silly goose of a schoolgirl had ever been so addled by the sight of her beloved. The gentleness and respect he had shown her from their wedding night on caused her both gratitude and frustration. How often she had bitten back the endearments she longed to utter or paused in the act of touching him. In many ways, Alf still served as the bridge between them and, perhaps, equally as a buffer. She didn't know how much longer she could live in this tension or how she and Seth could move beyond the logjam of their relationship. Yet she couldn't force the issue. Doing so might tear the fragile fabric of the accommodation they had made with one another.

Scooping out the last bits of stringy pumpkin, she wondered if this coming weekend would be any different. Seth planned to take Alf and her to the ranch to see the improvements being made to the house. Sophie had seemed delighted that there would be another woman in the home, and Seth had commented to her how pleased his father was that she would be living there when Sophie married. If only she didn't feel so guilty about leaving her father. Before she moved, she would have to make arrangements for a housekeeper. It would be strange not to be living with Papa. Only during the War Between the States, when he was serving in field hospitals, had they ever lived apart.

When she stepped outside to dump the pumpkin shell in the garbage heap, Alf came running over to her. "Go for a walk, Mama? I wanna see 'Vinia. I'll tell her 'bout Papa and fishing."

"I'm not sure she's at home, Alf."

He gripped her hand, "We can go see. C'mon."

She laughed at his insistence. "In a moment, son. Let me freshen up."

To Alf's delight, Aunt Lavinia was indeed at home.

While he rushed forward and hugged their hostess, Rose hung back, embarrassed that they had stopped by without notice. "I'm sure in St. Louis spontaneous calls are most irregular."

Lavinia patted Alf's head and then shooed him into the parlor where she kept some toys for him. "Ah, St. Louis. Yes, your servant would have delivered a note requesting to call. But here? Rose, I'm enjoying the informality. Besides," she smiled, "I don't have to worry about how I am dressed to receive. There is relief in that."

Lavinia summoned Hannah, who went to the kitchen and brought back some tea and wafer-thin cookies. "Anything else, ma'am?"

"No, thank you, Hannah. Perhaps you would like to take young Alf out to the carriage house?"

"Horses?" Alf said from across the room.

"Bright boy." Lavinia winked at Rose. "Go along with Hannah now." When they had left the room, the older woman turned to Rose. "Since you're here, I have several matters to discuss with you, dear. But first, how is marriage agreeing with you?"

What was there to say? That she didn't know… might never know? "Our temporary living arrangement seems to be working well. We are still getting accustomed to being together. Building our family will take time."

"Yes, such things do. You've undergone important changes lately. My counsel is patience and gratitude." She set down her teacup with a sigh. "I fear I was too impatient in my life. Too critical. Water under the bridge. No sense living with regret. This time here in the Flint Hills has been a breath of fresh air. I will be leaving soon. I have already missed the beginning of the St. Louis social season, something that would have been unthinkable to me in the past. I did so want to see you and Alf settled before I depart, though. I take the train a week from today, but before I go, I still require your advice concerning the kitchen of my new Flint Hills home. Do you recall our conversation?"

"I do, and although I am no expert, I shall happily offer my opinion."

"Good. You will not believe the progress Mr. Devane and his crew have made in a few short weeks. The house should be quite habitable by late spring. Could I pick you up this coming Monday? We can drop Alf off at Lily's and proceed to the site."

"I shall look forward to it." Rose never ceased to marvel at the change that had come over Aunt Lavinia. Kansas appeared to have given her a new lease on life.

"Now there is another matter I wish to raise." Lavinia picked up a cookie and nibbled daintily before continuing. "Your father."

"My father? What about him?"

"Years ago, I believe I quite hurt his feelings. In my youthful folly, I did not think he was good enough for my sister, your mother. Over time, we have made our peace, and I do hope that my being here and engaging with the family after so many years has ameliorated any awkwardness between us."

Rose had no idea where her aunt was heading. "I'm sure he is quite at peace about the matter."

"I hope so. I have grown very fond of him. When I leave Cottonwood Falls, I would like to know he is well situated."

"What do you mean?"

"In a few short weeks, you will be gone, dear. He will need tending."

"I had thought to engage a housekeeper."

Lavinia cocked an eyebrow. "Do you think that will be necessary?"

"Well, yes—"

Lavinia laughed a merry laugh. "Nonsense, child. Haven't you seen what I've seen?"

Rose smiled. "Bess Stanton?"

"Bess Stanton." Lavinia leaned forward in her chair. "I know Mathilda would approve, and it is clear Bess is devoted to your father. I suspect he cares a great deal for her. However, he may be uncomfortable confessing his feelings to you and Lily. I think we must help him along."

"I had no idea you were such a matchmaker, Aunt Lavinia."

"Not I, you. As Ezra's sister-in-law, it is not my place to insert my judgments into his life. But you? Ask him about Bess, Rose. That makes infinitely more sense than a…housekeeper."

Rose could hardly keep from chuckling. Lavinia made *housekeeper* seem like the last role on earth any woman would want to play. "Lily and I have discussed their relationship," she confessed. "We both see how happy and content they are with one another."

"He's waiting for you to approve."

As she thought about it, Rose had to agree—that's exactly what was going on. Her dear papa was putting his daughters' welfare first as he had done all his life. It was his turn now. "I hadn't thought of it quite that way, but you are right."

"Talk to him. Soon."

Rose was moved by the depth of her aunt's concern. "I will. Maybe even tonight. Thank you for reminding me of what I should have seen all along. I will miss you when you leave, just as Alf and all the rest of us will."

"Until the lilacs bloom, my dear niece. Until then."

Lavinia's words echoed in Rose's heart all the way home. The shadows had lengthened and a golden autumn glow touched the leaves and splayed across the road. If she couldn't smooth her own life in the way of love, surely she could pave her father's.

It was not until after putting Alf to bed that she had occasion to sit with her father at the kitchen table. He was compiling a list of medications to order from the supply house in Kansas City. She darned socks, watching him scrawl the names of various remedies on the paper in front of him. She studied his wrinkled face and balding head, grateful for all the love and guidance he had provided. Losing her mother had devastated her. How much more must Papa have suffered? Yet through everything, he had been a wise and loving force in her life. It was a very good God who had sent him as admirable a woman as Bess. She set aside the darning egg and laid a hand on his, stilling his movement. "Papa, could I ask you something?"

"Of course, my dear, anything."

"Are you in love with Bess?"

He stared at her, as if divining if she was serious. "What makes you ask such a thing?"

She screwed up her courage. "Bess is a wonderful woman and a genuine friend to me. Through some hard times, she has been here with us, often working quietly behind the scenes. I am extraordinarily fond of her." He opened his mouth to speak, but she went right on.

"I have watched the two of you together, sharing moments of laughter and friendship. I have seen the way you look at one another. Papa, one must never turn one's back on love." A fleeting grimace crossed her face. She should take her own advice. "All I'm trying to say is that if you and Bess were to marry, Lily and I would rejoice with you."

"You would?" The man seemed genuinely shocked. "But what about your mother—"

"Mother would be the first to shake her finger in your face and say, 'Ezra, you fool. Would you turn your back on love? Life is for the living.'"

He shook his head in wonder. "My Mathilda *would* say that, wouldn't she?" For a few moments he seemed lost in memory.

"Lily and I know how much you loved our mother. We also know that God has given you a rare second chance."

He swept one hand across his eyes, then gazed into hers. "Thank you, Rose."

Rose beamed. "You haven't yet answered my question, Papa."

The answer when it came was firm and sure. "Yes, dear daughter, I am in love with my generous and beautiful Bess."

Rose could hardly wait to tell Seth. And Lily. How odd. Spontaneously she had wanted to tell Seth the news, even before considering her own sister. That's the nature of marriage, she realized. *Please, God, help Seth and me to make love, rather than convenience or even friendship, the anchor of our marriage.*

Chapter Seventeen

After church the following Sunday, Andrew and Sophie went directly home while Seth gathered Alf and Rose and set out behind them in Ezra's borrowed buggy. The day was chilly but clear. The leaves barely clinging to the trees foretold the onset of winter. "I want you two to see the progress we've made on the house addition. I'm hoping to enclose it before the blizzards blow."

Alf jiggled with excitement. "I'll live with you one day, Papa Sett? Me and Mama at your house, right?"

Seth put an arm around the boy. "One day soon, son." He caught Rose's eye. "Will you mind being so far from town?"

"I like the countryside. I had been worried about Papa, but no more."

"Oh?

"I think very soon he will propose to Bess Stanton, and I do believe she will accept."

"I shouldn't be surprised. That match should ease your mind."

"It does."

Seth had wondered how Rose would deal with leaving Ezra and was relieved to hear such a practical, even romantic solution was at hand. If it was within his power, he wanted this upcoming move to go smoothly. Sophie and Pa were looking forward to the liveliness Alf would bring to the ranch, and Sophie had indicated she didn't mind at all sharing household duties, especially the cooking. Already on the weekends, he was the beneficiary of Rose's culinary talents. A lifetime of her food was a pleasant prospect.

"How are things on the ranch?" Rose asked.

"We're busy making plans for next spring, which pastures to use, whether we'll need to buy extra stock, ways to keep rustlers at bay."

Rose's eyes widened. "Rustlers? Is that a concern?"

"You never know. Open range like this, all kinds of folks drift through, some unfortunately up to no good. Once we're living at the ranch, I want to teach you how to use a shotgun. Sophie can shoot better than some men. I don't anticipate trouble, but it's best to be prepared just in case."

"I'd never thought..." She let her words die away.

He bit back an oath. More fool he. He'd frightened her just when he had hoped to impress her. He laid his gloved hand on hers. "I didn't mean to alarm you, Rose. Nobody's ever bothered the house, and I don't think they will, but I'd be a sorry excuse for a husband if I didn't do everything I can to secure your safety. And Alf's."

She clasped his hand. "I understand."

Nothing more was said during the last mile before home. Seth had noticed in the last couple of weeks that Rose seemed more reserved with him. Not rude, no.

Just…drawn into herself. Before, he'd always been able to talk freely with her. In fact, he'd looked forward to their conversations. She had a way of putting him at ease, even of making him feel good about himself. His mother had had that knack, too, always calling him her good big boy and even on her deathbed, trusting him to hold tiny Sophie.

Mama would've liked Rose. He wanted to be the kind of husband to her that his father had been to his mother. Yet Rose's reticence concerned him. Had he presumed too much by asking her to marry him? Was she regretting her decision? Looking out for Alf was one thing, but a lifetime partnership must seem quite another.

"The house. I see it." Alf pointed. "Maybe I'll see horses, too, Papa Sett? Patches and those other ones?"

"We should have time for that after I show you and your mama the new room."

When they walked from the barn to the house, Rose clutched his arm. "It's lovely out here, Seth. The house, the gardens, the views. Really lovely."

Alf had scampered on ahead, but now stopped in his tracks. "The new room…I spy it."

Seth led them to the construction site. The walls and roof were framed and some of the stonework was visible. "It's so big," Rose exclaimed. "And, oh, the window will overlook the flower garden." She whirled around. "You've thought of everything, even the luxury of a fireplace."

He put an arm around her waist. "I can't have my wife getting cold. Look there." He pointed to a small alcove off the room. "Alf will sleep in my old room, but this may someday hold a cradle."

How had that thought escaped his lips? He didn't dare turn to observe her reaction. Goliath had put his foot in his mouth once again. Instead of taking the bull by the horns, he needed to step back and let God work in their lives. One day, he prayed Rose would know how important she'd become to him.

"You're sure Sophie and your father will welcome our being here?"

"Welcome it? Come along with me and hear for yourself. They can't wait to have you and Alf here. Sophie is almost regretting leaving soon to marry Charlie. She's never had another woman in the house, you know, and she's looking forward to it and happy it's you."

Blushing, Rose looked up at him. "I'm glad," she said, before making one more inspection of the room.

Dinner went well, and surely Rose could tell from the lively conversation how much a part of all of them she was. Sophie had showed her where her name had already been inscribed in the family Bible. Now Pa settled with Alf to play checkers, so Seth approached Rose. "Would you favor a walk with me?"

She nodded and fetched her cloak. He shrugged into his coat and put on his hat as they went out the door. He searched the sky. The sun was low and wisps of clouds floated above the horizon. "I'll need to take you home soon."

"It will be good to stretch my legs before the buggy ride to town."

Arm in arm they strolled away from the house and up a small rise overlooking the ranch buildings. He wanted to ask her if she'd made a mistake throwing her lot in with him, but the words stuck in his throat, somehow seeming inappropriate. After the fact. If she had regrets, would she admit to them and would he even want to know? Their old ease with one another had vanished in the awkwardness of finding themselves suddenly man and wife. He thought about kissing her, showing her in a gesture how he felt about her. But if she rebuffed him?

At the top of the rise, he circled her waist and drew her close. "Are you disappointed that we won't have a home of our own?"

"Seth?" She seemed genuinely puzzled by the question. "It is not the building that makes a home, but the people within. I am so fond of your father and sister. And with Alf, you and I will make a home wherever we are."

"If you do want a new home one day, I will make it happen for you."

"I can't imagine a more pleasant house than the one Alf and I are moving into."

"Good." That one word was the last he felt capable of uttering. For the life of him, he couldn't grasp where the conversation could go from here. If not totally content, Rose seemed able to abide the prospect of a future with him. At this point, what more could he ask?

"I went to see Parson Dooley before we were married."

He drew in his breath, surprised and anxious.

"I confessed to him about my anger with God when Alf went missing. About how fulfilled I felt being someone's mother, and then how dashed I was to have that gift withdrawn." She turned to face him. "I was wrong to think God had tricked me or abandoned me. Our Alf has been restored to us, and you have generously taken us both on. I know marriage may not have been anything you'd even thought about, with me or anyone else, but I shall be eternally grateful that God moved you to offer yourself to Alf and me." She laid her hands on his chest and sought his eyes. "There. I needed to tell you what a fine man you are. I shall try always to honor your sacrifice by being a worthy wife."

"Sacrifice? That's what you think?" He stifled a bitter chuckle. She'd made a bargain with God. That was all. She'd said not one word about the possibility of loving him. A rare melancholy clouded his heart. "God's ways are more than mysterious, Rose. Sometimes they're downright confounding, but here's the thing—for better or worse, He's brought us to this place in our lives. All we can do is set forth in faith doing the best we can."

"In faith," she echoed. "In faith."

On the buggy ride back into Cottonwood Falls, they said little that didn't concern Alf. Far into the night, lying by his wife's side, Seth longed to gather her in his arms and convey the feelings he was unable to voice.

On Tuesday when Lavinia drove the two of them to the building site, Rose had to laugh. From top to toe, her aunt was bedecked as if preparing to call upon royalty. Diamonds glittered from her ear lobes and beneath her fur-lined cloak, her lush royal-purple merino dress highlighted the diamond and amethyst necklace she often wore. By contrast, Rose resembled a sparrow in her plain brown gown and serviceable cloak. "You look lovely, Aunt Lavinia, but hardly ready for the frontier."

"No matter. I have no place else to wear the finery I brought with me. Besides, it makes me feel good." Lavinia tapped Rose's knee. "But you are right. Next year I must invest in a more utilitarian wardrobe."

They had already dropped Alf at Lily's where they left the children creating a make-believe hideaway using a sheet draped over the kitchen table. After a cup of tea with Lily, they had set out again. For early November the day was mild, though a stout breeze caused them to gather the carriage blanket around their knees. "I had thought you'd have your man drive us today," Rose said.

"Sometimes I enjoy being at the reins, and this is one of my few chances before I leave for home at the end of the week."

"We will miss you."

"And I, you. Before you know it, though, it will be June and I'll return."

When they crested a hill about half a mile south of Caleb and Lily's house, Lavinia halted the buggy and pointed in the distance. Nestled in a grove of small trees overlooking the hills was the construction site. "What a beautiful vista, Aunt Lavinia! You couldn't have selected a better spot."

"I'm very pleased, Rose. Once I am settled as a part-time resident, I intend to discuss a cattle operation with Seth and Caleb. There's money to be made here, and I'd be a fool not to take advantage of that fact."

Rose looked at her aunt with fresh eyes. "You would want to be a business woman?"

Lavinia flicked the reins to start downhill. "I would relish it, my dear. One cannot live on bonbons and champagne alone."

Rose reflected on her earlier reservations about her high society aunt. In recent weeks she had come to regard her as resilient and independent. Who could have imagined it?

"Now then, my dear," Lavinia said as she stepped from the buggy and tied the reins to a tree, "I wanted to show you the place unimpeded by the workmen, who are at the quarry today with Mr. Devane. So we will have our run of the house."

Rose was impressed with the progress the construction crew had made. The first story floor was planked and the walls framed. The inviting front porch running the full width of the house seemed nearly complete. Rose turned to take in the panorama. "You will spend many happy hours rocking here and enjoying the view."

"I will be queen of all I survey," Lavinia said, nodding in agreement. "Now then, let me show you the house." They traversed through the suggestions of a parlor, informal sitting room, dining room and butler's pantry before arriving at the designated kitchen space. "What do you think, Rose?"

The room was large, and Rose took her time studying the placement of the windows and the access to the outdoors.

"I will spare no expense, dear."

"Very well, then. The sink might go under this window that looks out at the trees. A pleasant prospect. If you put the stove on the wall farthest from the dining room, the heat it puts out should not be a factor for your summertime guests. May I suggest you purchase a stove that has at least four burners and a spacious warming oven in addition to the bake oven? Also, there is room for a large work table to go in the center of the room. Perhaps your carpenters could make one with storage cabinets beneath. And over here, adjacent to the butler's pantry, I suggest a long counter where plates can be assembled for serving." Rose paused, then studied the wall opposite the proposed sink. "Perhaps it would be wise to put in another window there for cross-ventilation."

Lavinia clapped her hands. "My dear, I knew I could count on you for ideas I would never have imagined."

Rose felt her cheeks redden with pleasure. The kitchen she envisioned would be enviable. "It's going to be an elegant home."

"My prairie palace," Lavinia said, smiling in wonder.

They proceeded to walk around the exterior while Lavinia pointed to the planned location of the second-floor bedrooms and the summer porch extending from her upstairs sitting room. "It will be the talk of the county, and—" Rose started, then laid a finger to her lips. "Did you hear something?"

Lavinia cocked her head. "Nothing besides the wind in the trees and the nicker of our horse."

"Very well," Rose said trying to shake the sensation of being observed. "Where will you locate your stable?"

Lavinia led her behind the house and spread her arms. "There," she said, "just beyond that patch of cedars. Far enough from the house so unpleasant odors will not be a problem, but near enough for practicality."

Once again Rose's ears perked up. She could swear she heard twigs breaking. She faced the cedar trees, straining her senses. She could see nothing, yet the hairs on the back of her neck were standing on end. "Aunt Lavinia, I think we should leave now to get back to Alf in time to eat and then start for town."

"I suppose." Her aunt gazed around the property. "I could stay here for hours, though."

Rose controlled her impulse to run to the buggy and lash the horse to carry them away with dispatch. Was she silly to let her imagination run away with her? Yet something was not right. Not right at all.

With an irritating lack of haste, Lavinia made her way to the buggy. She had just untied the reins preparatory to climbing in beside Rose, when she stopped in her tracks. Rose followed her gaze and immediate prickles of fear engulfed her body. A thin man with filthy dungarees and muddy boots stood silhouetted against the cedars, a red bandanna covering his face except for his ferretlike eyes. But it was the pistol he held in his hand that terrified Rose. "Ladies, git your hands up." The man waved his gun to assure their obedience. "Tex, c'mon out. These heifers have got the message." He cackled in a way that froze Rose's blood.

Another taller man, wearing a soiled range coat, emerged from the brush, pointing a shotgun directly at them. "Don't be thinkin' yer running away. Ol' Tex don't mind none dispatching you to your Maker."

The first man approached Lavinia and jerked the reins from her hand. "Git in." He poked her with his gun. "We're goin' fer a little ride, gals."

"Now see here, sir." Lavinia's lips were clenched in outrage. "There must be some mistake."

The man used the pistol to goad Lavinia into the buggy. "No mistake," he said climbing onto the seat beside them, his foul odor further unnerving Rose. "Saddle up, Tex, and follow along to our camp."

Camp? Reaching for Lavinia's hand, Rose closed her eyes in frantic prayer. *Good Lord, deliver us. I haven't come this far to leave my Alf...and Seth.* Then with a lurch of the buggy, they were off...headed for what? It didn't bear considering.

Knowing Alf would be at Lily's this day, Seth rode out from the ranch after the midday meal in the hope of spending some time with the boy instead of having to wait until the weekend. When he arrived, the children were napping, so at Lily's suggestion, he prowled around in search of Caleb. He found him in the corral halter-training a colt. "Looks like a dandy," he said of the horse.

Caleb led the animal through two more circuits, then turned him loose and joined Seth, who was perched on the fence. "You do a fine job, brother, but I wouldn't expect any less of a former cavalry officer."

Caleb coiled the rope between his hands. "Nothing more important than a good mount."

"How old you reckon Alf needs to be for his first pony?"

"If you select a tractable animal, I figure in another year or so he'll be ready."

"He's sure keen to have one."

Caleb chuckled. "So were we, if I remember correctly." He made another loop in the rope. "You enjoying married life?"

"Hard to say, living in two different places." Seth studied his boots. "I reckon it'll get better."

"You didn't have any time for courtship. That's gotta be hard on you both."

"It was all suddenlike. You know me, Caleb. I don't expect much, but if I was gonna get married, it should've been for love."

Caleb clapped a hand on Seth's shoulder. "Love? You think there's no love? Thunderation, man, you've had your eyes on Rose since she first moved to town. I don't know what you call it, but I sure call it love."

"She's powerful important to me."

"So there. Enjoy it."

"I can't tell her. She just married me for Alf's sake." He hurried on. "And that's all right by me. I mean, we both think the world of that boy."

Caleb shoved his hat back on his head. "You are one dumb fella."

Seth cringed. Even his own brother echoed the school-yard taunts. *Dumb.* "What do you mean?"

Caleb threw up his arms. "The woman is mad for you, Seth. Anyone with any sense can see it. Pa and Sophie see it. Lily sees it. I see it. What's holding you back?"

Seth twiddled his thumbs between his knees. Could he believe Caleb? He wanted to. But if Rose loved him, why was she holding back? After several moments, he looked at his brother and gave the answer that cost him so dearly to admit. "I'm scared."

"Scared? You don't think I was scared when Lily traipsed off to St. Louis after I proposed? Scared when I traveled back there to tell her I loved her and to give her one more chance? Give us one more chance? Scared? I know all about that, brother. But here's what else I know. That's what love's about. Risk, man. You have to risk it all if you want the reward. It doesn't bear thinking what my life would have been like without Lily, but it didn't come easy. You gotta risk, Seth."

Seth had no answer, but Caleb had given him much to ponder. Even if words had been forthcoming, he would've been interrupted by Lily who was running toward them, trailed by the children. "Thank goodness I've found you close by. I'm worried."

Both men jumped to the ground. "Worried? About what?" Caleb asked.

"It's well past four and Lavinia and Rose left here before noon. They should've been back before now. I thought maybe they were waiting to return until the children awoke, but that was almost an hour ago. I'm afraid something's happened."

Seth started running for the barn before the words were out of his sister-in-law's mouth. He heard Caleb shouting to her, "We'll go look for them. Meanwhile, stay inside and lock the doors."

Both men leaped into the saddle and galloped away, heads bent low over their horses. Seth had never known such fear in his life, even when Alf had been taken. Then he could comfort himself that someone who loved Alf was behind the kidnapping. But now? There was no comfort. If something had happened to Rose… Whether it was the wind or tears that caused his eyes to water didn't matter, he loved that woman and a life without her…why, he couldn't fathom such an existence. He spurred Patches, throwing caution to the winds. Right behind him, he heard Caleb's horse snorting with exertion. Finally they crested the hill above Lavinia's property and looked down. Nothing.

They raced to a stop by the house and dismounted. Caleb began walking around, studying the ground. "Here," he called. "See the ruts in the grass. This is where the buggy was parked. I wonder if the horse bolted."

Seth ran one direction around the house and Caleb

the other, all the time calling Lavinia's and Rose's names. Only the wind, now picking up, answered, its mournful howl echoing that in Seth's chest. When they met up again, they looked at one another, grim-faced. "We'll try to follow the trail," Caleb said, remounting. Seth could only pray that Caleb's experience as an army scout would lead them to the women.

Rose clutched Lavinia's hand as the buggy went hurtling over the countryside, the horse urged on by the unrelenting whip administered by the ruffian sitting beside her. The man named Tex rode ahead of them, leading a second horse. With every lurch and bounce, Rose was sure they would be tossed out onto the hard ground…and with each turn of the wheels they were being transported farther and farther away from help. Rose's stomach seized with fear. Would she ever see Alf again? Or have the chance to make a real marriage with Seth?

"Try to keep calm," Lavinia said. "It's our only chance."

In hindsight, Rose recognized how careless it was of them to visit the building site alone, with no menfolk and no weapon. Lavinia was new to the territory, but Rose should have known better. Before this, the talk of desperadoes in the area had been just that—talk. Obviously, talk she'd too easily dismissed. If something happened to her… She bit her lip against the scream threatening to rip her lungs apart. Seth would care for Alf. Lily would help. As would others. But not seeing her boy again? Merely thinking about it was beyond bearing.

"Surely Lily will figure out we're in trouble," Lavinia tried to reassure her.

"But their home is miles from the sheriff."

"Shut your mouths," the driver snarled at them. "No talk."

Rose eyed Lavinia with alarm, but the older woman merely shrugged. How could she be so calm, Rose wondered.

After jolting down a rocky cow path, they approached a large rock formation, surrounded by cedars. Finally the buggy rolled to a halt. "Stay put." The driver aimed his pistol straight at them.

"Lester, I'll tie up the horses and then we can get on with it."

Lester. Rose hoped knowing their names might help apprehend them later, if she ever escaped their clutches.

Tex reappeared and unceremoniously lifted Lavinia from the buggy. Rose watched in horror as the man shoved her aunt to the ground and lashed her with a rope to a sturdy tree trunk. Before Rose could call out, Lester jabbed her with the gun. "Git out. No funny business. I've got you in my sights."

Rose's eyes darted around the scene, but no avenue of escape presented itself. She had no sooner hit the ground than Lester marched her to a tree adjacent to where Lavinia was secured. "You're next."

She felt the rough hemp biting into her wrists. This could not be happening. She couldn't just sit here. "Sir, I pray you, don't harm us. Take what you want, but leave us be. I have a small child who depends on me."

Tex chortled. "As if we care."

"You ladies think yer right fine." Lester lifted Lavinia's skirt above the ankle. "Fancy petticoats and all."

"Don't want no old woman," Tex said. "But this here young one—"

"Don't be ridiculous." Aunt Lavinia lifted her chin. "Take what you want from us, and then leave us be. Harming us will only get you in further trouble when you're caught, as I'm sure you will be."

"Oh, we'll take what we want all right, starting with this." Tex stepped forward and grabbed at Lavinia's fur-lined cloak that had slipped from her shoulders when they tied her up.

"And this," Lester grabbed at the ornate necklace, jerking it over Lavinia's head.

"You may as well have the earrings, too," Lavinia said. "Try not to wrench off my ears, sir."

"What about you?" Tex faced Rose. "What you got?"

"Nothing."

"Don't lie," Tex hunkered beside Rose, then jerked her head back by her hair.

"Unhand her," Lavinia shouted. "You have my jewels. If you leave us alone, I will tell you where you can find a significant sum of money."

"Money?" Tex leaped to his feet. "We had a little something more in mind, but…" He and Lester stepped a few paces away to confer. Rose glanced at Lavinia, who seemed ready to face whatever would happen next.

The two returned and stood over them, Lester brandishing his weapon. "Where?" Tex asked.

"If you look in my reticule, you will find some gold pieces, but there is more hidden inside the well behind my house. Under cover of dark, you should have no trouble lifting the lid and finding the packet attached to the wall about four feet down." Then she gave them directions to her residence. "Best go now, before we are discovered missing and a posse comes looking for us."

The two looked at one another, as if debating whether to stay and do more harm or go. Greed won out. Tex doffed his hat. "Have a good night with the coyotes." Then he guffawed. "All kind of critters come out in the dark." Then he moved away to roll up their tent.

Lester approached and stood menacingly over them. "You say anything about who we are, we'll come find you and it won't be so pretty then."

With that they unhitched the buggy horse and slapped him on the rump to shoo him off and then mounted their own horses and rode away. When the last sound of hoofbeats died, Lavinia muttered, "Good riddance."

"Is there really money in the well?"

Somehow Lavinia managed a wry smile. "Certainly not. My hope is that in the effort to reach the nonexistent packet, one of them will fall into the water. Also my man may very well hear them and apprehend them. Anything was better than having them stay here and act on any more nefarious impulses."

"We're very far from Lily's," Rose said.

"Your sister is no fool. She will surmise something has happened to us and roust the men to come looking for us."

"Oh, Aunt Lavinia, I pray it may be so."

"Prayer is a good idea. If ever we needed God, it would be now."

And so Rose began, tentatively at first and then more confidently. "Our Father who art in heaven…"

Their two voices, joined in supplication, gave Rose

hope, especially when they came to the line "deliver us from evil." When they finished, a silence fell, broken only by the rustling of the cedars in the wind.

"Now all we can do is wait."

Rose knew they must remain alert and positive. "If anyone can find us it is Caleb."

"And Seth."

"How would he receive word that we are missing? He's at the ranch," Rose reminded her aunt.

"Caleb will think of something."

"I'm cold. And I have my cloak, but they took yours."

"Perhaps we should get our minds off our discomfort. I think now might be a good time for me to tell you why your Alf is so important to me." Lavinia paused a long while, as if gathering her thoughts. "Mine has not been an altogether happy life. Louis and I were not able to have children. To compensate, I plunged into the whirlwind of St. Louis society. I distanced myself from other people's children, even convinced myself that I did not like children. In some ways, I felt isolated from the experiences of other women. It was only when Lily came to visit and I saw her courage and her love for Caleb that I was able to permit a small chink in my armor."

"So it must have disturbed you to see me, a spinster, being presented with the gift of a child," Rose murmured.

"At first, it seemed unfair that I should've been denied what God blessed you with. But then…then little Alf wrapped himself around my heart and Mattie endeared her sweet self to me. It came as a shock to me to realize that I could let down my guard and enjoy my great-niece and—nephew. That I wanted to."

"Thank you for telling me that. Your story helps me because there was a time when I was envious of Lily. She had a loving husband and a precious daughter. I had neither. It was especially the lack of a child that broke my heart."

"And that, I suspect, explains Bertha Britten's poisonous reactions. Perhaps, she, too, longs for a child she can never have."

Rose let her aunt's words sink in before replying. "I must exercise forgiveness rather than judgment."

"A difficult but important lesson in life, my dear." Aunt Lavinia struggled against her bonds and turned slightly toward Rose. "Now you have not only a child but a loving husband."

"A husband, at any rate."

"Child, whatever are you saying? That man adores you."

Rose swallowed nervously. "He has never told me so."

"I've noticed something about your Seth. Words do not come easily to him, but there are other ways to say 'I love you.' Through actions, Rose. Perhaps you need to spend some time thinking about the many ways Seth has demonstrated love. Don't fault him for not uttering the words."

Rose couldn't answer. Her mind was flooded with examples—Seth spending time with her on the porch, inventing excuses to come see Alf, complimenting her on her cooking, praying for a sick Alf when she could not and accompanying her to Council Grove. But most important? Proposing marriage in the attempt to save

Alf for her. Her eyes filled with tears. How could she ever have doubted his devotion?

The sun now sat just above the rim of the hills. What would night bring? If only she could have one more chance with Seth. One more day to tell him how much she loved him. One more evening to say prayers with Alf and tuck him into bed. *Forgive me, Lord, for withholding my love and for presuming to know Seth's heart. If it be Your will, preserve Lavinia and me this night from all dangers, so that we may be restored to live in the new day You have planned for us.*

Rose pulled her knees up against her chest and bowed her head over them in the effort to get warm. She had just nodded off when she heard Lavinia say, "Rose, do you hear that?"

Rose strained, listening to the night sounds. "What?"

"I thought I heard a horse."

"Pray God it is so." She straightened up, exerting all her senses in the effort to corroborate Lavinia's hopeful observation. Alas, it could as easily be Tex and Lester returning as the approach of rescuers. Then, borne on the wind, she thought she heard someone calling her name.

"Here! Over here!" she shouted at the top of her lungs.

"Caleb?" Lavinia called over and over.

Then at the top of the rise, Rose spotted two horses, immediately recognizing Patches. "Seth, oh, Seth!" In the dim twilight, she saw him, racing toward her, Caleb close behind. Caleb, she now saw, was leading their buggy horse. Seth wheeled to a stop right in front of her and slid from the saddle and in an instant was at her side, cradling her face as if examining it for injury.

"Dear, dear Rose. Are you hurt?"

She had hardly answered "no," when he was behind her releasing her hands from the rope. He pulled her to her feet, gently examining her chafed wrists. To the side she could see Caleb helping Aunt Lavinia to stand. Weak-kneed, Rose leaned against her husband's broad chest. "I am so glad to see you. I hoped you would come, but then it was getting dark and—"

"I've been out of my mind with worry. Rose, I don't know how I could go on without you. I knew I loved Alf, but never until this night did I realize that nothing and no one in my life is more important to me than you."

Rose lifted her head, startled to see tears running down her husband's cheeks. "Than me?"

"Rose, sweetheart. Have you any notion how much I love you?"

She reached up and wiped his tears with the tips of her fingers. "And I, you, my beloved husband. And I, you." Their embrace went on for what seemed both an eternity and mere seconds.

Finally turning to more practical matters, the men harnessed the buggy horse and helped the ladies onto the bench. Caleb nodded to Seth. "You go with the ladies. I'll bring Patches along."

Seth picked up the reins, and under Lavinia's approving glance, wrapped his free arm around his wife. Rose happily laid her head against his shoulder, knowing she would never ever forget this night when all the barriers between them came crashing down.

"All's well that ends well," Lavinia said by way of benediction.

Rose sighed contentedly. She couldn't agree more. The words! Her Seth had uttered the blessed words.

Epilogue

The Sunday after Christmas was cold but sunny, with slate-blue skies stretching as far as the eye could see. Remnants of a recent snow sat atop the hills like cake frosting, but the roads were clear. The bells Seth had attached to the horse's harness made the trip to town for services merrier than usual.

Seth eyed the horizon. "Even though the sheriff caught those two robbers, thanks to Lavinia's ruse about the well, I still want you to learn to protect yourself. The hired men are usually about the place if Pa and I aren't, but I don't want to take any chances with my family."

Rose nodded, then grinned. "It's prudent that I learn to handle a gun, but I'm probably more accurate with my iron skillet."

Seth laughed. "Remind me never to cross you when you're wielding such a weapon."

"That will never happen, dearest." Rose bundled Alf closer as she snuggled nearer to Seth. She was beside herself with excitement. Today Alf would be baptized, sealed as God's own.

"We've come a long way, haven't we?" she said to Seth.

He gazed down at her with his special smile that warmed her despite the freezing temperatures. "God has been good to us."

"Right now, I wonder how it was we ever doubted."

"We're human. In bad times, we get impatient—"

"And lose sight of God's timing." Rose closed her eyes, relaxing into her husband's shoulder. "'Our soul waiteth for the Lord,'" she murmured, quoting the psalmist.

"Faith," Seth said leaning down to kiss her forehead. "A lesson we must never forget."

"And one we will pass on to Alf."

Alf tugged on her cloak. "What about me, Mama? What about me?"

Rose smiled fondly. "Your papa and I were talking about how much we love you."

"God loves me, too, right?"

"He certainly does. And today He will give you your name."

"And everybody'll be there." In a singsong voice, he ticked them off. "Grandpapa Ezra, Grandpa Andrew, Aunt Sophie, Aunt Lily, Uncle Caleb and Mattie. But I wish 'Vinia was here."

"So do we, son, but you forgot to name someone," Seth reminded him.

Alf frowned in concentration, but then clapped his hands. "I know! Bess. She's gonna be my new grandma, right?"

"Soon, very soon." Rose pointed at the church coming into view. "And don't forget the other people who will be there for you today—all our friends in the town. Aren't we blessed?"

"We are," Seth whispered in her ear.

As they walked toward the church, the air was fragrant with wood smoke and cedar. Hanging above the door was a huge wreath of greenery bedecked with a red bow. Inside, the rest of the family had already gathered, saving seats on the front row for her, Seth and Alf. Seeing all their family gathered around them, Rose knew a contentment she had long sought. With her dear Seth at her side and her son growing into a fine young man, she lacked for nothing. And now? Beyond her wildest hopes, she was beginning to suspect that God had sent her one more blessing. It was too soon to be certain, so she had told no one, not even Seth. She raised a gloved hand to conceal a satisfied smile. In God's precious time she would know whether, come late summer, Alf would have a brother or sister.

The organ pealed with the strains of the opening hymn, and Rose stood with the congregation, singing with an abundance of gratitude. Seth put his arm around her, his deep bass ringing with conviction. "Hark, the herald angels sing!"

Following the sermon, Pastor Dooley stepped in front of the altar. "Today is a special day in the life of this congregation. Many of you know how God has acted in the life of young Alf. Sad circumstances for him, which could have ended very badly, have instead resulted in his finding a permanent, loving home with our friends Seth and Rose Montgomery. Today we welcome him into God's fellowship and bestow upon him the name he has chosen." The minister walked over to

Alf and took him by the hand and led him to the baptismal font. "Rose, Seth, please join us."

Alf stood in front of Rose and Seth. Rose laid a hand on his shoulder to calm him. After Pastor Dooley blessed the water and prayed, the moment came when he asked them to name the child. Before they could open their mouths, Alf blurted out, "Alfred Kellogg Montgomery."

Muffled laughter could be heard in the congregation. Then Rose and Seth repeated the name. "Alfred Kellogg Montgomery."

Seth picked up Alf and leaned him over the font as Pastor Dooley poured water over the boy's head and said in a clear voice, "I baptize thee Alfred Kellogg Montgomery in the name of the Father, the Son and the Holy Ghost."

When the rite had been completed, Alf put his little hands on Seth's cheeks and said loudly, "Now I be God's son. And yours. And we're a happy fambly 'cuz you love Mama, right?"

Seth found Rose's eyes over Alf's shoulder. "Yes, son, I do love your mama."

Looking at her two menfolk, Rose was nearly overcome with happiness.

"And, Mama, you love Papa Sett?"

Rose blinked away her tears. "Alfred Kellogg Montgomery, I love you and your dear papa with all my heart."

Seth held out his arm and drew her into a threeway embrace.

Pastor Dooley nodded approvingly, then turned to the congregation. "I can think of no better *Amen*."

The family and friends gathered in Christian fellowship must have agreed, for *Amen, Amen, Amen* rang from every corner of the church.

* * * * *

Author Note

For some, the Flint Hills of Kansas are an acquired taste. From my first introduction to that region when I attended college in Manhattan, Kansas, to spending time with friends who grew up in the area, to the pleasure of a recent visit to the Tallgrass Prairie National Preserve and charming, historic Cottonwood Falls, I have loved the area. In fact, my first book, *Mating for Life* (Harlequin Superromance, 1995), was also set in the Flint Hills.

What fun it has been, then, to relocate Rose and Ezra Kellogg from Fort Larned to Cottonwood Falls to reunite with Rose's sister, Lily, and her husband, Caleb Montgomery. Lily and Caleb found each other in *Into the Wilderness* (Harlequin Love Inspired Historical, 2013), and I long ago decided that Rose and Seth Montgomery needed their own love story. (Fortunately, my editors agreed.) Never ones to take the spotlight, Rose and Seth must overcome both their lack of self-confidence and the spiritual questions challenging them. Neither is looking for love, but isn't it usually the case that romance just happens to find people like them?

If you think Seth and Caleb's sister, Sophie, already has her happy ending, stay tuned. Her story is in the works. I have appreciated readers' positive responses to all the Kellogg-Montgomery characters. Some have even indicated they may make a real-life trip to Kansas as a result. I hope so.

Meanwhile, as always, I enjoy hearing your reactions to my books. I can be reached at lauraabbot@msn.com or on Facebook. My website address is www.lauraabbot.com.

Blessings,

Laura Abbot

P.S. An architectural wonder in its day, the Chase County Courthouse still stands and is open for tours. Where I have taken literary license with historical details, I have striven to remain faithful to the spirit of the place and the era.

Questions for Discussion

1. Rose regards herself as a Plain Jane. To what extent does her self-image affect her behavior and decisions? In your own life, how does self-image play a role?

2. Social standing and others' opinions of her are very important to Lavinia Dupree. How do these manifest themselves in her actions? Lily, in particular, sees through the facade her aunt adopts around others. In what ways is Lavinia's "mask" a self-protective device? How do others get through her mask to see the inner Lavinia? Do you ever wear "masks"? For what purposes? What would happen if others saw the "real you"?

3. Much like Rose, Seth has trouble believing others' high opinion of him. What in their pasts is responsible for such a lack of confidence? Why is coming to grips with the past an important step in facing the future?

4. Settling the West was fraught with challenges and hardships. In the book, how does the community help to make frontier life more bearable? In our modern world, where do you find a sense of community? Are we more or less likely to find it than Rose or Seth? Why?

5. What is the role of the Chase County Courthouse in the story? What does it tell us about the val-

ues and aspirations of those who settled in the Flint Hills?

6. What characteristics and actions show Rose and Seth to be admirable parental figures? What might we learn from them about parenting?

7. In the story, there are several sibling relationships (Rose and Lily, Seth and Caleb, Seth and Sophie, Caleb and Sophie). How would you characterize each relationship? If you have siblings, how has your relationship with them affected your life? What, if any, is the effect of birth order?

8. Both Rose and Seth have issues with God, His timing and His action in their lives. What led to such doubts? How do they overcome their lack of faith?

9. Periods of doubt or despair are often part of one's faith journey. Think about such "dark nights of the soul" in your own experience. What helped you deal with your questions? Where did you find God amid your doubt?

10. The main characters in the story have all been "scarred" in some way by events in their lives. What can we learn from the ways in which they coped with their problems? With which main character do you most closely identify? Why?

COMING NEXT MONTH FROM
Love Inspired® Historical

Available October 7, 2014

BIG SKY COWBOY
Montana Marriages
by Linda Ford

Cora Bell isn't looking for romance, and cowboy Wyatt Williams only wants to make a new start with his younger brother. But when Wyatt seeks temporary shelter on her family's farm, can he and Cora let their guards down to allow love in?

MARRIED BY CHRISTMAS
Smoky Mountain Matches
by Karen Kirst

Rebecca Thurston blames Caleb O'Malley for her broken engagement, but when he turns up at her door close to death, she can't turn her back. When rumors spread around town, will she be forced to marry the enemy?

SUITOR BY DESIGN
The Dressmaker's Daughters
by Christine Johnson

Seamstress Minnie Fox has her hopes set on being a star, but she can't help her attraction to a local mechanic caught up in a bootlegging scheme. Will she follow fame or fall for the boy next door?

THE NANNY ARRANGEMENT
by Lily George

Overwhelmed with caring for his baby niece, Paul Holmes is thrilled when Becky Siddons agrees to be her nursemaid. But he never expects to find feelings of love toward his charming new hire.

LIHCNM0914

REQUEST YOUR FREE BOOKS!

2 FREE INSPIRATIONAL NOVELS
PLUS 2
FREE
MYSTERY GIFTS

Love Inspired

HISTORICAL
INSPIRATIONAL HISTORICAL ROMANCE

YES! Please send me 2 FREE Love Inspired® Historical novels and my 2 FREE mystery gifts (gifts are worth about $10). After receiving them, if I don't wish to receive any more books, I can return the shipping statement marked "cancel." If I don't cancel, I will receive 4 brand-new novels every month and be billed just $4.74 per book in the U.S. or $5.24 per book in Canada. That's a saving of at least 21% off the cover price. It's quite a bargain! Shipping and handling is just 50¢ per book in the U.S. and 75¢ per book in Canada.* I understand that accepting the 2 free books and gifts places me under no obligation to buy anything. I can always return a shipment and cancel at any time. Even if I never buy another book, the two free books and gifts are mine to keep forever.

102/302 IDN F5CN

Name	(PLEASE PRINT)

Address	Apt. #

City	State/Prov.	Zip/Postal Code

Signature (if under 18, a parent or guardian must sign)

Mail to the Harlequin® Reader Service:
IN U.S.A.: P.O. Box 1867, Buffalo, NY 14240-1867
IN CANADA: P.O. Box 609, Fort Erie, Ontario L2A 5X3

Want to try two free books from another series?
Call 1-800-873-8635 or visit www.ReaderService.com.

* Terms and prices subject to change without notice. Prices do not include applicable taxes. Sales tax applicable in N.Y. Canadian residents will be charged applicable taxes. Offer not valid in Quebec. This offer is limited to one order per household. Not valid for current subscribers to Love Inspired Historical books. All orders subject to credit approval. Credit or debit balances in a customer's account(s) may be offset by any other outstanding balance owed by or to the customer. Please allow 4 to 6 weeks for delivery. Offer available while quantities last.

Your Privacy—The Harlequin® Reader Service is committed to protecting your privacy. Our Privacy Policy is available online at www.ReaderService.com or upon request from the Harlequin Reader Service.

We make a portion of our mailing list available to reputable third parties that offer products we believe may interest you. If you prefer that we not exchange your name with third parties, or if you wish to clarify or modify your communication preferences, please visit us at www.ReaderService.com/consumerschoice or write to us at Harlequin Reader Service Preference Service, P.O. Box 9062, Buffalo, NY 14269. Include your complete name and address.

LIH13R

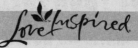
"**B**ad news," Cord said. "That was the wedding coordinator. She's quitting."

"Ouch. So now what?"

"I'm not sure."

"With no coordinator to help, will you call off the wedding?" Katie asked.

"No." There was too much at stake. The town needed this wedding and the money it would bring in. They had a bridge in need of repairs and a museum they couldn't finish without more funds. "I'll just figure out how to pull off a wedding for fifty couples, maybe get some media attention for Jasper Gulch and hopefully not mess up anyone's life."

"I think you'll do just fine. Remember, it's all about the dress."

"How long are you going to be in town, Katie?" He placed a hand on her back and guided her up the sidewalk.

"I'm not sure. I'm supposed to be helping my sister, but she seems to have escaped and left me here." She sighed and glanced at him.

"Do you think that as long as you're here…"

They were standing in front of the massive wooden doors that led to the church. She had a slightly red nose from the cool morning air and her lips were tinted with pink gloss. As long as she was there, she could be a friend. That wasn't what he'd planned to say, but the thought framed itself as a question in his mind.

She was studying his face, waiting for him to finish.

"Maybe you could help me with this wedding?"

"I thought maybe you wanted me to run interference and keep the single women at bay. 'Hands off Cord Shaw,' that kind of thing." As she said it, somehow her palm came to rest on his shoulder as if they'd been friends forever.

It was the strangest and maybe one of the best feelings. It tangled him up and made him lose track of the reality that he was standing in front of the church. The door could open at any moment. And for the first time in years, a woman had made him feel at ease.

Can rancher Cord Shaw and Katie Archer pull off
Jasper Gulch's latest centennial event without getting
their hearts involved? Find out in
HIS MONTANA BRIDE by Brenda Minton,
available October 2014 from Love Inspired.

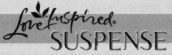
Danger and love go hand in hand in the small town
of Wrangler's Corner. Read on for a sneak preview of
THE LAWMAN RETURNS by Lynette Eason,
the first book in this exciting new series from
Love Inspired Suspense.

Sheriff's deputy Clay Starke wheeled to a stop in front of
the beat-up trailer. He heard the sharp crack, and the side
of the trailer spit metal.

A shooter.

The woman on the porch careened down the steps and
bolted toward him. Terror radiated from her. He shoved
open the door to the passenger side. "Get in!"

Breathless, she landed in the passenger seat and slammed
the door. Eyes wide, she lifted shaking hands to push her
blond hair out of her eyes.

Clay got on his radio and reported shots fired.

He cranked the car and started to back out of the drive.

"No! We can't leave!"

"What?" He stepped on the brake. "Lady, if someone's
shooting, I'm getting you out of here."

"But I think Jordan's in there, and I can't leave without
him."

"Jordan?"

"A boy I work with. He called me for help. I'm worried
he might be hurt."

Clay put the car back in Park. "Then stay down and let
me check it out."

"But if you get out, he might shoot you."

He waited. No more shots. "Stay put. I think he might be gone."

"Or waiting for one of us to get out of the car."

True. He could feel her gaze on him, studying him, dissecting him. He frowned. "What is it?"

"You."

He shot a glance behind them, then let his gaze rove the area until he'd gone in a full circle and was once again looking into her pretty face. "What about me?"

Red crept into her cheeks. "You look so much like Steven. Are you related?"

He stilled, focusing in on her. "I'm Clay Starke. You knew my brother?"

"Clay? I'm Sabrina Mayfield."

Oh, wow. Sabrina Mayfield. "Are you saying the kid in there knows something about Steven's death?"

"I don't know what he's doing here, but he called me and said he thought he knew who killed Steven and he needed me to come get him."

A tingle of shock raced through Clay. Finally. After weeks with nothing, this could be the break he'd been looking for. "Then I want to know what he knows."

Pick up THE LAWMAN RETURNS, available
October 2014 wherever
Love Inspired Suspense books are sold.

Love Inspired **HISTORICAL**

Big Sky Cowboy

by LINDA FORD

JUST THE COWBOY SHE NEEDED?

The last thing Cora Bell wants is a distracting cowboy showing up on her family's farm seeking temporary shelter. Especially one she is sure has something to hide. But she'll accept Wyatt Williams's help rebuilding her family's barn—and try not to fall once again for a man whose plans don't include staying around.

Since leaving his troubled past behind, Wyatt avoids personal entanglements. He just wants to make a new start with his younger brother. But there's something about Cora that he's instinctively drawn to. Dare this solitary cowboy risk revealing his secrets for a chance at redemption and a bright new future with Cora by his side?

Montana Marriages

Three sisters discover a legacy
of love beneath the Western sky

*Available October 2014 wherever
Love Inspired books and ebooks are sold.*

Find us on Facebook at
www.Facebook.com/LoveInspiredBooks

LIH28282